Six Feet of the Country

FIFTEEN SHORT STORIES BY

NADINE GORDIMER

1956

SIMON AND SCHUSTER • NEW YORK

"A Bit of Young Life," "Six Feet of the Country," "Clowns in Clover," "Out of Season," "The Smell of Death and Flowers," and "Which New Era Would That Be?" were originally published in *The New Yorker*. "Enemies" and "My First Two Women" were published in *The New Yorker* in different form under the titles, respectively, "A Sense of Survival" and "The Pretender."

"The Cicatrice" and "A Wand'ring Minstrel, I" were published originally in *Harper's*.

"Charmed Lives" was published originally in *Harper's Bazaar*.

"Happy Event" was published originally in *Charm*.

"Face from Atlantis" was published originally in *The Paris Review*.

FIRST PRINTING

LIBRARY OF CONGRESS CATALOG CARD NUMBER: 56-9927

MANUFACTURED IN THE UNITED STATES OF AMERICA

BY AMERICAN BOOK–STRATFORD PRESS, INC., NEW YORK

For my husband, Reinhold Cassirer

CONTENTS

Six Feet of the Country   1

Face from Atlantis   17

A Bit of Young Life   41

Enemies   57

Which New Era Would That Be?   69

Out of Season   87

My First Two Women   99

The White Goddess and the Mealie Question   115

Clowns in Clover   129

A Wand'ring Minstrel, I   139

Happy Event   151

Charmed Lives   169

Horn of Plenty   185

The Cicatrice   205

The Smell of Death and Flowers   215

Six Feet of the Country

My wife and I are not real farmers—not even Lerice, really. We bought our place, ten miles out of Johannesburg on one of the main roads, to change something in ourselves, I suppose; you seem to rattle about so much within a marriage like ours. You long to hear nothing but a deep satisfying silence when you sound a marriage. The farm hasn't managed that for us, of course, but it has done other things, unexpected, illogical. Lerice, who I thought would retire there in Chekhovian sadness for a month or two, and then leave the place to the servants while she tried yet again to get a part she wanted and become the actress she would like to be, has sunk into the business of running the farm with all the serious intensity with which she once imbued the shadows in a playwright's mind. I should have given it up long ago if it had not been for her. Her hands, once small and plain and well kept—she was not the sort of actress who wears red paint and diamond rings—are hard as a dog's pads.

I, of course, am there only in the evenings and on week ends. I am a partner in a luxury-travel agency, which is flourishing—needs to be, as I tell Lerice, in order to carry the farm. Still, though I know we can't afford it, and though the sweetish smell of the fowls Lerice breeds sickens me, so that I avoid going past their runs, the farm is beautiful in a way I had almost forgotten —especially on a Sunday morning when I get up and go out into the paddock and see not the palm trees and fishpond and imitation-stone bird bath of the suburbs but white ducks on the dam, the lucerne field brilliant as window dresser's grass, and the little, stocky, mean-eyed bull, lustful but bored, having his face tenderly licked by one of his ladies. Lerice comes out with her hair uncombed, in her hand a stick dripping with cattle dip. She will stand and look dreamily for a moment, the way she would pretend to look sometimes in those plays. "They'll mate tomorrow," she will say. "This is their second day. Look how she loves him, my little Napoleon." So that when people come out to see us on Sunday afternoon, I am likely to hear myself saying as I pour out the drinks, "When I drive back home from the city every day, past those rows of suburban houses, I wonder how the devil we ever did stand it. . . . Would you care to look around?" And there I am, taking some pretty girl and her young husband stumbling down to our riverbank, the girl catching her stockings on the mealie-stooks and stepping over cow turds humming with jewel-green flies while she says, ". . . the *tensions* of the damned city. And you're near enough to get into town to a show, too! I think it's wonderful. Why, you've got it both ways!"

And for a moment I accept the triumph as if I *had* managed it—the impossibility that I've been trying for all my life—just as if the truth was that you could get it "both ways," instead of finding yourself with not even one way or the other but a third, one you had not provided for at all.

But even in our saner moments, when I find Lerice's earthy enthusiasms just as irritating as I once found her histrionical ones, and she finds what she calls my "jealousy" of her capacity for enthusiasm as big a proof of my inadequacy for her as a mate as ever it was, we do believe that we have at least honestly escaped those tensions peculiar to the city about which our visitors speak. When Johannesburg people speak of "tension," they don't mean hurrying people in crowded streets, the struggle for money, or the general competitive character of city life. They mean the guns under the white men's pillows and the burglar bars on the white men's windows. They mean those strange moments on city pavements when a black man won't stand aside for a white man.

Out in the country, even ten miles out, life is better than that. In the country, there is a lingering remnant of the pretransitional stage; our relationship with the blacks is almost feudal. Wrong, I suppose, obsolete, but more comfortable all around. We have no burglar bars, no gun. Lerice's farm boys have their wives and their piccanins living with them on the land. They brew their sour beer without the fear of police raids. In fact, we've always rather prided ourselves that the poor devils have nothing much to fear, being with us; Lerice even keeps an eye on their children, with all the competence of a woman who has never had a child of her own, and she certainly doctors them all— children and adults—like babies whenever they happen to be sick.

It was because of this that we were not particularly startled one night last winter when the boy Albert came knocking at our window long after we had gone to bed. I wasn't in our bed but sleeping in the little dressing-room-*cum*-linen-room next door, because Lerice had annoyed me and I didn't want to find myself softening toward her simply because of the sweet smell of the talcum powder on her flesh after her bath. She came and woke me up. "Albert says one of the boys is very sick," she said. "I think you'd better go down and see. He wouldn't get us up at this hour for nothing."

"What time is it?"

"What does it matter?" Lerice is maddeningly logical.

I got up awkwardly as she watched me—how is it I always feel a fool when I have deserted her bed? After all, I know from the way she never looks at me when she talks to me at breakfast the next day that she is hurt and humiliated at my not wanting her—and I went out, clumsy with sleep.

"Which of the boys is it?" I asked Albert as we followed the dance of my torch.

"He's too sick. Very sick, *Baas*," he said.

"But who? Franz?" I remembered Franz had had a bad cough for the past week.

Albert did not answer; he had given me the path, and was walking along beside me in the tall dead grass. When the light of the torch caught his face, I saw that he looked acutely embarrassed. "What's this all about?" I said.

He lowered his head under the glance of the light. "It's not me, *Baas*. I don't know. Petrus he send me."

Irritated, I hurried him along to the huts. And there, on Petrus's iron bedstead, with its brick stilts, was a young man, dead. On his forehead there was still a light, cold sweat; his body was warm. The boys stood around as they do in the kitchen when it is discovered that someone has broken a dish—uncooperative, silent. Somebody's wife hung about in the shadows, her hands wrung together under her apron.

I had not seen a dead man since the war. This was very different. I felt like the others—extraneous, useless. "What was the matter?" I asked.

The woman patted at her chest and shook her head to indicate the painful impossibility of breathing.

He must have died of pneumonia.

I turned to Petrus. "Who was this boy? What was he doing here?" The light of a candle on the floor showed that Petrus was weeping. He followed me out the door.

When he were outside, in the dark, I waited for him to speak. But he didn't. "Now, come on, Petrus, you must tell me who this boy was. Was he a friend of yours?"

4

"He's my brother, *Baas*. He came from Rhodesia to look for work."

The story startled Lerice and me a little. The young boy had walked down from Rhodesia to look for work in Johannesburg, had caught a chill from sleeping out along the way, and had lain ill in his brother Petrus's hut since his arrival three days before. Our boys had been frightened to ask us for help for him because we had never been intended ever to know of his presence. Rhodesian natives are barred from entering the Union unless they have a permit; the young man was an illegal immigrant. No doubt our boys had managed the whole thing successfully several times before; a number of relatives must have walked the seven or eight hundred miles from poverty to the paradise of zoot suits, police raids, and black slum townships that is their *Egoli*, City of Gold—the Bantu name for Johannesburg. It was merely a matter of getting such a man to lie low on our farm until a job could be found with someone who would be glad to take the risk of prosecution for employing an illegal immigrant in exchange for the services of someone as yet untainted by the city.

Well, this was one who would never get up again.

"You would think they would have felt they could tell *us*," said Lerice next morning. "Once the man was ill. You would have thought at least—" When she is getting intense over something, she has a way of standing in the middle of a room as people do when they are shortly to leave on a journey, looking searchingly about her at the most familiar objects as if she had never seen them before. I had noticed that in Petrus's presence in the kitchen, earlier, she had had the air of being almost offended with him, almost hurt.

In any case, I really haven't the time or inclination any more to go into everything in our life that I know Lerice, from those alarmed and pressing eyes of hers, would like us to go into. She is the kind of woman who doesn't mind if she looks plain, or odd; I don't suppose she would even care if she knew how strange she looks when her whole face is out of proportion with urgent uncertainty. I said, "Now I'm the one who'll have to do all the dirty work, I suppose."

She was still staring at me, trying me out with those eyes— wasting her time, if she only knew.

"I'll have to notify the health authorities," I said calmly. "They can't just cart him off and bury him. After all, we don't really know what he died of."

She simply stood there, as if she had given up—simply ceased to see me at all.

I don't know when I've been so irritated. "It might have been something contagious," I said. "God knows." There was no answer.

I am not enamored of holding conversations with myself. I went out to shout to one of the boys to open the garage and get the car ready for my morning drive to town.

As I had expected, it turned out to be quite a business. I had to notify the police as well as the health authorities, and answer a lot of tedious questions: How was it I was ignorant of the boy's presence? If I did not supervise my native quarters, how did I know that that sort of thing didn't go on all the time? Et cetera, et cetera. And when I flared up and told them that so long as my natives did their work, I didn't think it my right or concern to poke my nose into their private lives, I got from the coarse, dull-witted police sergeant one of those looks that come not from any thinking process going on in the brain but from that faculty common to all who are possessed by the master-race theory—a look of insanely inane certainty. He grinned at me with a mixture of scorn and delight at my stupidity.

Then I had to explain to Petrus why the health authorities had to take away the body for a post-mortem—and, in fact, what a post-mortem was. When I telephoned the health department some days later to find out the result, I was told that the cause of death was, as we had thought, pneumonia, and that the body had been suitably disposed of. I went out to where Petrus was mixing a mash for the fowls and told him that it was all right, there would be no trouble; his brother had died from that pain in his chest. Petrus put down the paraffin tin and said, "When can we go to fetch him, *Baas?*"

"To fetch him?"

"Will the *Baas* please ask them when we must come?"

I went back inside and called Lerice, all over the house. She came down the stairs from the spare bedrooms, and I said, "*Now* what am I going to do? When I told Petrus, he just asked calmly when they could go and fetch the body. They think they're going to bury him themselves."

"Well, go back and tell him," said Lerice. "You must tell him. why didn't you tell him then?"

When I found Petrus again, he looked up politely. "Look, Petrus," I said. "You can't go to fetch your brother. They've done it already—they've *buried* him, you understand?"

"Where?" he said slowly, dully, as if he thought that perhaps he was getting this wrong.

"You see, he was a stranger. They knew he wasn't from here, and they didn't know he had some of his people here so they thought they must bury him." It was difficult to make a pauper's grave sound like a privilege.

"Please, *Baas*, the *Baas* must ask them." But he did not mean that he wanted to know the burial place. He simply ignored the

7

incomprehensible machinery I told him had set to work on his dead brother; he wanted the brother back.

"But, Petrus," I said, "how can I? Your brother is buried already. I can't ask them now."

"Oh, *Baas!*" he said. He stood with his bran-smeared hands uncurled at his sides, one corner of his mouth twitching.

"Good God, Petrus, they won't listen to me! They can't, anyway. I'm sorry, but I can't do it. You understand?"

He just kept on looking at me, out of his knowledge that white men have everything, can do anything; if they don't, it is because they won't.

And then, at dinner, Lerice started. "You could at least phone," she said.

"Christ, what d'you think I am? Am I supposed to bring the dead back to life?"

But I could not exaggerate my way out of this ridiculous responsibility that had been thrust on me. "Phone them up," she went on. "And at least you'll be able to tell him you've done it and they've explained that it's impossible."

She disappeared somewhere into the kitchen quarters after coffee. A little later she came back to tell me, "The old father's coming down from Rhodesia to be at the funeral. He's got a permit and he's already on his way."

Unfortunately, it was not impossible to get the body back. The authorities said that it was somewhat irregular, but that since the hygiene conditions had been fulfilled, they could not refuse permission for exhumation. I found out that, with the undertaker's charges, it would cost twenty pounds. Ah, I thought, that settles it. On five pounds a month, Petrus won't have twenty pounds—and just as well, since it couldn't do the dead any good. Certainly I should not offer it to him myself. Twenty pounds—or anything else within reason, for that matter —I would have spent without grudging it on doctors or medi-

8

cines that might have helped the boy when he was alive. Once he was dead, I had no intention of encouraging Petrus to throw away, on a gesture, more than he spent to clothe his whole family in a year.

When I told him, in the kitchen that night, he said, "Twenty pounds?"

I said, "Yes, that's right, twenty pounds."

For a moment, I had the feeling, from the look on his face, that he was calculating. But when he spoke again I thought I must have imagined it. "We must pay twenty pounds!" he said in the faraway voice in which a person speaks of something so unattainable that it does not bear thinking about.

"All right, Petrus," I said, and went back to the living room.

The next morning before I went to town, Petrus asked to see me. "Please, *Baas*," he said, awkwardly handing me a bundle of notes. They're so seldom on the giving rather than the receiving side, poor devils, that they don't really know how to hand money to a white man. There it was, the twenty pounds, in ones and halves, some creased and folded until they were soft as dirty rags, others smooth and fairly new—Franz's money, I suppose, and Albert's, and Dora the cook's, and Jacob the gardener's, and God knows who else's besides, from all the farms and small holdings round about. I took it in irritation more than in astonishment, really—irritation at the waste, the uselessness of this sacrifice by people so poor. Just like the poor everywhere, I thought, who stint themselves the decencies of life in order to insure themselves the decencies of death. So incomprehensible to people like Lerice and me, who regard life as something to be spent extravagantly and, if we think about death at all, regard it as the final bankruptcy.

The servants don't work on Saturday afternoon anyway, so it was a good day for the funeral. Petrus and his father had borrowed our donkey cart to fetch the coffin from the city, where, Petrus told Lerice on their return, everything was "nice"—the coffin waiting for them, already sealed up to save them from what must have been a rather unpleasant sight after two weeks' interment. (It had taken all that time for the authorities and the undertaker to make the final arrangements for moving the body.) All morning, the coffin lay in Petrus's hut, awaiting the trip to the little old burial ground, just outside the eastern boundary of our farm, that was a relic of the days when this was a real farming district rather than a fashionable rural estate. It was pure chance that I happened to be down there near the fence when the procession came past; once again Lerice had forgotten her promise to me and had made the house uninhabitable on a Saturday afternoon. I had come home and been infuriated to find her in a pair of filthy old slacks and with her hair uncombed since the night before, having all the varnish scraped off the living-room floor, if you please. So I had taken my No. 8 iron and gone off to practice my approach shots. In my annoyance, I had forgotten about the funeral, and was reminded only when I saw the procession coming up the path along the outside of the fence toward me; from where I was standing, you can see the graves quite clearly, and that day the sun glinted on bits of broken pottery, a lopsided homemade cross, and jam jars brown with rain water and dead flowers.

I felt a little awkward, and did not know whether to go on hitting my golf ball or stop at least until the whole gathering was decently past. The donkey cart creaks and screeches with every revolution of the wheels, and it came along in a slow, halting fashion somehow peculiarly suited to the two donkeys who drew it, their little potbellies rubbed and rough, their heads sunk between the shafts, and their ears flattened back with an air submissive and downcast; peculiarly suited, too, to the group of men and women who came along slowly behind. The patient ass. Watching, I thought, You can see now why the creature became a Biblical symbol. Then the procession drew level with me and stopped, so I had to put down my club. The coffin was taken down off the cart—it was a shiny, yellow-varnished wood, like cheap furniture—and the donkeys twitched their ears against the flies. Petrus, Franz, Albert, and the old father from Rhodesia hoisted it on their shoulders and the procession moved on, on foot. It was really a very awkward moment. I stood there rather foolishly at the fence, quite still, and slowly they filed past, not looking up, the four men bent beneath the shiny wooden box, and the straggling troop of mourners. All of them were servants or neighbors' servants whom I knew as casual, easygoing gossipers about our lands or kitchen. I heard the old man's breathing.

I had just bent to pick up my club again when there was a sort of jar in the flowing solemnity of their processional mood; I felt it at once, like a wave of heat along the air, or one of those sudden currents of cold catching at your legs in a placid stream. The old man's voice was muttering something; the people had stopped, confused, and they bumped into one another, some pressing to go on, others hissing them to be still. I could see that they were embarrassed, but they could not ignore the voice; it was much the way that the mumblings of a prophet, though not clear at first, arrest the mind. The corner of the coffin the old man carried was sagging at an angle; he seemed to be trying to get out from under the weight of it. Now Petrus expostulated with him.

The little boy who had been left to watch the donkeys dropped the reins and ran to see. I don't know why—unless it was for the same reason people crowd around someone who has fainted in a cinema—but I parted the wires of the fence and went through, after him.

Petrus lifted his eyes to me—to anybody—with distress and

11

horror. The old man from Rhodesia had let go of the coffin entirely, and the three others, unable to support it on their own, had laid it on the ground, in the pathway. Already there was a film of dust lightly wavering up its shiny sides. I did not understand what the old man was saying; I hesitated to interfere. But now the whole seething group turned on my silence. The old man himself came over to me, with his hands outspread and shaking, and spoke directly to me, saying something that I could tell from the tone, without understanding the words, was shocking and extraordinary.

"What is it, Petrus? What's wrong?" I appealed.

Petrus threw up his hands, bowed his head in a series of hysterical shakes, then thrust his face up at me suddenly. "He says, 'My son was not so heavy.'"

Silence. I could hear the old man breathing; he kept his mouth a little open, as old people do.

"My son was young and thin," he said at last, in English.

Again silence. Then babble broke out. The old man thundered against everybody; his teeth were yellowed and few, and he had one of those fine, grizzled, sweeping mustaches that one doesn't often see nowadays, which must have been grown in emulation of early Empire builders. It seemed to frame all his utterances with a special validity, perhaps merely because it was the symbol of the traditional wisdom of age—an idea so fearfully rooted that it carries still something awesome beyond reason. He shocked them; they thought he was mad, but they had to listen to him. With his own hands he began to prize the lid off the coffin and three of the men came forward to help him. Then he sat down on the ground; very old, very weak, and unable to speak, he merely lifted a trembling hand toward what was there. He abdicated, he handed it over to them; he was no good any more.

They crowded round to look (and so did I), and now they forgot the nature of this surprise and the occasion of grief to which it belonged, and for a few minutes were carried up in the delightful astonishment of the surprise itself. They gasped and flared noisily with excitement. I even noticed the little boy who had held the donkeys jumping up and down, almost weeping with rage because the backs of the grownups crowded him out of his view.

In the coffin was someone no one had ever seen before: a heavily built, rather light-skinned native with a neatly stitched scar on his forehead—perhaps from a blow in a brawl that had also dealt him some other, slower-working injury, which had killed him.

I wrangled with the authorities for a week over that body. I had the feeling that they were shocked, in a laconic fashion, by their own mistake, but that in the confusion of their anonymous dead they were helpless to put it right. They said to me, "We are trying to find out," and "We are still making inquiries." It was as if at any moment they might conduct me into their mortuary and say, "There! Lift up the sheets; look for him—your poultry boy's brother. There are so many black faces—surely one will do?"

And every evening when I got home, Petrus was waiting in the kitchen. "Well, they're trying. They're still looking. The *Baas* is seeing to it for you, Petrus," I would tell him. "God, half the time I should be in the office I'm driving around the back end of the town chasing after this affair," I added aside, to Lerice, one night.

She and Petrus both kept their eyes turned on me as I spoke, and, oddly, for those moments they looked exactly alike, though it sounds impossible: my wife, with her high, white forehead

13

and her attenuated Englishwoman's body, and the poultry boy, with his horny bare feet below khaki trousers tied at the knee with string and the peculiar rankness of his nervous sweat coming from his skin.

"What makes you so indignant, so determined about this now?" said Lerice suddenly.

I stared at her. "It's a matter of principle. Why should they get away with a swindle? It's time these officials had a jolt from someone who'll bother to take the trouble."

She said, "Oh." And as Petrus slowly opened the kitchen door to leave, sensing that the talk had gone beyond him, she turned away, too.

I continued to pass on assurances to Petrus every evening, but although what I said was the same and the voice in which I said it was the same, every evening it sounded weaker. At last, it became clear that we would never get Petrus's brother back, because nobody really knew where he was. Somewhere in a graveyard as uniform as a housing scheme, somewhere under a number that didn't belong to him, or in the medical school, perhaps, laboriously reduced to layers of muscle and strings of nerve? Goodness knows. He had no identity in this world anyway.

It was only then, and in a voice of shame, that Petrus asked me to try and get the money back.

"From the way he asks, you'd think he was robbing his dead brother," I said to Lerice later. But as I've said, Lerice had got so intense about this business that she couldn't even appreciate a little ironic smile.

I tried to get the money; Lerice tried. We both telephoned and wrote and argued, but nothing came of it. It appeared that the main expense had been the undertaker, and after all he had done his job. So the whole thing was a complete waste, even more of a waste for the poor devils than I had thought it would be.

The old man from Rhodesia was about Lerice's father's size, so she gave him one of her father's old suits, and he went back home rather better off, for the winter, than he had come.

Face from Atlantis

omehow it wasn't altogether a surprise when Waldeck Brand and his wife bumped into Carlitta at a theater in New York in 1953. The Brands were six thousand miles away from their home in South Africa, and everywhere they had visited in England and Europe before they came to America they had met Waldeck's contemporaries from Heidelberg whom he hadn't seen for twenty years and never had expected to see ever again. It had seemed a miracle to Waldeck that all these people, who had had to leave Germany because they were liberals (like himself), or Jews, or both, not only had survived transplantation but had thrived, and not only had thrived but had managed to do so each in the manner and custom of the country which had given him sanctuary.

Of course, Waldeck Brand did not think it a miracle that *he* had survived and conformed to a pattern of life lived at the other end of the world to which he had belonged. (Perhaps it is true, after all, that no man can believe in the possibility of his own failure or death.) It seemed quite natural that the gay young man destined primarily for a good time and, secondly, for the inheritance of his wealthy father's publishing house in Berlin should have become a director of an important group of gold mines in southernmost Africa, a world away from medieval German university towns where he had marched at the head of the student socialist group, and the Swiss Alps where he had skied and shared his log cabin with a different free-thinking

17

girl every winter, and the Kurfürstendamm where he had strolled with his friends, wearing elegant clothes specially ordered from England. Yet to him—and to his South African wife, who had been born and had spent the twenty-seven years of her life in Cape Town, looking out, often and often, over the sea which she had now crossed for the first time—it was a small miracle that his Heidelberg friend, Siggie Bentheim, was to be found at the foreign editor's desk of a famous right-of-center newspaper in London, and another university friend, Stefan Rosovsky, now become Stefan Raines, was president of a public-utility company in New York and had a finger or two dipped comfortably in oil, too. To Waldeck, Siggie was the leader of a Communist cell, an ugly little chap, best student in the *Institut fur Sozialwissenschaften,* whose tiny hands were dry-skinned and shrunken, as if political fervor had used up his blood like fuel. Stefan was the soulful-eyed Russian boy with the soft voice and the calm delivery of dry wit who tutored in economics and obviously was fitted for nothing but an academic career as an economist.

And to Eileen, Waldeck Brand's wife, both were people who lived, changeless, young, enviable, in a world that existed only in Waldeck's three green leather photograph albums. Siggie was the one who sat reading the *Arbeiterpolitik,* oblivious of the fact that a picture was being taken, in the photograph where a whole dim, underexposed room (Waldeck's at Heidelberg) was full of students. Eileen had been to a university in South Africa, but she had never seen students like that: such good-looking, happy, bold-eyed boys, such beautiful girls, smoking cigarettes in long holders and stretching out their legs in pointed-toed shoes beneath their short skirts. Someone was playing a guitar in that picture. But Siggie Bentheim (you could notice those hands, around the edges of the pages) read a paper.

Stefan was not in that picture, but in dozens of others. In particular, there was one taken in Budapest. A flashlight picture, taken in a night club. Stefan holds up a glass of champagne, resigned in his dinner suit, dignified in a silly paper cap. New Year in Budapest, before Hitler, before the war. Can you imagine it? Eileen was fascinated by those photograph albums and those faces. Since she had met and married Waldeck in 1952, she had spent many hours looking at the albums. When she did so, a great yawning envy opened through her whole body. She was young, and the people pictured in those albums were all, even if they were alive, over forty by now. But that did not matter; that did not count. That world of the photograph albums was not lost only by those who had outgrown it into middle age. It was *lost*. Gone. It did not belong to a new youth. It was not hers, although she was young. It was *no use* being young, now, in the Forties and Fifties. She thought of the green albums as the record of an Atlantis.

Waldeck had never been back to Europe since he came as a refugee to South Africa twenty years before. He had not kept up a regular correspondence with his scattered student friends, though one or two had written, at intervals of four or five years, and so for some, when Waldeck took his wife to Europe and America, he had the address-before-the-last, and for others the vaguest ideas of their whereabouts. Yet he found them all, or they found him. It was astonishing. The letters he wrote to old addresses were forwarded; the friends whom he saw knew where other friends lived, or at least what jobs they were doing, so that they could be traced that way, simply by a telephone call. In London there were dinner parties and plain drinking parties, and there they were—the faces from Atlantis, gathered together in a Strand pub. One of the women was a grandmother; most of the men were no longer married to women Waldeck remembered them marrying, and had shed their old political faiths along with their hair. But all were alive, and living variously, and in them was still the peculiar vigor that showed vividly in those faces, caught in the act of life long ago, in the photograph albums.

Once or twice in London, Waldeck had asked one old friend or another, "What happened to Carlitta? Does anyone know where Carlitta is?" Siggie Bentheim, eating Scotch salmon at Rules', like any other English journalist who can afford to, couldn't remember Carlitta. Who was she? Then Waldeck remembered that the year when everyone got to know Carlitta was the year that Siggie spent in Lausanne.

Another old friend remembered her very well. "Carlitta! Not in England, at any rate. Carlitta!"

Someone else caught the name, and called across the table, "Carlitta was in London, oh, before the war. She went to America thirteen or fourteen years ago."

"Did she ever marry poor old Klaus Schultz? My God, he was mad about the girl!"

"Marry him! No-o-o! Carlitta wouldn't marry him."

"Carlitta was a collector of scalps, all right," said Waldeck, laughing.

"Well, do you wonder?" said the friend.

Eileen knew Carlitta well, in picture and anecdote. Eileen had a favorite among the photographs of her, too, just as she had the one of Stefan in Budapest on New Year's Eve. The photograph was taken in Austria, on one of Waldeck's skiing holidays. It was a clear print and the snow was blindingly white. In the middle of the whiteness stood a young girl, laughing away from the camera in the direction of something or someone outside the picture. Her little face, burnished by the sun, shone dark against the snow. There was a highlight on each firm, round cheekbone, accentuated in laughter. She was beautiful in the pictures of groups, too—in boats on the Neckar, in the gardens of the *Schloss,* in cafés and at student dances; even, once, at Deauville, even in the unbecoming bathing dress of the time. In none of the pictures did she face the camera. If, as in the ski picture, she was smiling, it was at someone in the group, and if she was not, her black pensive eyes, her beautiful little firm-fleshed face with the short chin, stared at the toes of her shoes, or at the smoke of her cigarette, arrested in its climbing arabesque by the click of the camera. The total impression of all these photographs of the young German girl was one of arrogance. She did not participate in the taking of a photograph; she was simply there, a thing of beauty which you could attempt to record if you wished.

One of the anecdotes about the girl was something that had happened on that skiing holiday. Carlitta and Klaus Schultz, Waldeck and one of his girls had gone together to the mountains. ("Oh, the luck of it!" Eileen had said to Waldeck at this point in his story, the first time he related it. "You were eighteen? Nineteen? And you were allowed to go off on your first love affair to the mountains. Can you imagine what would have happened if I had announced to my parents that I was going off on a holiday with a young lover? And in Austria, and skiing . . ." Poor Eileen, who had gone, every year, on a five-day cruise along the coast to stay at a "family hotel" in Durban, accompanied by her parents and young brother and sister, or had been sent, in the winter vacation, with an uncle and cousins to hear the lions roar outside a dusty camp in the Kruger Park. She did not know which to envy Waldeck, Carlitta, and Klaus most—the sexual freedom or the steep mountain snows.) Anyway, it was on the one really long and arduous climb of that delightful holiday that Carlitta, who for some hours had been less talkative than usual and had fallen back a little, sat down in the snow and refused to move. Waldeck had lagged behind the rest of the party to mend a broken strap on his rucksack, and so it was that he noticed her. When he asked her why she did not hurry on with him to catch up with the other members of the party, she said, perfectly calm, "I want to sit here in the shade and rest. I'll wait here till you all come back."

There was no shade. The party intended to sleep in a rest hut up the mountain, and would not pass that way again till next day. At first Waldeck laughed; Carlitta was famous for her gaiety and caprice. Then he saw that in addition to being perfectly calm, Carlitta was also perfectly serious. She was not joking, but suffering from some kind of peculiar hysteria. He begged and begged her to get up, but she would not. "I am going to rest in the shade" was all she would answer. The rest of the party was out of sight and he began to feel nervous. There was only one thing he could try. He went up kindly to the beautiful little girl and struck her sharply, twice, in the face. The small head swung violently this way, then that. Carlitta got up, dusted the snow from her trousers, and said to Waldeck, "For God's sake, what are we waiting for? The others must be miles ahead."

"And when Klaus heard what had happened," Waldeck's story always ended, "he could scarcely keep himself from crying, he was so angry that *he* had not been the one to revive Carlitta, and Carlitta saw his nose pinken and swell slightly with the effort of keeping back the tears, and she noted how very much he must be in love with her and how easy it would be to torment him."

Wretched Klaus! He was the blond boy with the square jaw who always frowned and smiled directly into the camera. Eileen had a theory that young people didn't even fall in love like that any more. That, too, had gone down under the waves.

Waldeck and his young wife arrived in New York on a Tuesday. Stefan Raines came to take them out to dinner that very first night. Eileen, who had never seen him before in her life, was even more overjoyed than Waldeck to find that he had not changed. As soon as they came out of the elevator and saw him standing in the hotel lobby with a muffler hanging down untied on the lapels of his dark coat, they knew he had not changed. He wore the presidency of the public-utility company, the wealth and the Fifth Avenue apartment just as he had worn the paper cap in the Budapest night club on New Year's Eve long ago. Stefan's American wife was not able to accompany them that night, so the three dined alone at the Pierre. After dinner Stefan wanted to know if he should drive them to Times Square and along Broadway or anywhere else they'd read about, but they told him that he was the only sight they wanted to see so soon after their arrival. They talked for two hours over dinner, Stefan asking and Waldeck answering eager questions about the old Heidelberg friends whom Waldeck and Eileen had seen in London. Stefan went to London sometimes, and he had seen one or two, but many whom he hadn't been able to find for years seemed to have appeared out of their hiding places for Waldeck. In fact, there were several old Berlin and Heidelberg friends living in New York whom Stefan had seen once, or not at all, but who, on the Brands' first day in New York, had already telephoned their hotel. "We love Waldeck. Better than we love each other," said Stefan to his friend's wife, his black eyes looking quietly out over the room, the corners of his mouth indenting in his serious smile that took a long time to open out, brightening his eyes as it did until they shone like the dark water beneath a lamplight on a Venetian canal where Eileen had stood with her husband a few weeks before.

Eileen seemed to feel her blood warm in the palms of her hands, as if some balm had been poured over them. No man in South Africa could say a thing like that! The right thing, the thing from the heart. You had to have the assurance of Europe, of an old world of civilized human relationships behind you before you could say, simply and truthfully, a thing like that.

It was the moment for the mood of the conversation to take a turn. Waldeck said curiously, suddenly remembering, "And what ever became of Carlitta? Did you ever see Carlitta? Peter told me, in London, that she had come to live in America."

"Now that's interesting that you should ask," said Stefan. "I've wondered about her, too. I saw her once, twelve—more— thirteen years back. When first she arrived in America. She was staying quite near the hotel where you're living now. I took her out to lunch—not very sumptuous; I was rather poor at the time—and I never saw her again. She was beautiful. You remember? She was always beautiful—" he crinkled his eyes to dark slits, as if to narrow down the aperture of memory upon her— "even in a bad restaurant in New York, she was—well, the word my son would use is the best for her—she was terrific. Minute and terrific."

"That's it. That's it." Waldeck spoke around the cigar he held between his teeth, trying to draw up a light.

"We adored her," said Stefan, shaking his head slowly at the wonder of it.

"So you too, Stefan, you too?" said Eileen with a laugh.

"Oh, none of us was in love with Carlitta. Only Klaus, and he was too stupid. He doesn't count. We only adored. We knew it was useless to fall in love with her. Neither she nor we believed any one of us was good enough for her."

"So you don't think she's in New York?" asked Waldeck.

Stefan shook his head. "I did hear, from someone who knew her sister, that she had married an American and gone to live in Ohio." He stopped and chuckled congestedly. "Carlitta in Ohio. I don't believe it. . . . Well, we should move along from here now, you know. Sure there isn't *anywhere* you'd like to go before bedtime?"

The girl from South Africa remembered that one of the things she'd always wanted to do if ever she came to New York was to hear a really fat Negro woman singing torch songs, so Stefan took them to a place where the air-conditioning apparatus kept the fog of smoke and perfume and liquor fumes moving around the tables while an enormous yellow blubber of a woman accompanied her own voice, quakingly with her flesh and thunderously on the piano.

It was only two nights later that Eileen came out of the ladies' room to join her husband in a theater foyer during the interval and found him embracing a woman in a brown coat. As Waldeck held the woman away from him, by the shoulders, as if to take a good look at her after he had kissed her, Eileen saw a small face with a wide grin and really enormous eyes. As Eileen approached she noticed a tall, sandy-haired man standing by indulgently. When she reached the three, Waldeck turned to her with the pent-up, excited air he always had when he had secretly bought her a present, and he held out his hand to draw her into the company. In the moment before he spoke, Eileen felt a stir of recognition at the sight of the woman's hair, smooth brown hair in which here and there a gray filament of a coarser texture showed, refusing to conform to the classic style, center-parted and drawn back in a bun, in which the hair was worn.

"Do you know who this is?" said Waldeck almost weakly. "It's Carlitta."

Eileen was entitled to a second or two in which to be taken aback, to be speechless in the face of coincidence. In that moment, however, the coincidence did not even occur to her; she simply took in, in an intense perception outside of time, the woman before her—the brown coat open to show the collar of some nondescript silk caught together with a little brooch around the prominent tendons of the thin, creased neck; the flat, taut chest; the dowdy shoes with brown, punched-leather bows coming too high on the instep of what might have been elegant feet. And the head. Oh, that was the head she had seen before, all right; that was the head that, hair so sleek it looked like a satin turban, inclined with a mixture of coquetry, invitation, amusement and disdain toward a ridiculously long cigarette holder. That hair was brown, after all, and not the Spanish black of the photographs and imagination. And the face. Well, there is a stage in a woman's life when her face gets too thin or too fat. This face had reached that stage and become too thin. It was a prettily enough shaped face, with a drab, faded skin, as if it was exposed to but no longer joyously took color from the sun. Toward the back of the jaw line, near the ears, the skin sagged sallowly. Under the rather thick, attractive brows the twin caves of the eyes were finely puckered and mauvish. In this faded, fading face (it was like an old painting of which you are conscious that it is being faded away by the very light by which you are enabled to look at it) the eyes had lost nothing; they shone on, greedily and tremendous, just as they had always been, in the snow, reflecting the Neckar, watching the smoke unfurl to the music of the guitar. They were round eyes with scarcely any white to them, like the beautiful eyes of Negro children, and the lashes, lower as well as upper, were black and thick. Their assertion in that face was rather awful.

The woman who Waldeck said was Carlitta took Eileen's hand. "Isn't it fantastic? We're only up from Ohio this morning," she said, smiling broadly. Her teeth were small, childishly square and still good. On her neglected face the lipstick was obviously a last-minute adornment.

"And this is Edgar," Waldeck was saying, "Edgar Hicks. Carlitta's husband."

The tall, sandy-haired man shook Eileen's hand with as much flourish as a stage comedian. "Glad to know you," he said. Eileen saw that he wore sexagonal rimless glasses, and a clip across his tie spelled in pinkish synthetic gold "E.J.H."

"Carlitta Hicks—" Waldeck put out a hand and squeezed Carlitta's elbow. "I can't believe it."

"Sure is extraordinary," said Mr. Hicks. "Carlitta here and I haven't been up to New York for more than three years."

"*Ach,* no, darling," said Carlitta, frowning and smiling quickly. She used her face so much, no wonder she had worn it out. "Four at least. You remember, that last time was at Christmas." She added to Waldeck, "Once in a blue moon is enough for me. Our life . . ." She half lifted a worn hand, gave a little sudden intake of breath through her fine nostrils, as if to suggest that their life, whatever it was, was such that the pleasures of New York or anywhere else offered no rival enticement. She had still a slight German accent to soften the American pronunciation of her speech.

Everyone was incoherent. Waldeck kept saying excitedly, "I haven't been out of South Africa since I arrived there twenty years ago. I'm in New York two days and I find Carlitta!"

There was time only to exchange the names of hotels and to promise to telephone tomorrow. Then the theater bell interrupted. As they parted, Waldeck called back, "Keep Sunday lunch free. Stefan's coming. We'll all be together. . . ."

Carlitta's mouth pursed; her eyes opened wide in a pantomime "Lovely" across the crowd.

"And yet I'm not really entirely surprised," Waldeck whispered to his wife in the darkening theater. "It's been happening to us in one way or another all the time. What do you think of

27

the husband? What about Mr. Edgar Hicks from Ohio?" he added with a nudge.

In the dark, as the curtain rose, Eileen followed it with her eyes for a moment and then said, "I shouldn't have known her. I don't think I should ever have known her."

"But Carlitta hasn't changed at all!" said Waldeck.

Waldeck was on the telephone, talking to Stefan, immediately after breakfast next morning. Passing to and fro between the bedroom and the bathroom, Eileen could see him, his body hitched up onto the corner of the small desk, smiling excitedly at what must have been Stefan's quiet incredulity. "But I tell you he actually is some sort of farmer in Ohio. Yes. Well, that's what I wanted to know. I can't really say—very tall and fairish and thin. Very American. . . . Well, you know what I mean—a certain type of American, then. Slow, drawling way of speaking. Shakes your hand a long time. A week-end farmer, really. He's got some job with a firm that makes agricultural implements, in the nearby town. She said she runs pigs and chickens. Can you believe it? So is it all right about Sunday? I can imagine you are . . . *Ach*, the same old Carlitta."

Sunday was a clear, sharp spring day in New York, exactly the temperature and brightness of a winter day in Johannesburg. Stefan rang up to say he would call for the Brands at about eleven, so that they could drive around a little before meeting Carlitta and her husband for luncheon.

"Will it be all right if I wear slacks?" asked Eileen. She always wore slacks on Sundays in Johannesburg.

"Certainly not," said Stefan gravely. "You cannot lunch in a restaurant in New York in slacks."

Eileen put on a suit she had bought in London. She was filled with a childlike love and respect for Stefan; she would not have done the smallest thing to displease him or to prejudice his opinion of her. When he arrived to fetch the Brands he said, equally gravely, "You look very well in that suit," and led them to his car, where his wife, whom they had met in the course of the week, sat waiting.

His wife was perhaps an odd choice for Stefan, and then again perhaps she was not; she went along with the presidency, the wealth and the Fifth Avenue apartment, and left his inner balance unchanged. She was not so young as Eileen, but young, and a beauty. An American beauty, probably of Swedish or Norwegian stock. Hers was the style of blond beauty in which the face is darker than the hair, which was not dyed but real. It was clean and shiny and almost silvery-fair, and she wore it as such women do, straight and loose. She wore black, and when she stood up you noticed that hers was the kind of tall figure that, although the shoulders are broad and the breasts full, tapers to too narrow hips and too thin legs. Her eyes were green and brilliant, and crinkled up, friendly, and on the wrist of one beautiful ungloved hand she wore a magnificent broad antique bracelet of emeralds and diamonds. Otherwise she was unadorned, without even a wedding ring. As she shifted along the seat of the car, a pleasant fragrance stirred from her, the sort of fragrance the expensive Fifth Avenue stores were then releasing into the foyers of their shops, to convince their customers of the arrival of the time to buy spring clothes. When she smiled and spoke, in a soft American voice without much to say, her teeth showed fresh as the milk teeth of a child.

Eileen thought how different were this woman and herself (with her large, Colonial, blue-eyed, suburban prettiness) from the sort of girls with whom Waldeck and Stefan had belonged in the world that was lost to them—girls of the Twenties, restlessly independent, sensual and intellectual, citizens of the world with dramatic faces, girls such as Carlitta, inclining her dark Oriental head, had been.

The four drove through Central Park, rather threadbare after the snow and before the blossom. Then they went down to the East River, where the bridges hung like rainbows, glittering, soaring, rejoicing the heart in the sky above the water, where men have always expected to find their visions. They stopped the car at the United Nations building, and first walked along on the opposite side of the street, alongside the shabby, seedy shops, the better to see the great molten-looking façade of glass, like a river flowing upward, on the administrative block. The glass calmly reflected the skyline, as a river reflects, murky green and metallic, the reeds. Then they crossed the street and wandered about a bit along the line of flagstaffs, with the building hanging above them. The Brands resolved to come back again another day and see the interior.

"So far, there's nothing to beat your bridges," said Eileen. "Nothing."

They drove now uptown to an elegant, half-empty restaurant which had about it the air of recovering from Saturday night. There they sat drinking whisky while they waited.

"I don't know what we can do with the husband," said Waldeck, shrugging and giggling.

"That's all right," said Stefan. "Alice will talk to him. Alice can get along with anybody." His wife laughed good-naturedly.

"You know, he's *worthy* . . ." said Waldeck.

"I know," said Stefan, comforting.

"Same old Carlitta, though," said Waldeck, smiling reminiscently. "You'll see."

His wife Eileen looked at him. "Oh, she's not," she said, distressed. "She's not. Oh, how can you say that to Stefan?" The girl from South Africa looked at the two men and the woman who sat with her, and around the paneled and flower-decorated room, and suddenly she felt a very long way from home.

Just at that moment, Carlitta and Mr. Edgar Hicks came

across the room toward them. Stefan got up and went forward with palms upturned to meet them; Waldeck rose from his seat; a confusion of greetings and introductions followed. Stefan kissed Carlitta on both cheeks gently. Edgar Hicks pumped his hand. In Edgar Hicks' other hand was the Palm Beach panama with the paisley band which he had removed from his head as he entered. The hovering attendant took it from him and took Carlitta's brown coat.

Carlitta wore the niggly-patterned silk dress that had shown its collar under the coat the night at the theater, the same shoes, the same cracked beige kid gloves. But above the bun and level with the faded hairline, she had on what was obviously a brand-new hat, a hat bought from one of the thousands of "spring" hats displayed that week before Easter, a perky, mass-produced American hat of the kind which makes an American middle-class woman recognizable anywhere in the world. Its newness, its frivolous sense of its own emphemerality (it was so much in fashion that it would be old-fashioned once Easter was over) positively jeered at everything else Carlitta wore. Whether it was because she fancied the sun still painted her face the extraordinary rich glow that showed against the snow in the picture of herself laughing in Austria years ago, or whether there was some other reason, her face was again without make-up except for a rub of lipstick. Under the mixture of artificial light and daylight, faint darkening blotches, not freckles but something more akin to those liver marks elderly people get on the backs of their hands, showed on her temples and her jawline. But her eyes, of course, her eyes were large, dark, quick.

She and her husband consulted together over what they should eat, he suggesting slowly, she deciding quickly, and from then on she never stopped talking. She talked chiefly to her two friends Waldeck and Stefan, who sat on either side of her. Edgar Hicks, after a few trying minutes with Eileen, who found it difficult to respond to any of his conversational gambits, discovered that Alice Raines rode horses and, like a swamp sucking in fast all around its victim, involved her in a long, one-sided argument about the merits of two different types of saddle. Edgar preferred the one type and simply assumed that Alice must be equally adamant about the superiority of the other. Although his voice was slow, it was unceasing and steady, almost impossible to interrupt.

Eileen did not mind the fact that she was not engaged in conversation. She was free to listen to and to watch Carlitta with Stefan and Waldeck. And now and then Carlitta, forking up her coleslaw expertly as any born American, looked over to Eileen with a remark or query—"That's what *I* say, anyway," or "Wouldn't you think so?" Carlitta first told briefly about her stay in London when she left Germany, then about her coming to the United States, and her short time in New York. "In the beginning, we stayed in that hotel near Grand Central. We behaved like tourists, not like people who have come to stay. We used to go to Coney Island and rowing on the lake in Central Park, and walking up and down Fifth Avenue—just as if we were going to go back to Germany in a few weeks."

"Who's we?" asked Stefan. "Your sister?"

"No, my sister was living in a small apartment near the river. Klaus," she said, shrugging her worn shoulders with the careless, culpable gesture of an adolescent. Stefan nodded his head in confirmation toward Waldeck; of course, he remembered, Klaus had followed her or come with her to America. Poor Klaus.

"What happened to him?" asked Stefan.

"I don't know," she said. "He went to Mexico."

Her audience of three could guess very well how it had been. When she had tired of Coney Island and the outside of Fifth Avenue shops and the rowing in Central Park, Klaus had found

out once again that in the new world, as in the old, he had
nothing more than amusement value for her.

"After three months—" Carlitta had not paused in her narra-
tive—"I went to stay with my sister and brother-in-law—she
had been here some years already. But he got a job with a real-
estate scheme, and they went to live on one of the firm's housing
projects—you know, a little house, another little house next
door, a swing for the kids, the same swing next door. I came
back to New York on my own and I found a place in Greenwich
Village."

Ah, now, there was a setting in which one could imagine the
Carlitta of the photographs, the beautiful, Oriental-looking German girl from Heidelberg, with the bold, promising eyes. And
at the moment at which Eileen thought this, her ear caught the
drawl of Edgar Hicks. ". . . now, our boy's the real independent
type. Now, only the other day . . ." Edgar Hicks! Where had
Edgar Hicks come in? She looked at him, carefully separating
the flesh from the fine fringe of bone in his boiled trout, the knife
held deliberately in his freckled hand.

"Did you live in Greenwich Village?" Eileen said to him suddenly.

He interrupted his description of his boy's seat in the saddle
to turn and say, surprised, "No, ma'am, I certainly didn't. I've
never spent more than two consecutive weeks in New York in
my life." He thought Eileen's question merely a piece of tourist
curiosity, and returned to Alice Raines, his boy, and the saddle.

Carlitta had digressed into some reminiscence about Heidelberg days, but when she paused, laughing from Stefan to Waldeck with a faltering coquettishness that rose in her like a half-
forgotten mannerism, Eileen said, "Where did you and your
husband meet?"

"In a train," Carlitta said loudly and smiled, directed at her
husband.

He took it up across the table. "Baltimore and Ohio line," he said, well rehearsed. There was the feeling that all the few things he had to say had been slowly thought out and slowly spoken many times before. "I was sittin' in the diner havin' a beer with my dinner, and in comes this little person looking mighty proud and cute as you can make 'em . . ." So it went on, the usual story, and Edgar Hicks spared them no detail of the romantic convention. "Took Carlitta down to see my folks the following month and we were married two weeks after that," he concluded at last. He had expected to marry one of the local girls he'd been to school with; it was clear that Carlitta was the one and the ever-present adventure of his life. Now they had a boy who rode as naturally as an Indian and didn't watch television; he liked to raise his own chickens and have independent pocket money from the sale of eggs.

"Carlitta," Stefan said, aside, "how long were you in Greenwich Village?"

"Four years," she said shortly, replying from some other part of her mind; her attention and animation were given to the comments with which she amplified her husband's description of their child's remarkable knowledge of country lore, his superiority over town-bred children.

Eileen overheard the low, flat reply. Four years! Four years about which Carlitta had said not a word, four years which somehow or other had brought her from the arrogant, beautiful, "advanced" girl with whom Waldeck and Stefan could not fall in love because they and she agreed they were not good enough for her, to the girl who would accept Edgar Hicks a few weeks after a meeting on a train.

Carlitta felt the gaze of the girl from South Africa. A small patch of bright color appeared on each of Carlitta's thin cheekbones. Perhaps it was the wine. Perhaps it was the wine, too, that made her voice rise, so that she began to talk of her life on the

Ohio farm with a zest and insistence which made the whole table her audience. She told how she never went to town unless she had to; *never* more than once a month. How country people, like herself, discovered a new rhythm of life, something people who lived in towns had forgotten. How country people slept differently, tasted their food differently, had no nerves. "I haven't a nerve in my body, any more. Absolutely placid," she said, her sharp little gestures, her black eyes in the pinched face challenging a denial. "Nothing ever happens but a change of season," she said arrogantly to people for whom there were stock-market crashes, traffic jams, crowded exhibitions and cocktail parties. "Birth and growth among the animals and the plants. Life. Not a cement substitute." No one defended the city, but she went on as if someone had. "I live as instinctively as one of our own animals. So does my child. I mean, for one thing, we don't have to worry about clothes."

Eileen said rather foolishly, as if in reflex, "Stefan said I couldn't wear slacks to a New York restaurant today."

"Stefan was always a snob." Carlitta's little head struck like a snake.

Eileen was taken aback; she laughed nervously, looking very young. Carlitta grinned wickedly under the hat whose straw caught the light concentrically, like a gramophone record. Stefan's wife smiled serenely and politely, as if this were a joke against her husband. She had taken off the jacket of her suit, and beneath it she wore a fine lavender-colored sweater with a low, round neck. She had been resting her firm neck against her left hand, and now she took the hand away; hers was the kind of wonderful blood-mottled fair skin that dented white with the slightest pressure, filled up pink again the way the sea seeps up instantly through footprints in wet sand. She looked so healthy, so well cared for that she created a moment of repose around herself; everyone paused, resting his gaze upon her.

35

Then Carlitta's thin little sun-sallow neck twisted restlessly. "I don't know how you stand it," she said. "I don't know how you can live in New York year after year."

"We go away," Stefan said soothingly. "We go to Europe most summers, to Switzerland to my mother, or to Italy. Alice loves Italy."

"Italy," said Carlitta, suddenly turning over a piece of lobster on her plate as if she suspected that there must be something bad beneath it. "Spain."

"You remember how you went off to the Pyrenees?" Waldeck said to her. From his tone it was clear that this was quite a story, if Carlitta cared to tell it.

"You can't imagine how time flies on the farm," said Carlitta. "The years . . . just go. Sometimes, in summer, I simply walk out of the house and leave my work and go and lie down in the long grass. Then you can hear nothing, nothing at all."

"Maybe the old cow chewing away under the pear tree," said Edgar tenderly. Then with a chuckle that brought a change of tone: "Carlitta takes a big part in community affairs, too, you know. She doesn't tell you that she's on the library committee in town, and last year she was lady president of the Parent-Teacher Association. Ran a bazaar made around three hundred dollars." There was a pause. Nobody spoke. "I'm an Elk myself," he added. "That's why we're going to Philadelphia Thursday. There's a convention on over there."

Carlitta suddenly put down her fork with a gesture that impatiently terminated any current subject of conversation. (Eileen thought: she must always have managed conversation like that, long ago in smoky, noisy student rooms, jerking the talk determinedly the way she wanted it.) Her mind seemed to hark back to the subject of dress. "Last year," she said, "we invited some city friends who were passing through town to a supper party. Now it just so happened that that afternoon I could see a storm banking up. I knew that if the storm came in the night it was good-by to our hay. So I decided to make a hay-making party out of the supper. When those women came with their high-heeled fancy sandals and their gauzy frocks I put pitchforks into their hands and sent them out into the field to help get that hay in under cover. Of course I'd forgotten that they'd be bound to be rigged out in something ridiculous. You should have seen their faces!" Carlitta laughed gleefully. "Should have seen their shoes!"

The young girl from South Africa felt suddenly angry. Amid the laughter, she said quietly, "I think it was an awful thing to do. If I'd been a guest, I should flatly have refused."

"Eileen!" said Waldeck mildly. But Carlitta pointedly excluded from her notice the girl from South Africa, whom Waldeck was apparently dragging around the world and giving a good time. Carlitta was sitting stiffly, her thin hands caught together, and she never took her eyes off Alice Raines's luxuriantly fleshed neck, as if it were some object of curiosity, quite independent of a human whole.

"If only they'd seen how idiotic they looked, stumbling about," she said fiercely. Her eyes were extraordinarily dark, brimming with brightness. If her expression had not been one of malicious glee, Eileen would have said that there were tears in them.

After lunch, the Brands and the Raineses parted from the Hickses. Carlitta left the restaurant with Waldeck and Stefan on either arm, and that way she walked with them to the taxi stand at the end of the block, turning her small head from one to the other, tiny between them. "I just couldn't keep her away from her two boy friends today," Edgar said indulgently, walking behind with Eileen and Alice. At this point the thin, middle-aged woman between the two men dropped their arms, bowed down, apparently with laughter at some joke, in the extravagant fashion of a young girl, and then caught them to her again.

Edgar and Carlitta got into a taxi, and the others went in Stefan's car back to his apartment. It was three o'clock in the afternoon, but Stefan brought in a bottle of champagne. The weak sunlight coming in the windows matched the wine. "Carlitta," said Stefan before he drank. "Still 'terrific.' Beautiful." Eileen Brand, sitting on a yellow sofa, felt vaguely unhappy, as if she had wandered into the wrong room, the wrong year. She even shook her head sadly, so slowly that no one noticed.

"I told you, same old Carlitta," said Waldeck. There was a silence. "And that husband," Waldeck went on. "The life they lead. So unlike Carlitta."

"And because of that, so like her," said Stefan. "She always chose the perverse, the impossible. She obviously adores him. Just like Carlitta."

Eileen Brand wanted to stand up and beg of the two men, for their own sake—no, to save her, Eileen, from shame (oh, how could she know her reasons!)—*see* she is changed; see Carlitta is old, faded, exists, as Carlitta, no more!

She had stood up without knowing it. "What's the matter, Eileen?" Waldeck looked up. As she opened her mouth to tell him, to tell them both, a strange thing happened. It seemed that her whole mind turned over and showed her the truth. And the truth was much worse than what she had wanted to tell them. For they were right. Carlitta had not changed. They were right, but not in the way they thought. Carlitta had not changed *at all*, and that was why there was a sense of horror about meeting her; that was why she was totally unlike any one of the other friends they had met. Under that faded face, in that worn body, was the little German girl of the Twenties, arrogant in a youth that did not exist, confidently disdainful in the possession of a beauty that was no longer there.

And what did *she* think of Ohio? Of good Edgar Hicks? Even of the boy who raised chickens and didn't look at television?

"Nothing," said Eileen. "I'd like a little more wine."

It so happened that a day or two later, Stefan's business took him to Philadelphia. "Don't forget Carlitta and her husband are staying at the Grand Park," Waldeck said.

"Oh, I'll find them," said Stefan.

But when he came back to New York and dined with his wife, Waldeck and Eileen the same night, he seemed entirely to have forgotten his expressed intention. "I had a hell of a job dodging that Edgar Hicks," he said, by the way. "Wherever I went I seemed to bump into that Elk convention. They were everywhere. Everytime I saw a panama hat with a paisley band I had to double on my tracks and go the other way. Once he nearly saw me. I just managed to squeeze into an elevator in time."

And they all laughed, as if they had just managed it, too.

A Bit of Young Life

It was not yet half past nine and the cat from the bar still lay in the cane chair on the hotel veranda where she had spent the night, licking the short white fur that covered the kittens kicking in her belly.

On this Saturday, as on every other morning, the old ladies sat looking out into the bright haze that struck off the water along the Durban beach front. Soon the young men began to gather on the steps, smoking, and poking one another in the ribs as they roared with laughter, and scratching their chests through clinging polo shirts. The old ladies smiled indulgently, liking to see a bit of young life. "The boys," as the men called themselves, no matter what age they were, noticed the first girls passing on their way to town or to the beach: a beautiful pale blonde stepping along on her high heels like a well-bred poodle, and the arm-in-arm group from the even more expensive hotel next door, their bright faces disguised like dominoes' at a masked ball by the geometrical shapes of sunglasses. An Indian waiter came quickly the length of the veranda, flicking at the ash trays. The big doors leading to the dining room were bolted by the fat maître d'hôtel from Italy (how strange his Mediterranean voice sounded above the soft "prt-prt"—a quick, excited purr, rather than speech—of the Hindi dialects his waiters spoke), and the last stragglers from breakfast came out onto the veranda, a little feeble and wan from the gaiety of last night's club.

A Bit of Young Life

The cat ran in through the service door, shaking her bundle of kittens from side to side in her thin flanks.

It was going to be another hot day. By now, Indian venders, with the haggard heads of prophets, had started to pester along the balustrade, holding up trays of brass ornaments on which the sun leaped fiercely. Then the lily sellers ("Bundle of t'ree for two shilling—take them home, lady!"), and the whole life of the lily—whiskery roots, pearly bulb, tender stem, and gleaming petals, thin and brilliant as the wings of dragonflies—hung in the air for the moment of offering, still dripping from the river; they would never grow again anywhere.

Then came the double baskets of roses—peach and yellow and red—and nobody bought them, either. It seemed that nobody ever did, unless the honeymoon couple happened to be down, when, with bird noises of pleasure, the bride, her nose peeling and her hands burned to claws, would take away a bunch to put in a tooth glass.

It was at about this time every morning that the young mother and her baby boy came through the revolving doors and out onto the veranda. Every morning since Monday, when she had arrived, they had all watched her, holding the baby's hand—he in his little swimming trunks and mannish toweling gown and little boy's flop-brimmed hat like a daisy upside down on his head—and carrying under her other arm a trailing towel and a book and a beach bag with a red fish on it. She was slight and small; the baby was brown and fat. Her fragile, serious profile, beneath a wide hat, which sagged with the moistness of sea air, would be turned gently down to the child. "She looks like a child herself," one of the old ladies would say admiringly. "So young!" And then she would stir her fat columns of legs as if she were fancying herself as once, years back, just such a slip of a thing.

The boys would stop talking a moment as the young mother

passed, and then fade in again, talking in a lower key. She was attractive but withdrawn. "Why don't you speak to her, Ed?" one of them kidded that Saturday morning. (He enjoyed suggesting to others pleasures he would not dare attempt for himself.) "Go on. Speak to her in the lounge. Why don't you, Ed?" But Ed, the traveler in ladies' underwear who was taking a few days off midway on his usual southerly route, bit the end off his cigar and rearranged his navy silk scarf. "I got my own plans, thank you very much," he said, and certainly his was the room number most frequently called to answer the telephone. Here was the page now, a small Indian boy with a head of stiff black hair like porcupine quills and the voice of a ventriloquist's doll, shouting Ed's number along the veranda: "Tweu-oh-eight? . . . Tweu-oh-eight?"

The traveler turned indoors to take his call, but the rest of the boys, wondering if they should go down to the club for snooker, could still just see her at the corner, looking this way and that before she crossed in front of the stand of Zulu rickshaw boys, who rustled their peanut-shell anklets and agitated their horned and feathered heads as if a wind had suddenly taken them up. Evidently the baby was frightened, for she hurried him past, like a puppy dragged on a lead. And then she was gone. The beach was splattered with people like bright rags—so many children shouting, so many women lying face down, that no one knew where she had got to, or what magazine hid her.

But they all knew that at lunchtime she would appear again, sifting outlines of sand printing the passing of the baby's feet up the steps and over the red carpet and into the lift; she would hold him on her hip in the lift and he would look around with large, unblinking eyes, and sometimes she would wipe the sand from his moist little brow while he continued to stare, unmoved. A smell of sea and fresh flesh came from them both. Half an hour later, she would be sitting at her small table at the back of the dining room, her wet hair caught up at the back, like a horse's tail, her pale hands resting on the table in front of a glass of water.

To dinner she came rather late—she was never seen in the palm court, where the rest of the hotel silted in from five o'clock onward to drink beer or whisky, their sunburn shiny from the bath, their assorted shapes hidden in dark suits and rustling dresses—and she would walk the length of the dining room before them all with lightness, grace, and haste, as if, although she did not know them and sat alone, she did them the little courtesy of apologizing. Every night, she sipped one pale whisky, bending her slim neck to drink, her long earrings tipping, and after dinner she took coffee in the lounge, sitting back against the banked flowers near the magazine stands, so that the family parties, the old ladies, and the boys could have the larger and more prominent tables. There she would drink her coffee and then open her book, looking up frequently as the plump daughters came in to lean over their mothers' chairs a moment before leaving with their young student escorts. The older men—the boys—standing about touching cuffs and satin ties, looking at their watches, and hustling one another, would go off arguing over who was to pick up whom and in whose car, and the lounge, still floating with cigarette smoke, would empty slowly of all except the old ladies in black lace dresses, drumming their fingers absently between talk.

It was one of these old ladies who was the first to speak to the young woman. The lounge was full one evening and there was a vacant chair at her table. The old lady came to rest near it. "You're waiting for somebody, perhaps?" she asked tentatively.

The pretty, narrow, self-possessed face, which might have been rather frightening and haughty toward an old lady, dropped its look of aloof reserve, as if the girl had been unconscious of it, and opened into a smile of such warm pleasure and charm that the old lady was quite bewildered. Not only was she tolerated, she was welcomed, and spoken to with attention and interest. Her talk of the hotel food, the blood pressure that had brought her to stay on doctor's orders for three months, the hint or two about the qualities of her poor dead husband—she could tell them all without the harassing awareness of the listener's impatience to which she was accustomed when talking to other young people. And what sense of the present have old ladies to live on unless they collect living evidence of it in curiosity about young people's lives? "Tell me," said the old lady, "your husband's not here? You're all on your own, shame?"

She smiled. "All alone," she admitted. "But, of course, my baby."

"What a lovely little thing!" The old lady spoke as if she had never seen a baby before. "What a darling he is! I always watch you, you know, going out with him, and he's so fat! I hear him talking."

"Oh, he's learned to say everything since we've been here!" The young mother was excited; you could imagine her proudly writing it home; that would be the joy of it, really.

"What might your name be, if you'll excuse me?" The old lady hoped for an unrecognized daughter or niece of one of her cronies from upcountry. And she was not to be disappointed entirely. "Then your husband must be William Maisel's son," she said triumphantly when she heard the name. Well, no; old William was the husband's uncle, the young mother said.

"A very nice family, my dear, a very nice family." The old lady sat back and smiled satisfaction on the young woman's behalf. The young woman's smile deepened in frank acknowledgment of and apology for William Maisel's wealth and solidity. There followed a lot of questions about the ramifications of the house of Maisel—the older members, who had made the money out of hides; the middle-aged ones, who had trebled it on the stock exchange; and the young ones, who spent it becoming doctors and lawyers and even, in one instance, a painter. The young woman laughed, confused, and though she answered to the best of her knowledge, explained that really she saw them all only at weddings and other family gatherings. The old lady understood; a young wife feels strange in the first few years of her apprenticeship to her husband's family. But still, a Maisel, even if he was only old William's nephew instead of his son, would not marry *anybody*, that was certain.

"Well, of course, my dear girl—" The old lady gave her permission to the young woman to be excused; she must slip upstairs to see if the baby was asleep. And the old lady's eyes followed the small, slender figure in the swaying frock, making its way over the carpets. At the door of the lift, the young woman unexpectedly turned and smiled.

After that, everyone spoke to her. The honeymoon couple admired the baby in the lift. The mother shook her head in pleasurable denial of his obvious charm (sometimes, as now, she wore two pigtails when she went to the beach) and apologized for the noise he made in the early mornings; the honeymoon couple had the adjourning room. "Oh, but we never hear him, really!" the bride exclaimed. "We don't know how you do it, keeping him so quiet—we think it's wonderful!"

"It's a full-time job, I assure you," she said, and laughed with mock grimness.

"Wonderful! Not much of a holiday for you," said the bride, womanly and confidential. "I'd jolly well make sure my husband came along and did his share!" And they all laughed, including the husband, who by the same time the following year would be folding baby carriages and balancing napkin bags, as harassed as he was now tenderly amused.

"Where's the little chap?" people would call out at the most unlikely hours. "Dead to the world," the young woman would say, with a smile, going on her way with a new book in her hand.

Even the boys got to know her. It was the evening she wore her black dress—and she looked particularly young in black, as if her childlike boning, her gentle haughtiness, her tender air, showed up in direct ratio to the sophistication of her clothes. When she wore black, she wore all black; this dress sloped down around her shoulders, flowed out around her waist, was of a heavy material that had a somber voice as well as other qualities. She sat in it, with her hands, small and boneless as the hands in a Renaissance portrait, in her lap. She had finished both her after-dinner coffee and her book, and was simply looking around her at the lounge filled with people—without boldness, invitation, or embarrassment.

The traveler in ladies' underwear was sitting nearby, ordering a liqueur for himself and another of the boys. (He liked to think of himself as a bit of a connoisseur in most things.) While he was discussing the choice with the waiter, he sat facing the young woman, in the full line of her vision, and this made him feel that there was something rude about ordering refreshment under her very nose; he felt the guilty shyness that paralyzes a child dipping into a bag of sweets under the eyes of grownups, to whom he has been taught it should be offered first, and this emboldened him to do what he had wanted to do for a number of nights. "Excuse me," he said, getting up and pulling in his bottom stiffly, "but would you care to join us in a friendly liqueur? My friend and I here are just about to have one."

And again, rather astonishingly, she smiled—gave the full charm of her face to him like a gift. It was the pleasantest of shocks for Ed, since, for him, as it had been for the old lady, there was that about her that made one fear a rebuff; one did not know how to begin to talk to her, any more than one would know how to open a conversation with a nun or a member of a royal family. "Why, thank you," she said, and her chair was brought over, her drink was ordered, and there she sat, with the boys.

Two days of rain washed away any remaining stiffness. Shut in by such impenetrable sheets of gray water that it seemed the sea had come up silently over the promenade and the street and was looking in at the windows, they all huddled together in the coziness of electric light turned on at ten o'clock in the morning: old ladies, matrons and daughters, the boys, and, of course, the young mother, now wearing a downy sweater like a newly hatched chick. She sat with the old ladies and she sat with the boys, and this impartiality touched the old ladies and maddened and delighted the boys. "What's the matter with us?" they would chaff. "Would you rather talk knitting patterns than have us around you?" And she would get that teasing darkening of her eyes that was like a blush and go back to sit with them. They were admiring, they were lightly familiar, but always, as she counted up their scores when they played cards, or turned the stem of her whisky glass, the little hand, unobtrusive, dangling, one finger ringed, like a sapling, with a narrow wedding band, lay before them.

She was sitting with a group of the boys when one of them asked her, "How's your husband getting on without you? I'll bet he's lonely as hell."

"Is he a good-looking guy?" asked a second.

"You bet," said a third. "Trust her."

She said, "He's a big, fair man."

"What'd I tell you! See?"

"Better-looking than us?" They laughed.

"You not worried about leaving him at home?" said Ed watching her face. "Not afraid he'll run around?"

She did not answer but, looking straight at him and smiling deeply, shook her head very hard, so that her hair swung.

That decided him. "Crazy about the chap, huh?" he said wonderingly, sympathetic as well as curious.

"Oh, Ed, leave it alone, man. The girl's married. You can't ask things like that," one of the others said.

And all the boys laughed, turning away from something that was not for them to look at.

"Well, he's certainly got nothing to worry about with *you*," said Ed, thinking of the futile invitations to the club, to dinner, to the cinema he had given her in the past few days.

"But I've told you, honestly," she insisted, smiling and lifting her eyebrows with earnest concern. "It's not that. I wouldn't be silly about that. It's just that I can't go out at night and leave the baby."

"All right. I know," he said, with a laugh. "I don't blame you. You're just missing the guy badly. But it's silly, you know— there's no harm in a show, or a bit of dancing. I'm sure he wouldn't want you to mope around, going to bed in the evenings the way you do."

They all tried to get her to go out with them, but without success. She was charming, she was regretful, she was wistful—a young and pretty girl shut up in the hotel with a baby—but she gently refused. Her unavailability made the availability of others, of greater and more obvious attraction, pall. For the traveler, particularly, who "knew how to take a girl out," if you followed his meaning (flowers, fine dinners—the lot), and had a large and miscellaneous collection of terrific women (women with style, you know) in this as in every other town. Somehow he went reluctantly every night to call for the receptionists and models, with their big, dazzling bodies and their enthusiasm for being shown off in the best places. He wanted to go out with *her*, just once—this young woman whose only amorous tussle was rolling her baby over and over on the beach, nibbling his little neck while he laughed, who read so many books Ed had never heard of, who, despite her friendliness and courtesy and lack of affectation, unwittingly left an impress on him like the pressure of a seal: he saw it; it was the mark of someone too good for him. So, nightly, he sighed, straightened the carnation in his button hole, and went out into the town.

The old ladies, and even the matrons, who were a little suspicious of her, since they had daughters to arrange for, noticed with approval that she never went out with men.

"Well, they're very fine people, the Maisels," the old lady said, with the air of authority about the young woman that was growing upon her day by day. "You can't expect her to behave like a bit of rubbish, like those other young women. She's not the type, that's all there is to it. And he's a charming boy, the husband—" she was really beginning to believe that she knew him—"oh, charming! Nothing like it here." And she waved a fastidious hand at the boys—thickset, good-natured creatures, quite unaware of the scorn in which they were held.

It was true, other young women could take an example from her, the old ladies agreed. Still, it was a shame. Young couples should go away together. After all, she also wanted a bit of young life.

The young woman was the darling of the hotel. Yet she did not seem entirely happy. In fact, the more attention was centered on her, the more the baby was played with and presented with toys and the two of them were taken for drives and trips across the bay, and she was welcomed and invited to join groups at tea or drinks, the more frequently moods of pensiveness came upon her. Often, she would rest her chin on the head of the baby and look out to the sea; her mouth pulled a little at one corner, as if something tugged at her. If Ed was there, he would say at once, under the talk of others, "Feeling a bit blue?" Or

"Never mind, you'll appreciate him more when you get back to him." Then she would come to the surface with a little start, which he found delightful, and begin talking again.

In the early evening, sometimes, the mood lasted longer, and it seemed to the boys as if a kind of space cleared in the air around her. The talk of racing and the road and the stock exchange precluded any romantic nonsense, but, even when she was wearing her bare sun dress, the slope of her shoulders and the unconscious droop of her head, oval and smooth behind the curly fuzz of the baby's, suggested to them not the early Florentine madonnas of which they had never heard, but something further back even than that—the inspiration that gave rise to the paintings themselves.

Sometimes, too, there would show in her face a streak of strain, which, if the talk flagged for a moment, became the blankness of concealed distress. It was as if she had suddenly heard something that the talk usually managed to drown.

On the morning of the sixteenth day of the young woman's stay, Ed found her at the reception desk with a pile of notes under her hand. "Settling up your debts?" he asked, smiling. He knew he looked good in his blond Palm Beach trousers and that darkish shirt; a model had said to him the day before, "Ed, anyone can see you don't buy your clothes in *this* town." The young woman was pale, shadows showed under her eyes when she smiled, her hair was not as carefully done as usual; she had never looked more fascinating to him. "I've decided to go home," she said. "I'm paying up."

Home? It was a real pang that he felt, with his surprise. "But how long were you supposed to be here? You've got another two weeks!" he protested.

"I know," she said. "I'm—I'm suddenly fed up. I woke fed up with it. So I've managed to get a plane reservation and I'm going." She was obviously embarrassed; he had never heard her speak so jerkily and lamely before. She even tried a funny little laugh, which had to turn into a cough.

"Well, I'm damned!" he said.

But she simply stood there at the counter in embarrassment, offering no explanation.

"You're a silly girl," he went on. "Really, you're a silly girl. You'll get over it in a day or two and you'll enjoy the rest of your holiday. It's a shame for the kid, too. He's having a good time. And you can do with a bit of weight. What'll your husband say?"

She shook her head, catching her lower lip in a smile, like a guilty child.

"When you going?" he asked.

"I'm on the three-o'clock plane," she said.

"Go on," he said, urging her bluffly. "You phone them up and cancel it."

But she just stood there looking at him. "No." She smiled shyly, shakily. "I'm going."

"Look here," he said, taking her by the arm and looking around to see if anyone could overhear. He was entirely fatherly now. "I know how it is. It's just that we're not your sort, are we? You miss him, and you just haven't found any company your *own* sort."

She protested. "No, you've all been terribly nice. Everyone's been so nice." He looked into her face and she looked into his, smiling.

But suddenly he saw that the smile was merely something done with her face, and that, really, she was about to cry. It was incredible—not a thing she would ever do or he would ever be allowed to witness in *her*. He was so frightened that he drew back as if he had opened a door by mistake, and he suddenly gave in. "Look," he said. "Don't you worry about the airport.

I'll get the car round and take you and the kid. Now, what's
happening with the luggage? Will you get that ready, so that
we can send it on ahead?"

He arranged everything—saw that the keys of her cases were
in her handbag and her forwarding address left at the hotel,
even promised to send on to her some snapshots of the baby
that had been taken by the beach photographer a day or two
back and were not yet ready. The news of her imminent departure flew around the hotel by lunchtime. When she came down,
all ready to leave, in her black suit and an elegant hat that bent
back dramatically from her brow with a sweep of jet feathers,
there was somehow the unexpressed idea that she had been
recalled, and the drama of the idea, the sense of emotion out of
sight, made the other hotel guests feel a heightened touch of
regret. "We're going to lose you! What a *shame,* my dear" came
to her from all parts of the dining room. And the dear little
chap— Ah, there he was, adorable with his reddish-blond fluff
and the wide mouth that was not his mother's; he must look like
his daddy. ("Is it going to see its daddy again, then!") Even the
Indian waiters collected in the foyer around the hand luggage.
"Good-by, good-by, Big Man," they said to the baby. Then Ed's
Chrysler drew up twinkling at the door; the sun plunged a
thousand knives that glanced off its well-polished pate and
chromium flanks. She came down the steps with the child by the
hand, in her city clothes already a stranger to the humid, sea-
blown air, the rickshaw boys dozing in their shafts, and the yells
of paddling children. The baby boy turned around unprompted
and waved a fist. Then they were gone.

"Well," Ed said to her as they reached the airport, "in two
hours you'll be back home." Watching from the visitors' barrier,
he saw them cross the field and climb the steps into the plane
together. At the top, she turned, unconsciously duplicating the

53

child's gesture, and gave him a last little wave of her hand, unmistakable even in its black glove.

Among all the other people trooping away, he went slowly back to the car trying to decide whether he should spend the rest of the afternoon going for a swim or playing snooker. He settled on snooker. There was not even the scent of her left in the car, the way other women shed their perfume like bitches leaving a trail for the male.

By Tuesday morning, it was all out. The Johannesburg papers are flown down to the coast within an hour or two of issue, and everyone buys one as hungrily as if he were an exile instead of a willing holidaymaker. There it was, not even halfway down the matrimonial section of the court-judgments column along which everyone runs a half-hopeful eye: "Maisel versus Maisel. Hugh Watcham Maisel against Patricia Edwina Maisel (born van Helm)." And that very afternoon someone arrived at the hotel who knew the whole story—a most scandalous story. (The lives people live nowadays!) The wife had been carrying on with this other man ever since the baby was born, right in the house, under the husband's nose. (Oh, the child was the husband's, all right; apparently it was the image of him.) People said she lived with both of them at once for months on end—never turned a hair. Others blamed the husband; he should have thrown her out. Evidently the lover had originally been interested in her younger sister, which made it worse; she snatched him from under her sister's nose.

Then when, a day or two later, the papers reported the divorce proceedings in detail, the whole business was confirmed. The plaintiff this. The defendant that. Dirty business, said the boys wonderingly, crowding round the paper. The whole hotel, as if it had been stung, talked of nothing else. A kind of pyre of recollections and discussion piled up on her vanished presence, and went on smoking for days.

At home, five hundred miles away, the young woman sat and read about herself in the paper. The resort labels were peeling off her luggage in the steam of the bathroom, where it was stored on top of a cupboard. Sometimes she spent absent half hours gently rubbing the flaking brown skin that flew like powder from her arms.

In a day or two, an envelope came for her, postmarked "Durban" and addressed in an unfamiliar masculine handwriting. Inside were two postcard photographs of the baby.

Anonymous, dumb, it was a last protective touch on the elbow from Ed, the traveler in ladies' underwear. She took an odd comfort from it, and at the same moment became conscious of a guilt sharper, a burden of duplicity heavier, than she had felt for all the lies, the faithlessness, the cunning of her passion. A tear, which seemed to have the little tickling feet of a centipede, ran down the side of her nose.

Now no one had been spared—no one at all.

hen Mrs. Clara Hansen travels, she keeps herself to herself. This is usually easy, for she has money, has been a baroness and a beauty, and has survived dramatic suffering. The crushing presence of these states in her face and bearing is nearly always enough to stop the loose mouths of people who find themselves in her company. It is only the very stupid, the senile, or the self-obsessed who blunder up to assail that face, withdrawn as a castle, across the common ground of a public dining room.

Last month, when Mrs. Hansen left Cape Town for Johannesburg by train, an old lady occupying the adjoining compartment tried to make of her apologies, as she pressed past in the corridor, loaded with string bags and paper parcels, an excuse to open one of those pointless conversations between strangers which arise in the nervous moments of departure. Mrs. Hansen was giving last, calm instructions to Alfred, her Malay chauffeur and manservant, whom she was leaving behind, and she did not look up. Alfred had stowed her old calf cases from Europe firmly and within reach in her compartment, which, of course, influence with the reservation office had insured she would have to herself all the way. He had watched her put away, in a special pocket in her handbag, her train ticket, a ticket for her de-luxe bed, a book of tickets for her meals. He had made sure that she had her two yellow sleeping pills and the red pills—for that feeling of pressure in her head—lying in cotton wool in her silver pillbox. He himself had seen that her two pairs of spectacles, one for distance, one for reading, were in her overnight bag, and had noted that her lorgnette hung below the diamond bow on the bosom of her dress. He had taken down the folding table from its niche above the wash-basin in the compartment, and placed on it the three magazines she had sent him to buy at the bookstall, along with the paper from Switzerland that, this week, had been kept aside, unread, for the journey.

For a full fifteen minutes before the train left, he and his employer were free to ignore the to-and-fro of voices and luggage, the heat and confusion. Mrs. Hansen murmured down to him; Alfred, chauffeur's cap in hand, dusty sunlight the color of beer dimming the oil shine of his black hair, looked up from the platform and made low assent. They used the half sentences, the hesitations, and the slight changes of tone or expression of people who speak the language of their associa-tion in the country of their own range of situation. It was hardly speech; now and then it sank away altogether, into the minds of each, but the sounds of the station did not well up in its place. Alfred dangled the key of the car on his little finger. The old face beneath the toque noted it, and the lips, the infinitely weary corners of the eyes drooped in the indication of a smile. Would he really put the car away into the garage for six weeks after he'd seen that it was oiled and greased?

Unmindful of the finger, his face empty of the satisfaction of a month's wages in advance in his pocket, two friends waiting to be picked up in a house in the Malay quarter of the town, he said, "I must make a note that I mustn't send Madam's letters on after the twenty-sixth."

"No. Not later than the twenty-sixth."

Did she know? With that face that looked as if it knew everything, could she know, too, about the two friends in the house in the Malay quarter?

She said—and neither of them listened—"In case of need, you've always got Mr. Van Dam." Van Dam was her lawyer. This remark, like a stone thrown idly into a pool to pass the time, had fallen time and again between them into the widening hiatus of parting. They had never questioned or troubled to define its meaning. In ten years, what need had there ever been that Alfred couldn't deal with himself, from a burst pipe in the flat to a jammed fastener on Mrs. Hansen's dress?

Alfred backed away from the ice-cream carton a vendor thrust under his nose; the last untidy lump of canvas luggage belonging to the woman next door thumped down like a dusty animal at Mrs. Hansen's side; the final bell rang.

As the train ground past out of the station, Alfred stood quite still with his cap between his hands, watching Mrs. Hansen. He always stood like that when he saw her off. And she remained at the window, as usual, smiling slightly, inclining her head slightly, as if in dismissal. Neither waved. Neither moved until the other was borne out of sight.

When the station was gone and Mrs. Hansen turned slowly to enter her compartment to the quickening rhythm of the train, she met the gasping face of the old woman next door. Fat overflowed not only from her jowl to her neck, but from her ankles to her shoes. She looked like a pudding that had risen too high and run down the sides of the dish. She was sprinkling cologne onto a handkerchief and hitting with it at her face as if she were trying to kill something. "Rush like that, it's no good for you," she said. "Something went wrong with my son-in-law's car, and what a job to get a taxi! *They* don't care—get you here today or tomorrow. I thought I'd never get up those steps."

Mrs. Hansen looked at her. "When one is no longer young,

one must always give oneself exactly twice as much time as one needs. I have learned that. I beg your pardon." And she passed before the woman into her compartment.

The woman stopped her in the doorway. "I wonder if they're serving tea yet? Shall we go along to the dining car?"

"I always have my tea brought to me in my compartment," said Mrs. Hansen, in the low, dead voice that had been considered a pity in her day but that now made young people who could have been her grandchildren ask if she had been an actress. And she slid the door shut.

Alone, she stood a moment in the secretive privacy, where everything swayed and veered in obedience to the gait of the train. She began to look anxiously over the stacked luggage, her lips moving, but she had grown too set to adjust her balance from moment to moment, and suddenly she found herself sitting down. The train had dumped her out of the way. Good thing, too, she thought, chastising herself impatiently—counting the luggage, fussing, when in ten years Alfred's never forgotten anything. Old fool, she told herself, old fool. Her aging self often seemed to her an enemy of her real self, the self that had never changed. The enemy was a stupid one, fortunately; she merely had to keep an eye on it in order to keep it outwitted. Other selves that had arisen in her life had been much worse; how terrible had been the struggle with some of *them*!

She sat down with her back to the engine, beside the window, and put on her reading glasses and took up the newspaper from Switzerland. But for some minutes she did not read. She heard again inside herself the words *alone, alone*, just the way she had heard them fifty-nine years ago when she was twelve years old and crossing France by herself for the first time. As she had sat there, bolt upright in the corner of a carriage, her green velvet fur-trimmed cloak around her, her hamper beside her, and the locket with the picture of her grandfather hidden in her hand, she had felt a swelling terror of exhilaration, the dark, drowning swirl of cutting loose, had tasted the strength to be brewed out of self-pity and the calm to be lashed together out of panic that belonged to other times and other journeys approaching her from the distance of her future. *Alone, alone.* This that her real self had known years before it happened to her—before she had lived the journey that took her from a lover, or those others that took her from the alienated faces of madness and death—that same self remembered years after those journeys had dropped behind into the past. Now she was alone, lonely, lone—whatever you liked to call it—all the time. There is nothing of the drama of an occasion about it, for me, she reminded herself dryly. Still, there was no denying it, *alone* was not the same as *lonely;* even the Old Fool could not blur the distinction of that. The blue silk coat quivered where Alfred had hung it, the bundle of magazines edged along the table, and somewhere above her head a loose strap tapped. She felt again aloneness as the carapace that did not shut her off but shielded her strong sense of survival—against it, and all else.

She opened the paper from Switzerland, and, with her left foot (the heat had made it a little swollen) up on the seat opposite, she began to read. She felt lulled and comfortable and was not even irritated by the thuds and dragging noises coming from the partition behind her head; it was clear that that was the woman next door—*she* must be fussing with her luggage. Presently a steward brought a tea tray, which Alfred had ordered before the train left. Mrs. Hansen drew in her mouth with pleasure at the taste of the strong tea, as connoisseurs do when they drink old brandy, and read the afternoon away.

She took her dinner in the dining car because she had established in a long experience that it was not a meal that could be expected to travel train corridors and remain hot, and also because there was something shabby, something *petit bourgeois*, about taking meals in the stuffy cubicle in which you were also to sleep. She tidied her hair around the sides of her toque—it was a beautiful hat, one of four, always the same shape, that she had made for herself every second year in Vienna—took off her rings and washed her hands, and powdered her nose, pulling a critical, amused face at herself in the compact mirror. Then she put on her silk coat, picked up her handbag, and went with upright dignity, despite the twitchings and lurchings of the train, along the corridors to the dining car. She seated herself at an empty table for two, beside a window, and, of course, although it was early and there were many other seats vacant, the old woman from the compartment next door, entering five minutes later, came straight over and sat down opposite her.

Now it was impossible not to speak to the woman, and Mrs. Hansen listened to her with the distant patience of an adult giving half an ear to a child, and answered her when necessary, with a dry simplicity calculated to be far above her head. Of course, Old Fool was tempted to unbend, to lapse into the small boastings and rivalries usual between two old ladies. But Mrs. Hansen would not allow it, and certainly not with this woman— this acquaintance thrust upon her in a train. It was bad enough that, only the week before, Old Fool had led her into one of these pathetic pieces of senile nonsense, cleverly disguised—Old Fool could be wily enough—but, just the same, unmistakably the kind of thing that people found boring. It was about her teeth. At seventy-one, they were still her own, which was a self-evident miracle. Yet she had allowed herself, at a dinner party given by some young friends who were obviously impressed by her, to tell a funny story (not quite true, either) about how, when she was a week-end guest in a house with an oversolicitous hostess, the jovial host had hoaxed his wife by impressing upon her the importance of providing a suitable receptacle for their guest's teeth when she took them out overnight. There was a glass beside the jug of water on the bedside table; the hostess appeared, embarrassedly, with another. "But, my dear, what is the other glass for?" The denouement, laughter, etc. Disgusting. Good teeth as well as bad aches and pains must be kept to oneself; when one is young, one takes the first for granted, and does not know the existence of the others.

So it was that when the menu was held before the two women, Mrs. Hansen ignored the consternation into which it seemed to plunge her companion, forestalled the temptation to enter, by contributing her doctor's views, into age's passionate preoccupation with diet, and ordered fish.

"D'you think the fish'll be all right? I always wonder, on a train, you know . . ." said the woman from the next compartment.

Mrs. Hansen merely confirmed her order to the waiter by lowering her eyes and settling her chin slightly. The woman decided to begin at the beginning, with soup. "Can't go far wrong with soup, can you?"

"Don't wait, please," said Mrs. Hansen when the soup came.

The soup was watery, the woman said. Mrs. Hansen smiled her tragic smile, indulgently. The woman decided that she'd keep Mrs. Hansen company, and risk the fish, too. The fish lay beneath a pasty blanket of white sauce, and while Mrs. Hansen calmly pushed aside the sauce and ate, the woman said, "There's nothing like the good, clean food cooked in your own kitchen."

Mrs. Hansen put a forkful of fish to her mouth and, when she had finished it, spoke at last. "I'm afraid it's many years since I had my own kitchen for more than a month or two a year."

"Well, of course, if you go about a lot, you get used to strange food, I suppose. I find I can't eat half the stuff they put in front of you in hotels. Last time I was away, there were some days I didn't know what to have at all for lunch. I was in one of the

best hotels in Durban, and all there was was this endless curry
—curry this, curry that—and a lot of dried-up cold meats."

Mrs. Hansen shrugged. "I always find enough for my needs.
It does not matter much."

"What can you do? I suppose this sauce is the wrong thing
for me, but you've got to take what you get when you're traveling," said the woman. She broke off a piece of bread and passed
it swiftly around her plate to scoop up what was left of the
sauce. "Starchy," she added.

Mrs. Hansen ordered a cutlet, and, after a solemn study of
the menu, the other woman asked for the item listed immediately below the fish—oxtail stew. While they were waiting she
ate bread and butter, and, shifting her mouthful comfortably
from one side of her mouth to the other, accomplished a shift of
her attention, too, as if her jaw and her brain had some simple
mechanical connection. "You're not from here, I suppose?" she
asked, looking at Mrs. Hansen with the appraisal reserved for
foreigners and the license granted by the tacit acceptance of
old age on both sides.

"I have lived in the Cape, on and off, for some years," said
Mrs. Hansen. "My second husband was Danish, but settled
here."

"I could have married again. I'm not boasting, I mean, but I
did have the chance, if I'd've wanted to," said the woman.
"Somehow, I couldn't face it, after losing my first—fifty-two,
that's all, and you'd have taken a lease on his life. Ah, those doctors. No wonder I feel I can't trust them a minute."

Mrs. Hansen parted the jaws of her large, elegant black bag
to take out a handkerchief; the stack of letters that she always
had with her—new ones arriving to take the place of old with
every airmail—lay exposed. Thin letters, fat letters, big envelopes, small ones; the torn edges of foreign stamps, the large,

sloping, and small, crabbed hands of foreigners writing foreign tongues. The other woman looked down upon them like a tourist, curious, impersonally insolent, envious. "Of course, if I'd been the sort to run about a lot, I suppose it might have been different. I might have met someone really *congenial*. But there's my daughters. A mother's responsibility is never over—that's what I say. When they're little, it's little troubles. When they're grown up, it's big ones. They're all nicely married, thank God, but you know, it's always something—one of them sick, or one of the grandchildren, bless them . . . I don't suppose you've got any children. Not even from your first, I mean?"

"No," said Mrs. Hansen. "No." And the lie, as always, came to her as a triumph against that arrogant boy (Old Fool persisted in thinking of him as a gentle-browed youth bent over a dachshund puppy, though he was a man of forty-five by now) whom truly she had made, as she had warned she would, no son of hers. When the lie was said, it had the effect of leaving her breathless, as if she had just crowned a steep rise. Firmly and calmly, she leaned forward and poured herself a glass of water, as one who has deserved it.

"My, it does look fatty," the other woman was saying over the oxtail, which had just been placed before her, "My doctor'd have a fit if he knew I was eating this." But eat it she did, and cutlet and roast turkey to follow. Mrs. Hansen never knew whether or not her companion rounded off the meal with rhubarb pie (the woman had remarked, as she saw it carried past, that it looked soggy), because she herself had gone straight from cutlet to coffee, and, her meal finished, excused herself before the other was through the turkey course. Back in her compartment, she took off her toque at last and tied a gray chiffon scarf around her head. Then she took her red-and-gold Florentine-leather cigarette case from her bag and settled down to smoke her nightly cigarette while she waited for the man to come and convert her seat into the de-luxe bed Alfred had paid for in advance.

It seemed to Mrs. Hansen that she did not sleep very well during the early part of the night, though she did not quite know what it was that made her restless. She was wakened, time and again, apparently by some noise that had ceased by the time she was conscious enough to identify it. The third or fourth time this happened, she woke to silence and a sense of absolute cessation, as if the world had stopped turning. But it was only the train that had stopped. Mrs. Hansen lay and listened. They must be at some deserted siding in the small hours; there were no lights shining in through the shuttered window, no footsteps, no talk. The voice of a cricket, like a fingernail screeching over glass, sounded, providing, beyond the old woman's closed eyes, beyond the dark compartment and the shutters, a landscape of grass, dark, and telephone poles.

Suddenly the train gave a terrific reverberating jerk, as if it had been given a violent push. All was still again. And in the stillness, Mrs. Hansen became aware of groans coming from the other side of the partition against which she lay. The groans came, bumbling and nasal, through the wood and leather; they sounded like a dog with its head buried in a cushion, worrying at the feathers. Mrs. Hansen breathed out once, hard, in annoyance, and turned over; the greedy old pig, now she was suffering agonies of indigestion from that oxtail, of course. The groans continued at intervals. Once there was a muffled tinkling sound, as if a spoon had been dropped. Mrs. Hansen lay tense with irritation, waiting for the train to move on and drown the woman's noise. At last, with a shake that quickly settled into a fast clip, they were off again, lickety-lack, lickety-lack, past (Mrs. Han-

66

sen could imagine) the endless telephone poles, the dark grass, the black-coated cricket. Under the dialogue of the train, she was an unwilling eavesdropper to the vulgar intimacies next door; then either the groans stopped or she fell asleep in spite of them, for she heard nothing till the steward woke her with the arrival of early-morning coffee.

Mrs. Hansen sponged herself, dressed, and had a quiet breakfast, undisturbed by anyone, in the dining car. The man sitting opposite her did not even ask her so much as to pass the salt. She was back in her compartment, reading, when the ticket examiner came in to take her ticket away (they would be in Johannesburg soon), and, of course, she knew just where to lay her hand on it, in her bag. He leaned against the doorway while she got it out. "Hear what happened?" he said.

"What happened?" she said uncertainly, screwing up her face because he spoke indistinctly, like most young South Africans.

"Next door," he said. "The lady next door, elderly lady. She died last night."

"She died? That woman died?" She stood up and questioned him closely, as if he were irresponsible.

"Yes," he said, checking the ticket on his list. "The bed boy found her this morning, dead in her bed. She never answered when the steward came round with coffee, you see."

"My God," said Mrs. Hansen. "My God. So she died, eh?"

"Yes, lady." He held out his hand for her ticket; he had the tale to tell all up and down the train.

With a gesture of futility, she gave it to him.

After he had gone, she sank down on the seat, beside the window, and watched the veld go by, the grasses streaming past in the sun like the long black tails of the widow birds blowing where they swung upon the fences. She had finished her paper and magazines. There was no sound but the sound of the hurrying train.

When they reached Johannesburg she had all her luggage trimly closed and ready for the porter from the hotel at which she was going to stay. She left the station with him within five minutes of the train's arrival, and was gone before the doctor, officials, and, she supposed, newspaper reporters came to see the woman taken away from the compartment next door. What could I have said to them? she thought, pleased with her sensible escape. Could I tell them she died of greed? Better not to be mixed up in it.

And then she thought of something. Newspaper reporters. No doubt there would be a piece in the Cape papers tomorrow. ELDERLY WOMAN FOUND DEAD IN CAPE–JOHANNESBURG TRAIN.

As soon as she had signed the register at the hotel she asked for a telegram form. She paused a moment, leaning on the marble-topped reception desk, looking out over the heads of the clerks. Her eyes, which were still handsome, crinkled at the corners; her nostrils lifted; her mouth, which was still so shapely because of her teeth, turned its sad corners lower in her reluctant, calculating smile. She printed Alfred's name and the address of the flat in Cape Town, and then wrote quickly, in the fine hand she had mastered more than sixty years ago: "It was not me. Clara Hansen."

Which New Era Would That Be?

ake Alexander, a big, fat colored man, half Scottish, half African Negro, was shaking a large pan of frying bacon on the gas stove in the back room of his Johannesburg printing shop when he became aware that someone was knocking on the door at the front of the shop. The sizzling fat and the voices of the five men in the back room with him almost blocked out sounds from without, and the knocking was of the steady kind that might have been going on for quite a few minutes. He lifted the pan off the flame with one hand and with the other made an impatient silencing gesture, directed at the bacon as well as the voices. Interpreting the movement as one of caution, the men hurriedly picked up the tumblers and cups in which they had been taking their end-of-the-day brandy at their ease, and tossed the last of it down. Little yellow Klaas, whose hair was like ginger-colored wire wool, stacked the cups and glasses swiftly and hid them behind the dirty curtain that covered a row of shelves.

"Who's that?" yelled Jake, wiping his greasy hands down his pants.

There was a sharp and playful tattoo, followed by an English voice: "Me—Alister. For heaven's sake, Jake!"

The fat man put the pan back on the flame and tramped through the dark shop, past the idle presses, to the door, and flung it open. "Mr. Halford!" he said. "Well, good to see you. Come in, man. In the back there, you can't hear a thing." A young Englishman with gentle eyes, a stern mouth, and flat, colorless hair, which grew in an untidy, confused spiral from a double crown, stepped back to allow a young woman to enter ahead of him. Before he could introduce her, she held out her hand to Jake, smiling, and shook his firmly. "Good evening. Jennifer Tetzel," she said.

"Jennifer, this is Jake Alexander," the young man managed to get in, over her shoulder.

The two had entered the building from the street through an archway lettered "NEW ERA BUILDING." "Which new era would that be?" the young woman had wondered aloud, brightly, while they were waiting in the dim hallway for the door to be opened, and Alister Halford had not known whether the reference was to the discovery of deep-level gold mining that had saved Johannesburg from the ephemeral fate of a mining camp in the Nineties, or to the optimism after the settlement of labor troubles in the Twenties, or to the recovery after the world went off the gold standard in the Thirties—really, one had no idea of the age of these buildings in this run-down end of the town. Now, coming in out of the deserted hallway gloom, which smelled of dust and rotting wood—the smell of waiting—they were met by the live, cold tang of ink and the homely, lazy odor of bacon fat—the smell of acceptance. There was not much light in the deserted workshop. The host blundered to the wall and switched on a bright naked bulb, up in the ceiling. The three stood blinking at one another for a moment: a colored man with the fat of the man of the world upon him, grossly dressed—not out of poverty but obviously because he liked it that way—in a rayon sports shirt that gaped and showed two hairy stomach rolls hiding his navel in a lipless grin, the pants of a good suit, misbuttoned and held up round the waist by a tie instead of a belt, and a pair of expensive sports shoes, worn without socks; a young Englishman in a worn greenish tweed suit with a neo-

Edwardian cut to the vest that labeled it a leftover from under-graduate days; a handsome white woman who, as the light fell upon her, was immediately recognizable to Jake Alexander.

He had never met her before, but he knew the type well—had seen it over and over again at meetings of the Congress of Democrats, and other organizations where progressive whites met progressive blacks. These were the white women who, Jake knew, persisted in regarding themselves as your equal. That was even worse, he thought, than the parsons who persisted in regarding *you* as *their* equal. The parsons had had ten years at school and seven years at a university and theological school; you had carried sacks of vegetables from the market to white people's cars from the time you were eight years old until you were apprenticed to a printer, and your first woman, like your mother, had been a servant, whom you had visited in a back-yard room, and your first gulp of whisky, like many of your other pleasures, had been stolen while a white man was not looking. Yet the good parson insisted that your picture of life was exactly the same as his own: *you* felt as *he* did. But these women—oh, Christ!—these women felt as *you* did. They were sure of it. They thought they understood the humiliation of the pure-blooded black African walking the streets only by the per-mission of a pass written out by a white person, and the guilt and swagger of the colored man light-faced enough to slink, fugitive from his own skin, into the preserves—the cinemas, bars, libraries that were marked "EUROPEANS ONLY." Yes, breathless with stout sensitivity, they insisted on walking the whole teeter-totter of the color line. There was no escaping their understand-ing. They even insisted on feeling the resentment *you* must feel at their identifying themselves with your feelings. . . .

Here was the black hair of a determined woman (last year they wore it pulled tightly back into an oddly perched knot; this year it was cropped and curly as a lap dog's), the round, bony brow unpowdered in order to show off the tan, the red mouth, the unrouged cheeks, the big, lively, handsome eyes, dramatically painted, that would look into yours with such intelligent, eager honesty—eager to mirror what Jake Alexander, a big, fat slob of a colored man interested in women, money, brandy, and boxing, was feeling. Who the hell wants a woman to look at you honestly, anyway? What has all this to do with a *woman*—with what men and women have for each other in their eyes? She was wearing a wide black skirt, a white cotton blouse baring a good deal of her breasts, and earrings that seemed to have been made by a blacksmith out of bits of scrap iron. On her feet she had sandals whose narrow thongs wound between her toes, and the nails of the toes were painted plum color. By contrast, her hands were neglected-looking—sallow, unmanicured—and on one thin finger there swiveled a huge gold seal ring. She was beautiful, he supposed with disgust.

He stood there, fat, greasy, and grinning at the two visitors so lingeringly that his grin looked insolent. Finally he asked, "What brings you this end of town, Mr. Halford? Sight-seeing with the lady?"

The young Englishman gave Jake's arm a squeeze, where the short sleeve of the rayon shirt ended. "Just thought I'd look you up, Jake," he said, jolly.

"Come on in, come on in," said Jake on a rising note, shambling ahead of them into the company of the back room. "Here, what about a chair for the lady?" He swept a pile of handbills from the seat of a kitchen chair onto the dusty concrete floor, picked up the chair, and planked it down again, in the middle of the group of men, who had risen awkwardly, like zoo bears to the hope of a bun, at the visitors' entrance. "You know Maxie Ndube? And Temba?" Jake said, nodding at two of the men who surrounded him.

Alister Halford murmured with polite warmth his recognition

72

of Maxie, a small, dainty-faced African in neat, businessman's dress, then said inquiringly and hesitantly to Temba, "Have we? When?"

Temba was a colored man—a mixture of the bloods of black slaves and white masters, blended long ago, in the days when the Cape of Good Hope was a port of refreshment for the Dutch East India Company. He was tall and pale, with a large Adam's apple, enormous black eyes, and the look of a musician in a jazz band; you could picture a trumpet lifted to the ceiling in those long yellow hands, that curved spine hunched forward to shield a low note. "In Durban last year, Mr. Halford, you remember?" he said eagerly. "I'm sure we met—or perhaps I only saw you there."

"Oh, at the Congress? Of course I remember you!" Halford apologized. "You were in a delegation from the Cape?"

"Miss—?" Jake Alexander waved a hand between the young woman, Maxie, and Temba.

"Jennifer. Jennifer Tetzel," she said again clearly, thrusting out her hand. There was a confused moment when both men reached for it at once and then hesitated, each giving way to the other. Finally the handshaking was accomplished, and the young woman seated herself confidently on the chair.

Jake continued, offhand, "Oh, and of course Billy Boy—" Alister signaled briefly to a black man with sad, blood-shot eyes, who stood awkwardly, back a few steps, against some rolls of paper—"and Klaas and Albert." Klaas and Albert had in their mixed blood some strain of the Bushman, which gave them a batrachian yellowness and toughness, like one of those toads that (prehistoric as the Bushman is) are mythically believed to have survived into modern times (hardly more fantastically than the Bushman himself has survived) by spending centuries shut up in an air bubble in a rock. Like Billy Boy, Klaas and Albert had backed away, and, as if abasement against the rolls

73

of paper, the wall, or the window were a greeting in itself, the two little colored men and the big African only stared back at the masculine nods of Alister and the bright smile of the young woman.

"You up from the Cape for anything special now?" Alister said to Temba as he made a place for himself on a corner of a table that was littered with photographic blocks, bits of type, poster proofs, a bottle of souring milk, a bow tie, a pair of red braces, and a number of empty Coca-Cola bottles.

"I've been living in Durban for a year. Just got the chance of a lift to Jo'burg," said the gangling Temba.

Jake had set himself up easily, leaning against the front of the stove and facing Miss Jennifer Tetzel on her chair. He jerked his head toward Temba and said, "Real banana boy." Young white men brought up in the strong Anglo-Saxon tradition of the province of Natal are often referred to, and refer to themselves, as "banana boys," even though fewer and fewer of them have any connection with the dwindling number of vast banana estates that once made their owners rich. Jake's broad face, where the bright-pink cheeks of a Highland complexion—inherited, along with his name, from his Scottish father—showed oddly through his coarse, coffee-colored skin, creased up in appreciation of his own joke. And Temba threw back his head and laughed, his Adam's apple bobbing, at the idea of himself as a cricket-playing white public-school boy.

"There's nothing like Cape Town, is there?" said the young woman to him, her head charmingly on one side, as if this conviction was something she and he shared.

"Miss Tetzel's up here to look us over. She's from Cape Town," Alister explained.

She turned to Temba with her beauty, her strong provocativeness, full on, as it were. "So we're neighbors?"

74

Jake rolled one foot comfortably over the other and a spluttering laugh pursed out the pink inner membrane of his lips.

"Where did you live?" she went on, to Temba.

"Cape Flats," he said. Cape Flats is a desolate colored slum in the bush outside Cape Town.

"Me, too," said the girl, casually.

Temba said politely, "You're kidding," and then looked down uncomfortably at his hands, as if they had been guilty of some clumsy movement. He had not meant to sound so familiar; the words were not the right ones.

"I've been there nearly ten months," she said.

"Well, some people've got queer tastes," Jake remarked, laughing, to no one in particular, as if she were not there.

"How's that?" Temba was asking her shyly, respectfully.

She mentioned the name of a social rehabilitation scheme that was in operation in the slum. "I'm assistant director of the thing at the moment. It's connected with the sort of work I do at the university, you see, so they've given me fifteen months' leave from my usual job."

Maxie noticed with amusement the way she used the word "job," as if she were a plumber's mate; he and his educated African friends—journalists and schoolteachers—were careful to talk only of their "professions." "Good works," he said, smiling quietly.

She planted her feet comfortably before her, wriggling on the hard chair, and said to Temba with mannish frankness, "It's a ghastly place. How in God's name did you survive living there? I don't think I can last out more than another few months, and I've always got my flat in Cape Town to escape to on Sundays, and so on."

While Temba smiled, turning his protruding eyes aside slowly, Jake looked straight at her and said, "Then why do you, lady, why *do* you?"

"Oh, I don't know. Because I don't see why anyone else—any one of the people who live there—should have to, I suppose." She laughed before anyone else could at the feebleness, the philanthropic uselessness of what she was saying. "Guilt, what-have-you . . ."

Maxie shrugged, as if at the mention of some expensive illness, which he had never been able to afford and whose symptoms he could not imagine.

There was a moment of silence; the two colored men and the big black man standing back against the wall watched anxiously, as if some sort of signal might be expected, possibly from Jake Alexander, their boss, the man who, like themselves, was not white, yet who owned his own business, and had a car, and money, and strange friends—sometimes even white people, such as these. The three of them were dressed in the ill-matched cast-off clothing that all humble workpeople who are not white wear in Johannesburg, and they had not lost the ability of primitives and children to stare, unembarrassed and unembarrassing.

Jake winked at Alister; it was one of his mannerisms—a bookie's wink, a stage comedian's wink. "Well, how's it going, boy, how's it going?" he said. His turn of phrase was barroom bonhomie; with luck, he *could* get into a bar, too. With a hat to cover his hair, and his coat collar well up, and only a bit of greasy pink cheek showing, he had slipped into the bars of the shabbier Johannesburg hotels with Alister many times and got away with it. Alister, on the other hand, had got away with the same sort of thing narrowly several times, too, when he had accompanied Jake to a shebeen in a colored location, where it was illegal for a white man to be, as well as illegal for anyone at all to have a drink; twice Alister had escaped a raid by jumping out of a window. Alister had been in South Africa only eighteen months, as correspondent for a newspaper in England, and because he was only two or three years away from under-graduate escapades, such incidents seemed to give him a kind of nostalgic pleasure; he found them funny. Jake, for his part, had decided long ago (with the great help of the money he had made) that he would take the whole business of the color bar as humorous. The combination of these two attitudes, stemming from such immeasurably different circumstances, had the effect of making their friendship less self-conscious than is usual between a white man and a colored one.

"They tell me it's going to be a good thing on Saturday night?" said Alister, in the tone of questioning someone in the know. He was referring to a boxing match between two colored heavyweights, one of whom was a protégé of Jake's.

Jake grinned deprecatingly, like a fond mother. "Well, Pikkie's a good boy," he said. "I tell you, it'll be something to see." He danced about a little on his clumsy toes, in pantomime of the way a boxer nimbles himself, and collapsed against the stove, his belly shaking with laughter at his breathlessness.

"Too much smoking, too many brandies, Jake," said Alister.

"With me, it's too many women, boy."

"We were just congratulating Jake," said Maxie in his soft, precise voice, the indulgent, tongue-in-cheek tone of the protégé who is superior to his patron, for Maxie was one of Jake's boys, too—of a different kind. Though Jake had decided that for him being on the wrong side of a color bar was ludicrous, he was as indulgent to those who took it seriously and politically, the way Maxie did, as he was to any up-and-coming youngster who, say, showed talent in the ring or wanted to go to America and become a singer. They could all make themselves free of Jake's pocket, and his printing shop, and his room with a radio in the lower end of the town, where the building had fallen below the standard of white people but was far superior to the kind of thing most coloreds and blacks were accustomed to.

"Congratulations on what?" the young white woman asked.

She had a way of looking up around her, questioningly, from face to face, that came of long familiarity with being the center of attention at parties.

"Yes, you can shake my hand, boy," said Jake to Alister. "I didn't see it, but these fellows tell me that my divorce went through. It's in the papers today."

"Is that so? But from what I hear, you won't be a free man long," Alister said teasingly.

Jake giggled, and pressed at one gold-filled tooth with a strong fingernail. "You heard about the little parcel I'm expecting from Zululand?" he asked.

"Zululand?" said Alister. "I thought your Lila came from Stellenbosch."

Maxie and Temba laughed.

"Lila? *What* Lila?" said Jake with exaggerated innocence.

"You're behind the times," said Maxie to Alister.

"You know I like them—well, sort of round," said Jake. "Don't care for the thin kind, in the long run."

"But Lila had red hair!" Alister goaded him. He remembered the incongruously dyed, artificially straightened hair on a fine colored girl whose nostrils dilated in the manner of certain fleshy water plants seeking prey.

Jennifer Tetzel got up and turned the gas off on the stove, behind Jake. "That bacon'll be like charred string," she said.

Jake did not move—merely looked at her lazily. "This is not the way to talk with a lady around." He grinned, unapologetic.

She smiled at him and sat down, shaking her earrings. "Oh, I'm divorced myself. Are we keeping you people from your supper? Do go ahead and eat. Don't bother about us."

Jake turned around, gave the shrunken rashers a mild shake, and put the pan aside. "Hell, no," he said. "Any time. But—" turning to Alister—"won't you have something to eat?" He looked about, helpless and unconcerned, as if to indicate an ab-

78

sence of plates and a general careless lack of equipment such as white women would be accustomed to use when they ate. Alister said quickly, no, he had promised to take Jennifer to Moorjee's.

Of course, Jake should have known; a woman like that would *want* to be taken to eat at an Indian place in Vrededorp, even though she was white, and free to eat at the best hotel in town. He felt suddenly, after all, the old gulf opening between himself and Alister: what did *they* see in such women—bristling, sharp, all-seeing, knowing women, who talked like men, who wanted to show all the time that, apart from sex, they were exactly the same as men? He looked at Jennifer and her clothes, and thought of the way a white woman could look: one of those big, soft, European women with curly yellow hair, with very high-heeled shoes that made them shake softly when they walked, with a strong scent, like hot flowers, coming up, it seemed, from their jutting breasts under the lace and pink and blue and all the other pretty things they wore—women with nothing resistant about them except, buried in white, boneless fingers, those red, pointed nails that scratched faintly at your palms.

"You should have been along with me at lunch today," said Maxie to no one in particular. Or perhaps the soft voice, a vocal tiptoe, was aimed at Alister, who was familiar with Maxie's work as an organizer of African trade unions. The group in the room gave him their attention (Temba with the little encouraging grunt of one who has already heard the story), but Maxie paused a moment, smiling ruefully at what he was about to tell. Then he said, "You know George Elson?" Alister nodded. The man was a white lawyer who had been arrested twice for his participation in anti-discrimination movements.

"Oh, George? I've worked with George often in Cape Town," put in Jennifer.

"Well," continued Maxie, "George Elson and I went out to one of the industrial towns on the East Rand. We were interviewing the bosses, you see, not the men, and at the beginning it was all right, though once or twice the girls in the offices thought I was George's driver—'Your boy can wait outside.'" He laughed, showing small, perfect teeth; everything about him was finely made—his straight-fingered dark hands, the curved African nostrils of his small nose, his little ears, which grew close to the sides of his delicate head. The others were silent, but the young woman laughed, too.

"We even got tea in one place," Maxie went on. "One of the girls came in with two cups and a tin mug. But old George took the mug."

Jennifer Tetzel laughed again, knowingly.

"Then, just about lunchtime, we came to this place I wanted to tell you about. Nice chap, the manager. Never blinked an eye at me, called me Mister. And after we'd talked, he said to George, 'Why not come home with me for lunch?' So of course George said, 'Thanks, but I'm with my friend here.' 'Oh, that's O.K.,' said the chap. 'Bring him along.' Well, we go along to this house, and the chap disappears into the kitchen, and then he comes back and we sit in the lounge and have a beer, and then the servant comes along and says lunch is ready. Just as we're walking into the dining room, the chap takes me by the arm and says, 'I've had *your* lunch laid on a table on the stoep. You'll find it's all perfectly clean and nice, just what we're having ourselves.'"

"Fantastic," murmured Alister.

Maxie smiled and shrugged, looking around at them all. "It's true."

"After he'd asked you, and he'd sat having a drink with you?" Jennifer said closely, biting in her lower lip, as if this were a problem to be solved psychologically.

"Of course," said Maxie.

Jake was shaking with laughter, like some obscene Silenus.

There was no sound out of him, but saliva gleamed on his lips, and his belly, at the level of Jennifer Tetzel's eyes, was convulsed.

Temba said soberly, in the tone of one whose good will makes it difficult for him to believe in the unease of his situation, "I certainly find it worse here than at the Cape. I can't remember, y'know, about buses. I keep getting put off European buses."

Maxie pointed to Jake's heaving belly. "Oh, I'll tell you a better one than that," he said. "Something that happened in the office one day. Now, the trouble with me is, apparently, I don't talk like a native." This time everyone laughed, except Maxie himself, who, with the instinct of a good raconteur, kept a polite, modest, straight face.

"You know that's true," interrupted the young white woman. "You have none of the usual softening of the vowels of most Africans. And you haven't got an Afrikaans accent, as some Africans have, even if they get rid of the Bantu thing."

"Anyway, I'd had to phone a certain firm several times," Maxie went on, "and I'd got to know the voice of the girl at the other end, and she'd got to know mine. As a matter of fact, she must have liked the sound of me, because she was getting very friendly. We fooled about a bit, exchanged first names, like a couple of kids—hers was Peggy—and she said, eventually, 'Aren't you ever going to come to the office yourself?' " Maxie paused a moment, and his tongue flicked at the side of his mouth in a brief, nervous gesture. When he spoke again, his voice was flat, like the voice of a man who is telling a joke and suddenly thinks that perhaps it is not such a good one after all. "So I told her I'd be in next day, about four. I walked in, sure enough, just as I said I would. She was a pretty girl, blond, you know, with very tidy hair—I guessed she'd just combed it to be ready for me. She looked up and said 'Yes?,' holding out her hand for the messenger's book or parcel she thought I'd brought.

81

I took her hand and shook it and said, 'Well, here I am, on time—I'm Maxie—Maxie Ndube.' "

"What'd she do?" asked Temba eagerly.

The interruption seemed to restore Maxie's confidence in his story. He shrugged gaily. "She almost dropped my hand, and then she pumped it like a mad thing, and her neck and ears went so red I thought she'd burn up. Honestly, her ears were absolutely shining. She tried to pretend she'd known all along, but I could see she was terrified someone would come from the inner office and see her shaking hands with a native. So I took pity on her and went away. Didn't even stay for my appointment with her boss. When I went back to keep the postponed appointment the next week, we pretended we'd never met."

Temba was slapping his knee. "God, I'd have loved to see her face!" he said.

Jake wiped away a tear from his fat cheek—his eyes were light blue, and produced tears easily when he laughed—and said, "That'll teach you not to talk swanky, man. Why can't you talk like the rest of us?"

"Oh, I'll watch out on the 'Missus' and 'Baas' stuff in future," said Maxie.

Jennifer Tetzel cut into their laugher with her cool, practical voice. "Poor little girl, she probably liked you awfully, Maxie, and was really disappointed. You mustn't be too harsh on her. It's hard to be punished for not being black."

The moment was one of astonishment rather than irritation. Even Jake, who had been sure that there could be no possible situation between white and black he could not find amusing, only looked quickly from the young woman to Maxie, in a hiatus between anger, which he had given up long ago, and laughter, which suddenly failed him. On his face was admiration more than anything else—sheer, grudging admiration. This one was the best yet. This one was the coolest ever.

"Is it?" said Maxie to Jennifer, pulling in the corners of his mouth and regarding her from under slightly raised eyebrows. Jake watched. Oh, she'd have a hard time with Maxie. Maxie wouldn't give up his suffering-tempered blackness so easily. You hadn't much hope of knowing what Maxie was feeling at any given moment, because Maxie not only never let you know but made you guess wrong. But this one was the best yet.

She looked back at Maxie, opening her eyes very wide, twisting her sandaled foot on the swivel of its ankle, smiling. "Really, I assure you it is."

Maxie bowed to her politely, giving way with a falling gesture of his hand.

Alister had slid from his perch on the crowded table, and now, prodding Jake playfully in the paunch, he said, "We have to get along."

Jake scratched his ear and said again, "Sure you won't have something to eat?"

Alister shook his head. "We had hoped you'd offer us a drink, but—"

Jake wheezed with laughter, but this time was sincerely concerned. "Well, to tell you the truth, when we heard the knocking, we just swallowed the last of the bottle off, in case it was someone it shouldn't be. I haven't a drop in the place till tomorrow. Sorry, chappie. Must apologize to you, lady, but we black men've got to drink in secret. If we'd've known it was you two . . ."

Maxie and Temba had risen. The two wizened colored men, Klaas and Albert, and the somber black Billy Boy shuffled helplessly, hanging about.

Alister said, "Next time, Jake, next time. We'll give you fair warning and you can lay it on."

Jennifer shook hands with Temba and Maxie, called "Good-by! Good-by!" to the others, as if they were somehow out of earshot in that small room. From the door, she suddenly said to Maxie, "I feel I must tell you. About that other story—your first one, about the lunch. I don't believe it. I'm sorry, but I honestly don't. It's too illogical to hold water."

It was the final self-immolation by honest understanding. There was absolutely no limit to which that understanding would not go. Even if she could not believe Maxie, she must keep her determined good faith with him by confessing her disbelief. She would go to the length of calling him a liar to show by frankness how much she respected him—to insinuate, perhaps, that she was *with him*, even in the need to invent something about a white man that she, because she herself was white, could not believe. It was her last bid for Maxie.

The small, perfectly made man crossed his arms and smiled, watching her out. Maxie had no price.

Jake saw his guests out of the shop, and switched off the light after he had closed the door behind them. As he walked back through the dark, where his presses smelled metallic and cool, he heard, for a few moments, the clear voice of the white woman and the low, noncommittal English murmur of Alister, his friend, as they went out through the archway into the street.

He blinked a little as he came back to the light and the faces that confronted him in the back room. Klaas had taken the dirty glasses from behind the curtain and was holding them one by one under the tap in the sink. Billy Boy and Albert had come closer out of the shadows and were leaning their elbows on a roll of paper. Temba was sitting on the table, swinging his foot. Maxie had not moved, and stood just as he had, with his arms folded. No one spoke.

Jake began to whistle softly through the spaces between his front teeth, and he picked up the pan of bacon, looked at the twisted curls of meat, jellied now in cold white fat, and put it down again absently. He stood a moment, heavily, regarding them all, but no one responded. His eye encountered the chair that he had cleared for Jennifer Tetzel to sit on. Suddenly he kicked it, hard, so that it went flying onto its side. Then, rubbing his big hands together and bursting into loud whistling to accompany an impromptu series of dance steps, he said "Now, boys!" and as they stirred, he planked the pan down on the ring and turned the gas up till it roared beneath it.

aroline Hunter has everything. Nobody in Johannesburg says it grudgingly; everybody likes Caroline—she has that, too. "The only thing Carrie has missed in life is wanting something she can't have," I remember Greta Falk saying to me one day, and we both laughed.

Greta spoke without envy, because she happens to be one of those curious people who truly, sincerely have a taste only for what everyone else does not seem to want—one of those people, normal themselves, who are a gift to the misfits of this world, animate and inanimate; who conduct successful love affairs with men or women so neurotic or repulsive that no one else could tolerate them; who serenely endure lengthy marriages with partners so dull that others can scarcely bear with them for an evening; who buy houses in which no one else would be comfortable, in areas where no one else would care to live. Greta is an Austrian who came to South Africa as a young woman with an attractive and charming husband; he immediately established himself as a successful lawyer, and Greta left him for a weedy, myopic flute player in the municipal orchestra, who has never married her.

I agreed with Greta's remark about Carrie without envy, because apparently I am one of those women who have always been resigned to the limitations of their lot. The fact that I use the very word "lot," connoting life as something apportioned, arbitrarily limited at different levels for individual beings, will tell

87

you all about me. I am the kind known as "a wonderful person"—
person, mark you, not woman, for that might suggest a splendid
femininity, something enviable. "Lottie's a wonderful person,"
my friends say, and they mean that I am as likable, cheerful,
and uncomplaining now—with my sickly, irascible, and unsuc-
cessful husband, whom I have had to support for many years,
and my two sons, whom I have managed to bring up with almost
as much indulgence as my rich friends have lavished on theirs—
as I was when we were girls and everyone was sincerely pleased
that I managed to find a husband in spite of my prematurely
matronly figure, my thin hair, and my good-natured, comedian's
elongated jaw, inherited from my father, which was, alas, all he
had to leave me.

It so happens that Greta Falk was one of the two women invited, along with me, to lunch at Caroline's last month. The
other was Dolly Best, and she, I might add, would never envy
anyone anything but the capacity to find something enviable;
she is one of those women—rich, of course—who never have been
able to find anything they really wanted. When we were young,
Dolly had the money, the freedom, the European tours everyone else longed for; she married a man whose face, intellect,
and position in society were what she knew to be the ideal of
her friends. By now, she has tried the bearing of children, good
works, a career, a lover—everything that she has observed trans-
forming the lives of her friends into ecstasy or despair. All this,
she has coolly noted, has touched her no deeper than the mauve
or blue rinse with which her hairdresser changes the appearance
of her now fading hair from one week to the next.

Caroline rather likes these ladies' lunches of hers. I know that
every few months I am invited, and when I go, I usually find a
similar group of old friends—such as Greta and Dolly and I were
that day—who seldom meet anywhere else. For Dolly and Caroline and I were "girls together" and we have all known Greta

since we were young women. You will hear in the typical ab-
breviation of our names the unmistakable ring of our generation;
we are the Dollys and Carries and Lotties of the Twenties. Of
us all, Caroline has undoubtedly worn the best. Greta was once
as good-looking as she, but Greta now has the perpetually
strained look of the woman who has determinedly put herself
just outside the milieu to which she belongs, and besides, at
forty-four, hair has suddenly shown itself above her beautiful
mouth; the grotesque carnival of middle age has daubed Greta
with a mustache. Dolly was never particularly pretty, except for
her eyes—their shrewd, dreary look of appraisal is all that is left
of them now—and she wears the make-up and the clothes that
busy cosmeticians and couturiers choose for her. And I—well,
ugly women often seem to improve with the years, since middle
age has little to take away from them anyway, so one might say
that the contrast between Caroline and myself is no greater, if
no less, than it has ever been. At forty-six, I am perhaps less
offensively plain than I was at twenty-six—that is all. As with
most homely businesswomen, the improvement brought about
in my appearance by well-fitting clothes and careful hairdress-
ing is not due to any illusion that I may after all be able to make
myself more attractive as a woman, but is merely intended to
make me less offensive in the eyes of my customers and my employers. I am well aware that I have always looked rather like
a horse; and I don't mind nearly so much as I used to.

 That day we gathered to lunch with Caroline, she was looking beautiful. Greta Falk and I had both come from our offices,
with hastily washed hands and hastily powder-dabbed noses;
Dolly, who was there before us and already sipping a sherry,
had let her hairdresser arrange her hair in a way that was meant
for somebody else's face. But Caroline smelled as if she had
bathed at her leisure in roses, and her hands fascinated me—
each oval, pale, shining nail fresh as the inside of a sea shell.

against her smooth-fleshed fingers, the ring with the amethysts and the two pear-shaped diamonds (from her first husband) perfectly in place on her right hand, and the new, thin platinum wedding band never slipping from its proper level between white knuckle and white joint on her left hand. They were hands that did nothing; they lived, like cats, in her lap. Caroline wore, as usual, one of those low-cut dresses that showed off her neck— lovely still, though the clear flesh had thickened and softened, and trembled very slightly when she swallowed—and the first swell of her breasts was still small, though the curve was the immobile one of artifice. She had had her hair cut very short since any of us had seen her last. "But it's been this way for four months!" she exclaimed disbelievingly when we spoke of it. Yet it was true; we hadn't seen her for four months, then. "One just doesn't realize how time flies," said Greta helplessly.

The truth of it was that since Caroline's remarriage she had withdrawn a little from her old friends and from certain aspects of her old way of life. I thought that I detected her consciousness of this in her disbelieving tone, her look of innocence, and I found something rather touching in the embarrassment at the back of the subterfuge; Caroline, at forty-seven, thought it might seem a little ridiculous to let the old friends of her girlhood and first marriage realize that she had gone through all over again, out of season, that period of withdrawal from the world that comes at the beginning of life with the beloved.

Yet though Greta's commonplace remark remained uncommented on and, for a moment or two, everyone sipped at her sherry, the fact was there, rising up in the minds of all of us. Caroline had secured for herself again what the rest of us had put behind us, if we ever had had it at all.

At twenty, Caroline had married William Dalberg, a man fourteen years older than herself, who adored and indulged her. They had two sons and a life of ease and happiness, and by no stretch of sensibility could she be said to have suffered any denial by reason of the difference in years, except that because William reached middle age fourteen years before she did, she was left without him fourteen years sooner than she should have been, for he died suddenly of one of those businessmen's diseases, which decree that such men shall have only half a lifetime. He left her as rich as he had kept her while he lived, and, being a beautiful woman who had enjoyed life, she soon consoled herself and began to enjoy it again. She had two love affairs that I know of, and several times there were rumors that she was about to marry again, always some suitable man, mature, of social stature—in fact, a replacement of William. But she never did marry any of them, and in the meantime her sons grew up. Then, two years ago, at a house party given by one of her young daughters-in-law, Caroline met Gideon Hunter, a thirty-one-year-old Canadian who had been to Cambridge and had once sailed from somewhere to somewhere (I forget the details, but know they were adventurous) in a ketch he had built himself. They became lovers, and after a year the young man went back to Canada. There was nothing broken or tragic about Caroline after what everyone took to be the breakup of this rather curious affair. But then, why should there have been? Caroline had had affairs before, and was wise enough to know how to take them and how to leave them. She continued to go to her usual parties and on her usual holidays, and had her usual number and variety of escorts—men her own age again, or older. And then, six months ago, Gideon Hunter came back from Canada, and Caroline invited some people to one of her cocktail parties, at which the guests discovered that Gideon Hunter and Caroline were married—had been married that morning. (I was not invited to the party, but by noon the next day half a dozen people had said to me, "Have you heard . . . ?")

Within a few weeks, all of us who had not done so already

91

met Gideon. After one met him, all that one had said or prevented oneself from saying, and all that one had been unable to prevent oneself from thinking, was silenced. Gideon was attractive, undoubtedly a personality, undoubtedly sound and likable. He was not even, it appeared, a penniless young man; he did not have the wealth of Caroline, of course, but he had a very good position with a firm importing chemicals and, in addition, represented a chemical factory owned by his family in Quebec.

"How's Bunny?" asked Caroline now, turning to Greta, perhaps merely because Greta's remark about the flight of time had remained dangling in the air but perhaps also, subconsciously, to make a move of cozy, indulgent solidarity toward Greta, who, too, had made her choice of a man in defiance of probability. If there was a pleasant guilt in the confidential turn of Caroline's soft body, there was also gentle triumph; she and Greta had something shared, from which Dolly Best and I were automatically excluded. Shared? But how could one compare the possession of Bunny, the flute player, with his myopia and his delicate stomach, with the possession of a Gideon Hunter! No, Caroline's kindness, her desire not to appear too singularly fortunate in the eyes of her poorly endowed friends, succeeded only in emphasizing the nature of the gap between their lives and her own. Her face, as she nodded interestedly in reply to Greta's account of an argument the flute player had had with his conductor, had the look of the child in the schoolyard who pretends that the cake he is turning over in his mouth is the same as the bread his companions are munching.

"It really is a disgrace. This is no country for an artist, you know, Greta, my dear," Caroline said. She smiled inquiringly at Dolly and me. (Caroline still has her own teeth, I saw, though they look thinner, sharper on the edges than I remember them when we were young.) "Sherry, anyone? Come along, Lottie."

While she filled our glasses, Caroline went on, "Greta, he should go overseas, shouldn't he?"

"Of course," said Greta, raising her strongly marked, handsome eyebrows and letting her shoulders fall, as if she saw before her eyes the thin, reedy genius of her lover, cast down in waste. And we all accepted the tacit deceit, though all of us, including Greta, knew that it would be quite impossible for the flute player to live anywhere but where Greta could help to support him.

"Aren't they good?" said Caroline gaily as she saw me lean forward to help myself to another canapé. "I've gone quite mad about them since we tasted them at the Barlows'. Gideon wants them made every evening."

"How is Gideon, anyway?" said Dolly, sounding bored. Dolly has a horror of the polite social formula of inquiring after the health of various members of a family, and when she feels compelled to get it over with, it always shows in her voice.

Caroline had risen to ring for a servant. She paused with her hand on the bell, smiling. The flesh of her neck pinkened slightly. "Oh, wonderful," she said. "He's in Rhodesia, you know. Flew up on Wednesday week."

"Oh, he's not here?" Greta said.

"Really?" I said. "That's interesting. Perhaps he'll see Donnie up there. Donnie and Isabel are spending three weeks with Isabel's people in Salisbury." Donnie is my elder son.

Caroline had rung the bell, but she continued to linger at the wall for a moment, as if not wanting to deflect the turn of the conversation from something that pleased her so much. "No, Lottie, I'm afraid not. I don't think he's going to Salisbury this time. He'll probably stay in Bulawayo, and then go straight up to Ndola and the Copper Belt. Perhaps even to the Belgian Congo."

"I think I'd like to go to Elisabethville sometime," Dolly was saying. "They tell me it's gay. Probably overrated. South Africans have only got to go somewhere where they hear French or Portuguese instead of English and they'll come back and tell you it's gay. Look at Lourenço Marques—wretched, provincial little town."

"But the bullfight!" said Greta. "The bullfight!"

"Oh, I don't think you'd be disappointed in the Belgian Congo," said Caroline. "Gid's been to Elisabethville several times, and he found it charming. Very European."

"But he likes Lourenço Marques, doesn't he?" said Dolly.

"Well, so do I," Caroline admitted, with a laugh. "I'm afraid Europe hasn't spoiled me at all."

"How long will Gideon be away, Carrie?" I asked.

"A month, at least," she said, pulling a little face. "He's been gone nearly two weeks already. He's so funny. One day I get a letter telling me how beastly it is and how he can't stick it, and then he phones me—he phoned me on Saturday at some absurd hour in the morning—and says how delightful the people are and how the only problem is to get any sleep at all."

Greta and I laughed with her.

While we were talking, one of Caroline's servants appeared at the door in answer to her summons. "Wilson," she said, smiling, "tell cook to try and be prompt, please. Two of my guests have to get back to their offices. Tell her we're ready now." To Greta and me, she added, "I know how awful it is to eat against time."

The African, in his stiffly pressed white suit, was trying to attract Caroline's attention to a bundle of letters he had put down on a small table. "Oh, thank you, Wilson," she said, snatching up the bundle as he left the room. "Bills, bills . . ." She smiled at us out of her beautiful green eyes, which are still, in their framework of mascaraed lashes and faintly bluish, greased lids, so bright that they seem faceted. Her fingers dealt deftly with the thin envelopes, stopped. "Ah, a letter," she said. "It's Gid." She took a step or two back, and leaned against the mantel. "D'you mind if I have a quick look?"

"Oh, do, do!" "Of course not." We all murmured away her apologies.

"Look at this." She was smiling, the delicate movement under her lowered eyelids showing her progress over the page. He *is* going to Salisbury, Lottie, so I'll tell him about Donnie and Isabel.... And he's changed his hotel.... This one much better. Met some delightful people called— What is this? Wellfeet, or Wellfleet—I can't make it out. Knew his mother in Canada.... That's about all." And then she began to read from the letter: " 'Next time I have to come up, you really must come with me. On Sunday, I spent the whole day on a magnificent farm about sixty miles out—sat in a garden blazing with every imaginable color, rode, when it was cool, a white mare Angus brought out for himself specially, from England. Lovely creature. Then in the evening we swam, and the sky was smoky with pink light— can't describe it. Little night club on Saturday also very good, rather drunken. And the business side goes swimmingly. I really was wise to come; personal contact is the thing. We'll come up again together in September. I miss you terribly and I want you in my arms—' " Caroline broke off, giving a little guilty, dismissing shrug, a giggle, as though she had let out a hiccup instead of an indiscretion. We three guests tried to look as if we were not looking at her—as if we had not heard. I saw the dent in Greta's chin deepen a moment—was she suppressing a tremble?—and, strangely, at the corners of Dolly's mouth there was a little wry smile, an admiring, reluctant recognition, as if she had met a ghost when she didn't believe in ghosts. Caroline smilingly bit her underlip in apology but not in embarrassment. And then, like a woman who has so many jewels that she can afford to be careless of them, she put the letter lightly aside on a chest of drawers near her hand and led us in to lunch, talking and laughing. Sitting opposite her, I watched her, at the head of her beautiful table, in her beautifully proportioned dining room, direct the serving of a dish of game that scented the room with wine.

"Really, Carrie," said Dolly, "this duck is quite remarkable."

"Caroline *always* has the most wonderful cooks," said Greta, in the tone of a simple statement of incontrovertible fact. "That's all there is to it." And Caroline, exquisitely fair and well preserved, delicately animated by the sherry that had coarsened the faces of Greta, Dolly, and me, laughed and deprecated with the pleasing modesty of the unassailable.

In the middle of the pleasant feminine companionability of our luncheon, I was thoroughly irritated to find myself attacked by one of my bouts of hay fever; it may have been caused by some unfamiliar herb in the food. At any rate, I had to excuse myself from the table and go to the living room to get from my handbag the phial of pills I carry in anticipation of one of these attacks. I took a pill and sat down on a sofa, closing my streaming eyes and trying to control my desire to sneeze. After a few minutes, the attack subsided, and I took out my powder compact to conceal the tear marks left on my face. I had the feeling of idle exhaustion that comes after the relief of some physical discomfort, and as I strolled slowly across the room toward the door, I saw Caroline's letter from her young husband lying open on the bureau, and I went over and held it in my hand a moment. I lifted the top pages and looked at the last one, in an impulse to see his name, his signature, there: Gideon. As if the sight of the signature, the symbol of this young man revealed to my eyes, might also convey what it was to have a young man like that in one's life—to know him, in love. And because one's eye is trained in the habit of running along a line of print or writing, I read the last lines of the letter, without guilt or a sense of what I was doing; in any case, they were the lines that Caroline had read

96

aloud: "Next time I have to come up, you really must come with me. On Sunday, I spent the whole day on a magnificent farm about sixty miles out—sat in a garden blazing with every imaginable color, rode, when it was cool, a white mare Angus brought out for himself specially, from England. Lovely creature. Then in the evening we swam, and the sky was smoky with pink light —can't describe it. Little night club on Saturday also very good, rather drunken. And the business side goes swimmingly. I really was wise to come; personal contact is the thing. We'll come up again together in September. Love, Gideon."

That was all. I read it again, because there was something about it that bothered me—bothered my ear with a certain lack, or difference, like a phrase of music in which a note is silent.

And when I read it again, I saw that, indeed, that was all.

I put the letter back again just as I had found it, and when I walked back into the dining room, Caroline's beautiful face, hardly spoiled by the fans of fine skin opening and closing at the corners of her eyes, welcomed me with pleasure and concern. "Darling, are you all right?" she was saying. "Darling—but *can't* you do something about it?"

My First Two Women

J have been trying to remember when and where I saw my father's second wife for the first time. I must have seen her frequently, without singling her out or being aware of her, at many of those houses, full of friends, where my father and I were guests in the summer of 1928. My father had many friends, and it seems to me (I was not more than four years old at the time) that, at week ends at least, we were made much of at a whole roster of houses, from tiny shacks, which young couples had "fixed up" for themselves, to semi-mansions, where we had two guest rooms and a bathroom all to ourselves. Whether we sat under a peach tree on painted homemade chairs at a shack, or around the swimming pool on cane chaises-longues at a mansion, the atmosphere of those Saturdays and Sundays was the same: the glasses of warm beer, full of sun, into which I sometimes stuck a finger; the light and color of a Johannesburg summer, with thousands of midges, grasshoppers and other weightless leaping atoms exploding softly over your face as you lay down on the grass; the laughter and voices of the men and women, as comforting and pleasant as the drunken buzz of the great bluebottles that fell sated from rotting fruit, or bees that hung a moment over your head, on their way to and fro between elaborate flowering rockeries. She must have been there often—one of the women who would help me into the spotted rubber Loch Ness monster that kept me afloat, or bring me a

99

lemonade with a colored straw to drink it through—so often that
I ceased to see her.

During the months of that summer, I lived at one or another
of those friends' houses, along with the children of the house;
sometimes my father stayed there with me, and sometimes he
did not. But even if he was not actually living in the same place
with me, he was in and out every day, and the whole period has
in my mind the blurring change and excitement of a prolonged
holiday—children to play with, a series of affectionate women
who arranged treats, settled fights, and gave me presents. The
whereabouts of my mother were vague to me and not particularly troubling. It seems to me that I believed her not to be back
yet from her visit to my grandmother in Kenya, and yet I have
the recollection of once speaking to her on the telephone, as if
she were in Johannesburg after all. I remember saying, "When
are you coming back?" and then not waiting for her to answer
but going on, "Guess what I've got in my hand?" (It was a frog,
which had just been discovered to have completed its metamor-
phosis from a tadpole in a tin basin full of stones and water.)

The previous winter, when my mother had gone to Kenya, my
father and I had lived in our house, my parents' own house,
alone. This was not unusual; I am aware that I had been alone
with him, in the care of servants, time and again before that. In
fact, any conception I have in my mind of my mother and father
and me living together as a family includes her rather as a presence—rooms that were hers, books and trinkets belonging to
her, the mute testimony of her grand piano—rather than a flesh-
and-blood actuality. Even if she *was* there she did little or nothing of an intimate nature for me; I do not connect her with meal
or bath times. So it came about, I suppose, that I scarcely understood, that summer, that there was a real upheaval and change
over my head. My father and I were never to go back to that
house together. In fact, we both had left it for good; even

though I, before the decision was to be made final for me, was to return for a few weeks, it was not to the *same house*, in any but the brick-and-mortar sense, and my position in it and the regrouping of its attention in relation to me were so overwhelmingly changed that they wiped out, in a blaze of self-importance and glory, the dim near babyhood that had gone before.

For, suddenly, in a beautiful autumn month (it must have been March), I found myself back in our house with my mother. The willows around the lawn were fountains spouting pale-yellow leaves on the grass that was kept green all year round. I slept with my mother, in her bed. Surely I had not done so before. When I said to her, "Mummy, didn't I used to sleep in the nursery before you went to Kenya?" she pushed up my pajama jacket and blew in my navel and said, "Darling, I really have no idea where your Daddy put you to sleep while I was away."

She had short, shiny black hair cut across her forehead in a fringe. She took me to the barber and had my hair, my black hair, cut in a fringe. (Daddy used to brush my hair back, first dipping the brush in water. "Water dries out the hair," she said.) We would get out of her car together, at the houses of friends, and she would walk with me slowly up the path toward them, hand in hand. We looked exactly alike, they all said, exactly alike; it was incredible that a small boy could look so much the image of his mother.

My mother would put me up on the long stool beside her while she played the piano; I had never been so close to a piano while it was being played, and sometimes the loud parts of the music swelled through my head frighteningly, like the feeling once when I slipped through my Loch Ness monster and went under in a swimming pool. Then I got used to the sensation and found it exciting, and I would say to her, "Play loudly, Mummy. Make it boom." Sometimes she would stop playing suddenly and whirl around and hold me tight, looking out over my head at the guests who had been listening. I would hear the last reverberation die away in the great rosewood shape behind us while silence held in the room.

My mother walked up and down a room when she talked, and she talked a great deal, to people who seemed to have no chance to answer her, but were there to listen. Once, in the bathroom, I threw a wet toy and it hit my African nanny on the mouth, and when she smacked my behind and I yelled, my mother rushed in and raged at her, yelling as loudly as I did. My mother was beautiful when she was angry, for she was one of those women who cry with anger, and her eyes glistened and her natural pallor was stained bright with rising blood.

She took me to a circus. She took me to a native mineworkers' "war" dance. She came home from town with a pile of educational toys and sat over me, watching, while I hesitated, caught her long, black, urging eye, brilliant as the eye of an animal that can see in the dark, and then, with a kind of hypnotized instinct born of the desire to please, fitted the right shape on the right peg.

There were still a few leaves, like droplets not yet shaken off, on the twigs of the willows when my clothes and toys were packed up again and my father came to fetch me away.

This time I went to the sea, with the family of three little boys and their mother, with whom I had stayed before. I had a wonderful time, and when I came back, it was to a new house that I had never seen. In it were my father and his second wife.

I was not surprised to see this woman, and, as I have said, she was not a stranger to me. I liked her, and, made gregarious by the life of the past year, asked, "How much days can Deb stay with us?"

"For always," said my father.

"Doesn't she ever have to go home?"

"This is her home, and yours, and Daddy's."

"Why?"

"Because she is married to me now, Nick. She is my wife, and husbands and wives love each other and live together in the same house."

There was a pause, and when I spoke again, what I said must have been very different from what they expected. They did not know that while I was on holiday at the sea I had been taken, one rainy afternoon, along with the older children, to the cinema. There I had seen, in all the rose and crystalline blur of Technicolor, a man and woman dance out beneath the chandeliers of a ballroom. When I had asked what they were doing, I was told that this was a wedding—the man and the woman had just been married.

"Do you mean like this?" I asked my father and my stepmother, taking my father's hand, bending my knees, and shaping out my arms in a jiglike posture. I hopped around solemnly, dragging him with me.

"Dancing?" guessed my father, mystified and affectionate, appealing to his wife.

"Oh, that's wonderful!" she cried in sudden delight. "Bless his formal heart! A real wedding!"

There followed a confusion of hugging, all around. I was aware only that in some way I had pleased them.

I was now nearly five years old and due to begin going to school. My stepmother took me to town with her, and together we bought the supplies for my birthday party, and my school uniform, and a satchel with a fancy lock—soon to be stained as greasy as an old fish-and-chip wrapping with the print of successive school lunches—and the elaborate equipment of pencil sharpeners, erasers and rulers indispensable to the child who has not yet learned to write. Deb understood what a birthday party for a five-year-old boy should be like. She had ideas of

her own, and could sway a wavering torment of indecision between candleholders in the guise of soldiers or elephants, im-
parting to the waverer a comforting sense of the rightness of the
final choice, but she also knew when to efface her own prefer-
ences entirely and let me enjoy my own choice for my own un-
explained reasons. In fact, she was so good at the calm manage-
ment of the practical details of my small life that I suppose I
quickly assumed this stability as my right, and took it altogether
for granted, as children, in their fierce unconscious instinct for
personal salvation, take all those rights which, if withheld from
them, they cannot consciously remark, but whose lack they ex-
hibit and revenge with equal unconscious ferocity. Of course
Deb bought neat and comfortable clothes for me, found the
books I would best like to hear her read from, took me with her
on visits that would be interesting to me, but left me at home to
play when she was going where there would be nothing to
amuse me; she always had, hadn't she, right from the first day?

The children at school wanted to know why I called my
mother "Deb." When I said that she was not my mother, they
insisted that she must be. "Are you my mother now, Deb?" I
asked her.

"No," she said. "You know that you have your own mother."

"They say you must be, because you live with Daddy and me."

"I'm your second mother," she said, looking to see if that
would do.

"Like my godmother?"

"That's right."

I dashed off to play; it was perfectly satisfactory.

There came a stage when school, the preparation for which
had been so enjoyable, palled. I suppose there must have been
some incident there, some small failure which embarrassed or
shamed me. I do not remember. But I know that, suddenly, I
didn't want to go to school. Deb was gentle but insistent. I re-

member my own long, sullen silence one day, after a wrangle of
"Why?s" from me and firm explanations from her. At last I said,
"When I'm at my mother's I stay home all the time."

My stepmother was squatting on her heels in front of a low
cupboard, and her eyes opened up toward me like the eyes of
those sleeping dolls which girl children alternately lower and
raise by inclining the doll's body, but her voice was the same as
usual. "If you lived with your mother now, you would go to
school just as you do here," she said.

I stood right in front of her. She looked up at me again, and I
said, "No I wouldn't." I waited. Then I said, "She lets me do
what I like." I waited again. "I can even play her piano. She's
got a big piano. As big as this room."

My stepmother went on slowly putting back into the cupboard the gramophone records she had been sorting and cleaning. Standing over her, I could see the top of her head, an unfamiliar aspect of a grownup. It was then, I think, that I began
to see her for the first time, not as one of the succession of pretty
ladies who petted and cared for me, but as Deb, as someone
connected in wordless depths with my father and me, as my
father and I and, yes, my mother were connected. Someone who
had entered, irrevocably, the atavistic tension of that cunning
battle for love and supremacy that exists between children and
parents sometimes even beyond the grave, when one protago-
nist is dead and mourned, and lives on in the fierce dissatisfac-
tion of the other's memory.

She was a fair woman, this Deb, this woman beloved of my
father; on all faces there is some feature, some plane that catches
the light in characteristic prominence of that face, and on her
face, at that moment and always, it was her long golden eyebrows, shining. They were bleached from much swimming, but
her dull, curly hair, always protected from sun and water by a
cap, hung colorless and nowhere smooth enough to shine. The

face was broad and brown across strong cheekbones, and she had a big, orange-painted mouth, the beautiful underlip of which supported the upper as calmly as a carved pediment. Her eyes, moving from record to cupboard, lowered under my presence, were green or blue, depending upon what color she wore. As she squatted, her knees, with thighs and calves showing under the short skirt, closed back against each other like the blades of a knife, were particularly pretty—smooth and pink-skinned, with a close speckling of dainty freckles, like the round tops of her arms and her long calves. She was the sort of fair woman who would never be called a blonde.

Deb. I knew what it smelled like in that pink freckled neck. I knew the stiff and ugly ears that she kept hidden under that hair, and that sometimes, when she was hot and lifted her hair off her neck a moment for coolness, were suddenly discovered.

I shall never forget the feeling I had as I stood there over her. If I search my adult experience as a man to approximate it, I can only say that now it seems to me that physically it was rather like the effect of the first drink you take after a long wet day of some strenuous exercise—rowing or hunting. It was a feeling of power that came like an inflow of physical strength. I was only five years old, but power is something of which I am convinced there is no innocence this side of the womb, and I knew what it was, all right; I understood, without a name for it, what I had. And with it came all the weapons—that bright, clinical set that I didn't need to have explained to me, as my father had had to explain to me the uses of the set of carpenter's tools I had been given for my birthday. My hand would go out unfalteringly for these drills and probes, and the unremembered pain of where they had been used on me would guide me to their application.

"Deb," I said, "why didn't Daddy marry my mother?"

"He did," she said. "Once he was married to her. But they were not happy with each other. Not like Daddy and me—and

you. Not happy together like us." She did not ask me if I remembered this, but her voice suggested the question, in spite of
her.

Daddy. My mother. My mother was simply a word I was
using at that moment. I could not see her in my head. She was
a mouth moving, singing; for a second she sat at the piano,
smiled at me, one of her swift, startling smiles that was like
someone jumping out of concealment and saying "Boo!" Inside
me, it gave me a fright. If my dog had been there, I would have
pulled back his ears, hard, to hear him yelp. There was Deb,
squatting in front of me. I said, "My mother's got a piano as
big as this house. I want to go and stay with her."

Deb got up from the floor and rubbed down her thighs.
"Soon," she said. "You'll go on a visit soon, I'm sure. Let's see if
tea's ready." We did not take each other's hand, but walked out
onto the porch side by side, with a space between us.

It was after that day that I began to be conscious of the relationship between my father and Deb. This was not the way he
and those others—the pretty, helpful friends who were the
mothers of my friends—had behaved toward each other. I
watched with unbiased interest, as I would have watched a bird
bringing his mate tidbits where she balanced on our paling
fence, when my father ate an apple bite-and-bite-about with this
woman, or, passing her chair at breakfast, after he had kissed
me good-by in the morning, paused to press his cheek silently,
and with closed eyes, against hers. In the car, I noticed that she
rested her hand on his knee as he drove. Sometimes, in the evenings, both she and I sat on his lap at once.

There were no images in my memory to which to match
these. They were married, Deb and my father. This behavior
was marriage. Deb herself had told me that marriage once had
existed between my father and my mother. One day I came

home from a visit to my mother and remarked, conversationally, in the bedroom Deb and my father shared, "My mother's got a bed just like yours, Deb, and that's where Daddy and she used to sleep when he lived there, didn't you, Daddy?"

It was Sunday, and my father still lay in bed, reading the paper, though Deb's place was empty and she was gathering her clothes together before she went off to the bathroom. He said, "No, son. Don't you remember? Mine was the room with the little balcony."

"Oh, yes," I said. "Of course, I know." All at once I remembered the smell of that rather dark, high room, a smell of shirts fresh from the iron, of the two leather golf bags in the corner, and some chemical with which the carpet had been cleaned. All this—the smell of my father—had disappeared under the warmer, relaxing and polleny scents of the room he now shared with a woman, where peach-colored dust from her powder settled along his hairbrushes, and the stockings she peeled off retained the limp, collapsed semblance of her legs, like the newly shed skin of a snake I had come upon in the bush when I was on holiday at the sea.

I think that there must have been something strongly attractive to me in the ease of this feminine intimacy to which my father and I found ourselves admitted with such naturalness. Yet because it was unfamiliar, the very seductiveness of its comfort seemed, against the confusion of my short life, a kind of disloyalty, to which I was party and of which I was guilty. Disloyalty—to what? Guilty—of what?

I was too young for motives; I could only let them bubble up, manifest in queer little words and actions. I know that that Sunday morning I said stoutly, as if I were explaining some special system of living, "There we each had our *own* rooms. Everybody slept in their own room."

Before the end of the first year of the marriage that power

that had come to me like a set of magical weapons, the day when my stepmother knelt before me at the record cupboard, became absolute. It crushed upon my little-boy's head the vainglory and triumph of the tyrant, crown or thorn. I was to wear it as my own for the rest of my childhood.

I was cuddling Deb, secure in her arms one day, when I said, out of some gentle honey of warmth that I felt peacefully within me, "I'm going to call you Mummy because I love you best." I am sure that she knew that the statement was not quite so stunning and meaningful as it sounds now, out of the context of childhood. Quite often, she had heard me say of an animal or a new friend, "You know whom I love. I love only Eddie." (Or "Sam," or "Chris.") Sometimes the vehement preference was expressed not out of real feeling for the friend or animal in question, but out of pique toward some other child or animal. At other times it was merely an unreasonable welling up of wellbeing that had to find an object. But I had never before said this particular thing to her. I felt her thighs tighten suddenly beneath me; all four fingers and the thumb of her hand seized round my arm. She shook back her hair fumblingly and held her face away from mine to look at me; she was awkward with joy. I looked up into the stare of her eyes—grown-up eyes that fell before mine—and in me, like milk soured by a flash of lightning, the sweet secretion of affection became insipid in the fearful, amazed thrill of victim turned victor.

That was our story, really, for many years. My father and Deb were deeply in love and theirs was a serene marriage. The three of us lived together in amity; it was a place of warmth for a child to grow in. I visited my mother at regular, if widely spaced, intervals. I went to her for short periods at Christmas, birthdays, and during holidays. Thus along with her, with that elegant black head and those hard wrists volatile with all the wonderful bracelets she had picked up all over the world, went excitement and occasion, treats and parties, people who exclaimed over me, and the abolishment of that guillotine of joys, bedtime. Sometimes the tide of grown-up activities would pass on over my head and leave me stranded and abandoned on a corner of somebody's sofa, rubbing my eyes against the glare of forgotten lights. It did not matter; the next day, or the day after that, I was sure to be delivered back to Deb and my father and the comfort of my child's pace.

Thus it was, too, that along with home and Deb and my father went everyday life, the greater part of life, with time for boredom, for transgressions and punishments. When I visited my mother for a week end or a day I was on my best behavior, befitting a treat or an occasion; I was never with her long enough to need chastisement. So when, at home, I was naughty and my father or Deb had to punish me, I would inflame myself against them with the firm belief that my mother would never punish me. At these times of resentment and injury, I would see her clearly and positively, flaming in the light of a Christmas tree or the fiery ring of candles on a birthday cake, my champion against a world that would not bend entirely to my own will. In the same way, for the first few days after my return from a visit to her, everything about the way she lived and the things about her were lit up by the occasion with which my visit had coincided; her flat (when I was seven or eight she moved into a luxurious penthouse in a block overlooking a country club) was like the glowing cardboard interior of the king's castle, carried away in my mind from a pantomime matinee. "There's a swimming pool right on top of the building, on the roof garden," I would tell Deb. "I swim there every morning. Once I swam at night. My mother lets me. The lift doesn't go up to the top—you have to walk the last flight of stairs from the twelfth floor." "My mother's got a car with an overhead drive. Do you know what that is, Deb? It means you don't have to change the gears with your hands." "I wish we had a swimming pool here. I don't like this old house without even a swimming pool."

Deb always answered me quietly and evenly. Never, even when I was very young, did she try to point out rival attractions at home. But in time, when I grew older and was perhaps eleven or twelve, I struggled against something that went more than quiet—went dead—in her during these one-sided conversations. I felt not that she was not listening, but that she was listless, without interest in what I said. And then I did not know at whom the resentment I suddenly felt was directed, whether at my mother—that glossy-haired kingfisher flashing in and out of my life—for having a roof-garden swimming pool and a car without gears, or at Deb, for her lack of attention and negative reaction to my relation of these wonders. This reaction of hers was all the more irking, and in some vague, apprehensive way dismaying, when one remembered the way she watched and listened to me sometimes, with that look in her eyes that wanted something from me, wondered, hesitated, hopeful—that look I had known how to conjure up ever since the first day when I suggested I would call her my mother, and that, in perverse, irresistible use of the same power, I had also known how never to allow to come to articulacy, to emotional fulfillment, between us. The business of my calling her mother, for instance; it had come up several times again, while I was small. But she, in the silence that followed, had never managed anything more than, once, an almost unintelligibly murmured "If you like." And I, once the impulsive, casually pronounced sentence had exploded and left its peculiar after-silence, had dropped my avowal as I left a toy, here or there, for someone else to pick up in house or garden. I never did call her mother; in time, I think I should have been surprised to hear that there had ever been any question that she should be anything else but "Deb."

I was strongly attached to her, and when, at twelve or thirteen, I entered adolescence and boarding school at the same
time, there was in fact a calm friendship between us unusual
between a woman, and a boy walking the knife edge dividing
small-boy scorn of the feminine from awakening sex interest. I
suppose if she had been truly in the position of a mother, this
relationship would not have been possible. Her position must
have been curiously like that of the woman who, failing to secure as a lover the man with whom she has fallen in love, is
offered instead his respect and his confidences.

I was fifteen when I asked the question that had taken a
thousand different forms—doubts, anxieties, and revenges—all
through my life but had never formulated itself directly. The
truth was, I had never known what that question *was*—only felt
it, in all my blood and bones, fumbled toward it under the kisses
of people who loved me, asked it with my seeking of my father's
hands, the warmth of Deb's lap, the approval of my form
master's eye, the smiles of my friends. Now it came to me matter-
of-factly, in words.

I was home from school for the week end, and there had been
guests at lunch. They had discussed the divorce of a common
friend and the wrangle over the custody of the children of the
marriage. One of the guests was a lawyer, and he had gone into
the legal niceties in some detail. After the guests had gone, my
father went off for his nap and Deb and I dragged our favorite
canvas chairs out onto the lawn. As I settled mine at a comfortable angle, I asked her, curiously, "Deb, how was it that my
mother didn't get me? The custody of me, I mean."

She thought for a moment, and I thought she must be trying
how best to present some legal technicality in a way that both
she and I would understand.

"I mean, their divorce was an arranged thing, wasn't it—one

of those things arranged to look like desertion that Derrick spoke about? Why didn't my mother get me?" The lawyer had explained that where parents contested the custody, unless there was some strong factor to suggest that the mother was unsuitable to rear a child, a young child was usually awarded to her care.

Then quite suddenly Deb spoke. Her face was red and she looked strange, and she spoke so fast that what she said was almost blurted. "She gave you up."

Her face and tone so astonished me that the impact of what she had said missed its mark. I stared at her, questioning.

She met my gaze stiffly, with a kind of jerky bravado, intense, looking through me.

"How do you mean?"

"Voluntarily. She gave you over to your father."

The pressure in her face died slowly down; her hands moved, as if released, on the chair arms. "I should never have told you," she said flatly. "I'd promised myself I never should."

"You mean she didn't want me?"

"We don't know what her reasons were, Nick. We can't know them."

"Didn't try to get me?"

There was a long silence. "We made up our minds. We decided it was best. We decided we would try and make your relationship with her as normal as possible. Never say anything against her. I promised myself I wouldn't try—for myself. I often wanted to tell you—oh, lots of things. I wanted to punish you for what I withheld for your sake. I wanted to hurt you; I suppose I forgot you were a child. . . . Well, what does it matter anyway? It's all worked itself out, long ago. Only I shouldn't have told you now. It's pointless." She smiled at me, as at a friend who can be counted on to understand a confession. "It didn't even give me any pleasure."

My stepmother talked about this whole situation in which we had all lived as if it were something remembered from the past, instead of a living situation out of the continuity of which I was then, at that moment, beginning my life as a man. All worked itself out, long ago. Perhaps it had. Yes, she was right. All worked itself out, without me. Above and about me, over my head, saving me the risk and the opportunity of my own volition.

My mother? That black-haired, handsome woman become rather fleshy, who, I discovered while I sat, an awkward visitor among her admiring friends (I had inherited her love of music), sang off-key.

But it was not toward her that I felt anger, regret, and a terrible, mournful anguish of loss, which brought up from somewhere in my tall, coarse, half-man's, half-child's body what I was alarmed to recognize as the raking turmoil that precedes tears.

"We're really good friends, aren't we?" said my stepmother lovingly, with quiet conviction.

It was true: that was what we were—all we were.

I have never forgiven her for it.

The White Goddess and the Mealie Question

D. B. Landsdorf is just one more reason why my life in Johannesburg is so complicated. There are reasons enough, heaven knows, and most of them are artists or foreigners, or both, or art collectors, refugees *and* members of the best practically extinct European families—all at once.

You see, I am an ordinary South African girl who might have married a mine manager (he is now doing awfully well on the new Free State gold fields) or an estate agent (I hear he has a charming house overlooking the sea at Durban), but I chose an Austrian art dealer named Kurt Breslauer. And why? At the mention of that name, anyone who knows him will say at once, "Oh, but he's a darling!" And he is. That's why. He looked, when I met him, like a great clumsy spaniel who, as a treat, has just been allowed into the living room. It sounds ridiculous to say it, but this muscleless hulk of a man is the only person I've ever seen in my life whose eyes are starry—really starry, the way they describe the eyes of unbearably beautiful heroines in cheap novels. Yes, those very large, loving and intelligent eyes of my husband were starry, and they still are.

But, of course, he's not an art dealer any more. That didn't last very long. I don't think he ever really was an art dealer by profession, but simply a man who had grown up in a house full of treasures and who wanted to continue to have them about him in a country and a way of life where that house did not exist. When I married him he had been in South Africa for four

115

years, and he still had the larger part of the packing cases full of furniture and carpets and *objets d'art* that was all that was left of one of the best families in Austria.

My first dressing table was a pretty, rickety thing that had once belonged to an empress of Austria. Our fish servers, I remember, and our soup tureen bore the crest of George III. We had Cloisonné, and Sèvres, and Chippendale, and heaven knows what else, and how I used to show it all off to the girls who *had* married mine managers and estate agents! It's all gone long ago now, sold or exchanged for other "treasures" which again in their turn have been sold or exchanged. And Kurt has been a motorcar salesman, a representative of a firm of chemical engineers, an indent agent and an importer of Italian textiles. Currently he's selling venetian blinds, which suddenly have become the mark of the successful in Johannesburg suburbia (I hope television doesn't come here too soon and supersede the distinction of discreetly veiled windows with the newer distinction of weird contraptions on the roof).

D. B. Landsdorf is left over from the old art-dealing days. I suppose he would have had some sort of place in our lives anyway, since he belongs to the *Kaffeehaus* coterie of European exiles in which we move, Kurt nostalgically, I bewilderedly, the eternal foreigner in my own country; but if he hadn't been Kurt's partner in the art-dealing business, if they hadn't purred together over bits of faded tapestry and blowzy gilt chairs, lost money together, failed together, I don't suppose we'd have had D. B. tottering around under my feet for the rest of our lives, the way we do. You see, Dr. Landsdorf is old and poor and out of place, and consequently irritating, but at the same time he is also terribly fragile and terribly intellectual, and consequently rather awe-inspiring. Perhaps I've caught this feeling from the others, who find it hard to credit that this brittle effigy in a worn, dun-colored raincoat is the remaining substance of the art critic, philosopher and editor whose name rang so impressive a peal in their heads during their youth in Europe.

After the demise of the art business, D. B. Landsdorf couldn't turn to motorcars or venetian blinds, and he just gets along somehow, doing a bit of translation here and there, writing an occasional article on Sanskrit or Japanese industrialism or the influence of Wagnerian myth on the mind of prewar German youth—the sort of thing that may find a corner in the week-end edition of a Johannesburg newspaper eager to demonstrate the catholicity of its appeal. Nobody knows quite what he lives on; only that it's obvious he doesn't live on much. He has the slow-moving, insectlike head of the creature who is eating less and less, and indeed the capacity of his stomach seems to be shrinking all the time, for when you ask him home to a good dinner, he simply shifts it from one side of his plate to the other. You can see him at regular hours in a small coffee shop in one of the side streets of Johannesburg, padded about with the *New York Times*, the *Manchester Guardian*, *Le Monde* and the *Frankfurter Zeitung* sticking out of various pockets, and very likely he will be in the act of tearing the wrapper off the latest issue of the *New Statesman* over his cup of black coffee. He is pale gray and all skull and no flesh or hair to speak of, and his eyes are so far gone in his head that they look like vanishing lights in a tunnel. When he speaks his voice seems to be an echo rather than a voice. But there is life in him yet, all right, and speak he does, whenever he can get himself a platform and a table with a carafe and glass on it and an audience trapped on the other side. Then he will intone for an hour, hollow, scholarly, and inaudible beyond the second row, humming and ha-ing, stumbling and er-ing, on some subject that reveals his desire to create within himself a synthesis between the old world of which he has been disinherited and the new world which he finds on his hands.

He is filled with a solemn sense of responsibility toward the brash problems of South Africa; he doesn't want to live in the past. At the same time, he clings to the past as the only means by which the hotchpotch of our way of life here in South Africa may be fitted into the all-powerful realm of nineteenth-century reason by which he has lived so long. This produces some odd results on the lecture platform. As Kurt says, rolling those eyes, "Kant and the Mealie Question." ("Mealie" is the South African name for maize, staple food of the African population.) And that's no joke, either. Old D. B. really did give a talk under that title. Though sometimes we make a kind of game out of it: "Schopenhauer and the Lobola Question" ("Lobola" is the dowry, usually a cow or two, that African men give to their brides' fathers), "Agterskot, and Some Patterns of Neo-Fascism in Germany Today" ("Agterskot" is the bonus wool farmers get from the government when we have a record wool clip).

All about as unfunny, to the uninitiated, as most family jokes. But at least this may serve to show you what a trying person Dr. Landsdorf must be to have around, especially when your husband adores him, feels somehow responsible for him because they failed together in the art business, and this husband is, in any case, a person of the most muddled quixotic notions.

Yet I must admit that there have been even worse trials in my life than D. B. He goes on longer, that's all. From time to time, really big short-term crises have come up. One thing you must say about Dr. Landsdorf, unless you count "Kant and the Mealie Question": he's a fairly quiet and inoffensive nuisance. Not so some others. You've probably guessed that I'm talking of women now; Kurt says you can hear the change in my voice. You see, Kurt likes women. I mean precisely what I say; he doesn't— I think—philander. But unlike the more direct Colonial, the South African male who regards women as a choice of mates, but doesn't take women into account any more than he would parakeets when choosing friends, Kurt actually likes women as *people*. Not that any woman would be likely to be jealous of the woman of whom I'm thinking now. She almost broke up our marriage for different reasons, and one of them was that she came into our life at what was a particularly bad patch, anyway.

Our third daughter, Isabella, was only two or three months old. Like an impatient little ship tearing gaily away from its moorings to be off into the great world, she had got herself born in about an hour, and in her haste had done me some damage. I had gone off rather gloomily to the hospital to be patched up, knowing we couldn't afford the bill. The art-dealing business was down to its last unsalable Staffordshire dog, Kurt was going through one of his phases of dreamy optimism, my parents had paid the rent for nearly half a year. Kurt's phases of optimism, I should explain, always coincide with the decline of our fortunes and the energetic exchange of our few useful possessions for pieces of ancient knickknackery which, in this mood, Kurt believes will be worth a fortune if we "hang on for the right buyer." Since the birth of the baby I had seen the dining-room table twice changed under my very eyes, the living-room carpet replaced by two minute silk mats ("The only things of their kind in the Southern Hemisphere!"), and a bureau with really deep drawers, in which I had kept all the baby's clothes, exchanged for a ridiculous clock with a gilt bear dancing for the amusement of porcelain figurines every time the hour struck.

And when I came back from the hospital, my walnut desk was gone. Of all the things that had moved in and out of our house over eight years, that desk was the one that had endured. It was the one thing that *belonged* to me. The one object I'd had time to make my own. In my mind, it stood outside the continual shift and change of the interior against which I lived.

In its place was a two-foot-high white porcelain figure of a Chinese woman holding a basket of fish.

Kurt smiled at me mournfully and blinked his great eyes at

the figure in rapture and said, "That is the most beautiful thing I have ever seen in my life. That is perfection."

I suppose it was beautiful. I don't know. I don't think I ever saw it; only as the objective manifestation of my hatred for it.

Kurt loved it so much that he sometimes moved it into the bedroom at night, so that when he woke in the morning he would see it. *I* used to see it, gleaming whitely in the dark, when I got up to feed the baby while he slept.

You can imagine, then, how I felt when I came back from a morning's shopping in town one day and found the head of the figure broken off and lying neatly beside it, on the living-room floor. It was almost as if I had stuck pins into the wax effigy of an enemy and then walked in and found the enemy herself lying dead. I was triumphant and guilty, afraid and joyous, all at once. I gave our African servant girl—who, I almost believed, had been the instrument of my malice toward the figure—a half hour of furious reproach (she was leaving anyway because Kurt put too many shirts in the wash) and waited for Kurt to come home.

But my poor Kurt was heartbroken. Not angry, simply heartbroken, the way a man is heartbroken who finds that a woman whom he worships has been unfaithful to him. The figure had been perfection to him, his white goddess, and by losing perfection it affronted and disillusioned him. He had the head stuck on again by the old Belgian china mender who was another of his favorite lame dogs, but it was small consolation to him. He had fallen out of love with the white goddess, and he blamed her for it. He could never forget that the crack was *there*. And so the triumph I had wanted to savor again, before him, was somehow empty and disgruntled, and oddly became something else: a new resentment toward the wretched china figure, because now it had not only become worthless but also had had the effrontery to betray my Kurt.

My real triumph came later.

But let me explain first that this broken love affair of my husband's did not improve our relations. If I was angry with the white goddess for her behavior toward him, this did not mean that I was any the more reconciled to the impossible way he was conducting our life at the time. And things got worse instead of better. About five or six months after this, just when Isabella was creating nightly hell over her teeth, Kurt and a woman painter named Clara Netletter found each other. As I've said before, she was not a woman you would be jealous of; in fact, she did not look like a woman at all, to me. When I say that she was mannish, I don't mean that she in the least resembled one of those girlish-looking men one sees around; I mean that she looked like a *man*. She was immensely tall and hard-bodied and she wore a big watch with a wide leather strap, and she cracked her knuckles when she talked. Her hair stood up, bushy, curly and gray, cropped behind the ears and wild on top, like a cartoon professor's. She painted tremendous abstract pictures (she was supposed to have studied under Prampolini in Italy) and she collected antiques. She was very rich, and very shrewd about the sale and purchase not only of antiques but also of stocks and shares. She had the great patience of the truly acquisitive, and it was said that she would wait years for a change in the family fortunes of a house where she had noted there was some bibelot that she wanted; then she would walk in holding her checkbook and get it at her own price.

That, of course, was precisely what she was doing to us. Kurt wouldn't see it, but it was true, all right. And most of the time she wasn't even paying us in money, but in pictures—*her* pictures. You see, Kurt suddenly had got the idea into his head that he was, as it were, living on the fruits of the past; if he were a true lover of art, an aesthete of real vision and in the tradition of his forefathers, who had bought the beautiful things of their own time to hand down to the reverence of future generations, he would deal not only in beauty that had been confirmed by the perspective of the years, but also would boldly predict future judgments by buying up the art of his own day. Well!

In practice, this was the way it worked out. On weekdays, instead of looking for a job which would do something toward supporting us, he would sit in a coffee shop (the same one where you can always find old Landsdorf, but D. B. was away at the time) with Clara Netletter, discussing art and life. Then on Saturday afternoons Clara's little car would draw up at the gate, and she would stride into the house, knocking on the door and walking in at the same time, and blink at me twice, the way a very busy person with much on his mind might acknowledge the presence of a child or a servant. Kurt would be in the act either of lugging away from its accustomed position some piece of furniture that she wanted to buy, or getting hammer and nails ready to put up a picture of hers he had taken in exchange for something else. If he'd had a tail I suppose he'd have been wagging it. As it was, he was dreamy, excited, vague, talking his head off and pulling the house to pieces to show her how old this varnish was, or the exquisite graining of that. He tripped over the children as if they were floor mops, broke up their dolls' tea parties and wrecked their jigsaw puzzles. "I believe you have three children," Clara Netletter said to me once, the way you might remark that you'd heard that someone did barbola work.

While she and Kurt were closeted together, I would take the children out for a walk around the block. If, when we turned the corner, the little car was still outside our gate, we would go around once again. And again. The baby didn't mind, but the two little girls got bored and begged me to take them to the park. But I wouldn't. I wasn't going anywhere; I was simply waiting for Clara Netletter to go.

Sometimes Kurt would sit in the car talking to her before she

drove off. About the theory of art as understood by Clara Netletter. I couldn't hear what they were saying, but I could *see*,
from the bluff, intense angle of Clara's masculine forearm leaning on the steering wheel, the cocked look about the back of
that poor idiot Kurt's head. I would push the squeaky old per-
ambulator shatteringly through the gateway, sending the shaky
gate clanging and swinging against its supports—the rude, dull,
vulgar intrusion of domesticity itself. Of course, I never turned
to look, but I could picture the impatient twitch of Clara Netletter's handspun-clad shoulder, the shuddering pluck at her
sensibility.

As the pram rolled up the passage toward the children's room,
I would see it: the clean oval on the living-room wall where the
mauve Venetian lamp had been hanging when I went out, or
the rough frame—Clara's frames were always made of sacking,
or sugar-cane husks, or something vastly amusing like that—en-
closing yet another oblong of the stretched shapes, like those
the children made when they pulled gum back and forth between their teeth and thumb and forefinger, which were Clara's
mode of expression in paint. Later, while I bathed the children
and cooked supper, I would push half a dozen times past Kurt
where he stood, bulky and helpless, pondering his latest acquisi-
tion from Clara Netletter, his newest act of faith as a prophet
of art. "Excuse *me*." He would shift obediently aside, only to be
bumped again from *that* angle in a few minutes.

"She's a very clever woman, although she's so terribly ugly,"
he often said wilily to me during these days, fancying himself
to be a man who understood the minds of women.

"I wouldn't care if she were a gargoyle itself. No consolation
to me when I see her wheedling out of you the last few salable
things you've got, in exchange for the outpourings of her mal-
formed soul. Look at those pictures of hers. Can't you recognize
a grandiose fraud when you see one, or doesn't your taste func-

tion after the eighteenth century, like those people who simply don't hear any music later than Bach? And suppose she were any good, which even Isabella could see she isn't, what good will it do us to own a picture that will be worth twenty thousand pounds in 2054?"

These conversations didn't get us anywhere, not even so far as the divorce court, though I felt that we were circling around it once or twice. "*Haeschen, haeschen,*" Kurt would say at last, gently shocked, as if unable to believe in my behaving like this. His large blue eyes drooped toward their fat creases at the outer corners, sheepish and smiling.

I got so tired of Clara Netletter that I began to think quite nostalgically about old D. B. Landsdorf, and to wish that he were in Johannesburg to take up some of Kurt's time, instead of in Cape Town, where he had been gone several months, sponsored by some cultural society or other to start up a magazine that was to be a hybrid between *The Sewanee Review, Encounter,* and *Der Monat.* One Saturday afternoon I pushed the pram around the block five times without once seeing where I was going, crying all the way and not caring who saw me. The fifth time around, the little car was gone, and I trailed clumsily into the house with my brood, feeling flat and mournful and at peace. It was winter, and cold. The boards of the passage proclaimed their chill bareness as we came in over them.

Kurt came out of the kitchen, as if we had caught him up to something. He was on a diet again then, and I thought that he had been filching some forbidden food from the refrigerator. "Clara's gone," he said, smiling almost shyly.

I didn't answer.

"She said to say good-by to you."

"First time she's bothered, I'm sure."

"But this time she's really gone. She's leaving Johannesburg and going back to her house at the sea."

Before I could react to this piece of good news, I happened to notice something different about the wall above the telephone table, which stood in the angle where the passage made a turn toward the bedrooms. It was a new canvas by Clara Netletter. The biggest yet in my husband's collection. I was suddenly furious. "So, I see she didn't fail to lay the last of her abstract cuckoo eggs in my nest! Kurt, you *idiot!*"

He smiled at me. Oh, Kurt's patient, sheepish, maddening smiles. "Don't worry," he said. "I've got a buyer for it already. I can get three hundred pounds for it tomorrow, if I want to."

"Yes, I can imagine. Three buyers. And what did you give her for it, if I may ask? I can't imagine we've anything left that she'd consider worthy exchange for that monster."

Kurt came up and lifted my hair back behind my left ear (I flinched like a fly-plagued horse). "Darling," he said—he wore a look of conspiratorial shrewdness on his fat face, the way a baby looks in a top hat—"I gave her the white porcelain Chinese figure."

My ears, nipped by the cold, and my nose, tender from crying, burned with a slow, tingling blush. It was as if Kurt suddenly had made a passionate declaration of love for me in front of the children. Indeed, the presence of the two little girls, and even the baby, looking up at me, embarrassed and confused me. Keeping my head down, so that Kurt couldn't see whether I was giggling or on the verge of tears, or both, I jostled pram and children into their room. The white goddess! That damn smooth, serene face that used to gleam out at me in the middle of the night. Kurt's perfect beauty. The creature who let him down by having her neck broken. The white goddess, given away by him. And to Clara Netletter. Fobbed off—good riddance, twice good riddance—to Clara Netletter. Oh, here was *my* satisfaction in something perfect! I *was* crying and giggling at the same time.

Of course, things didn't remain on that hysterical plane. The Kurt Breslauers of this world don't really change in a day, or ever. But as each Saturday without her passed, the constricting tensions of Clara Netletter snapped from me one by one, and, every day, the house without the white goddess was a place where I could stroll from room to room, taking deep breaths and stretching my arms pleasurably. Kurt and I could even talk about them now, the white goddess and Clara Netletter. "Did she know about the mended neck?" I whispered to Kurt one night after we had put out the light above our bed. It was a question I had been wanting to ask for a long time. The mattress squeaked as Kurt turned over slowly, like a whale surfacing, and he chuckled. "I didn't tell her," he said softly. In complete accord, we slept.

Of course, we were still poor. We still lived, as my mother always says, pressing her left hand to that particular bone in her corset behind which she believes her heart to be imprisoned, "from hand to mouth, my dear, from hand to mouth." Shortly after this, Kurt got the job of representative of a firm of chemical engineers, which I mentioned before, and then, when that wasn't any good, an Italian ex-count he met at the coffee shop gave him some agencies for textiles.

It was when Kurt had been in the textile business for about five months and before it began to go wrong that old D. B. Landsdorf turned up in Johannesburg again. There was his hesitant, fluttering voice over the telephone one evening, back from Cape Town. It was I who answered the call. "Dr. Landsdorf! It's a surprise to hear your voice again. What are you doing here? How's the magazine?"

I should have known better than to ask. The magazine was not. D. B. Landsdorf was right back where he always had been, "looking around" again. I was sorry, I assured him. (I had been sorry so many times before.) It was nice to have him back in

Johannesburg, anyway. Oh, yes . . . er-er . . . he was glad . . . er-er, . . . to . . . um . . . be back. He must come to dinner sometime, perhaps next week? Oh, yes, he would like that, it was most kind. He was especially keen to see Kurtchen, because he had something he wanted to show him. I called Kurt to the telephone. When he had finished speaking to old D. B. he came back into the dining room with his eyes soft with pleasure.

"So the boy friend's back," I said, smiling at him.

"*Ach*, he's so excited," said Kurt, ignoring, in a manner typical of himself and Dr. Landsdorf, the failure of the magazine. "He's bought something, some art treasure. A wonderful thing, he says. He won't tell me anything about it until I've seen it. It's something he picked up in Cape Town, apparently."

I was not alarmed by Kurt's interest. I was lulled, as—weak woman, with all my experience of him—I have never learned not to be, by the precarious current security, this time the Italian textile business.

My poor Kurt could not wait to see his friend's work of art. He telephoned me next day from the textile sample rooms, to say that he was bringing D. B. home for dinner. I put a chicken on to boil, thinking of old D. B.'s delicate stomach. The two men came home at about six, and I happened to go out onto the veranda to bring in the baby's playpen just after the little car which the textile people provided for Kurt had drawn up at the gate. Kurt's elephantine beam and the bony curve of old Dr. Landsdorf's bent stick of a back showed them to be busy getting something out of the boot. I hastily dumped the playpen indoors, and as I came back into the passage, Kurt and D. B. Landsdorf were entering through the front door, carrying between them a large cardboard packing case whose contents evidently had been inspected and rather hastily put back—the two sides of the lid peaked up, and some straw was hanging out.

"What's that?" I said, following them as they carried it into

127

the living room. "Oh, how exciting! You've brought your find to show me, Dr. Landsdorf."

"Madam Breslauer," he said, between the parenthesis of his withered cheeks, "er-er most kind . . . You are always . . . Dinner, it may be a trouble . . . ?"

"*Haeschen*," said Kurt. "He bought it from Clara Netletter in Cape Town last week. He persuaded her to sell it. He bought it half with his last check from the magazine, but as her price was very high and that wasn't enough, he borrowed the other half of the money."

While he spoke, Kurt lifted the white porcelain Chinese figure out of the straw and set it down on the hall table, not three yards from its old place.

M̃ost women have a parting shot—the eternal revival of a past injustice which they use ruthlessly and indiscriminately, to end all arguments. My mother's was our Uncle Chookie. No matter how wrong she was (and being daily indoctrinated by her in the absolute rightness of everything she said and did, we never dreamed of thinking she was wrong), she put herself in the right at the end of every argument by flinging at my father, "And in all these years you never once offered to send my poor brother a ten-shilling postal order!" There, of course, she *was* right. He never had. And so, whatever the matter of the argument, we saw from my father's inability to counter the fact of this one neglect that he was wrong, wrong again, and my mother the injured.

The silence of the end of the argument hung in the air like steam in the street after a summer rainstorm—the silence of Uncle Chookie, produced in all its unfailing power. For, of course, we knew it was Uncle Chookie of whom my mother spoke, although she never mentioned him by name and she had two other brothers. Uncle Chookie's real name was Bernard, like my brother's, but I suppose the childish appellation had been given Uncle Chookie when he was a baby, as such names are given to so many, pending the time when he should grow up into the other. He is about forty in my memory, so that must be about the age he was when we children began to notice him first, but because we had never known him when he was younger, or by any other name, there seemed to us nothing incongruous about knowing as "Uncle Chookie" this tall, already gray-haired, bent man—bent not of his own volition but as our tall hollyhocks were bent after hard rain. His long hands touched everything—even your own when you greeted him—uncertainly, and they smelled, not as our father's did, of tobacco and news-print and petrol, but of soap, like a woman's. Uncle Chookie had large, gray eyes—mournful eyes, as we called them, like my mother's and mine—and around them a recess of delicate, dark-ened skin. But that was as far as the family likeness went; he was loose-boned where my mother was small and neat, he was slow of movement where she was quick, and, above all, he was silent; she had a high clear voice and talked all the time. When he was in our house he seemed like a shadow of my mother—a silent creature, looking out of her eyes, sitting where she sat, following her quietly from room to room.

He came to spend a fortnight with us in Johannesburg every year, and in between these visits we children never saw him, though once a month or so my mother would bake a cake in the evening, put out her things for an early start the next morning, and say—to our native maid, or to an aunt—on the telephone—"I'm going to poor Chookie tomorrow, you know. I feel I must, though it's such a drag." Then, before the three of us left for school in the morning, she would be gone to catch an early train to the Northern Transvaal town where Uncle Chookie lived—rather poorly, we gathered, but decently enough. "Of course, he's got his own room," we had overheard her telling someone once. "A few of his own things and a spirit stove for tea and so on, and there's another man next door—a schoolteacher, he was, I believe—also very nice, poor thing, and Chookie shares a bit of cake with him, and if *he* gets anything, he always takes some in to Chookie."

We children looked forward to Uncle Chookie's fortnight,

though once it came, there was little to distinguish it from any other fortnight; it merely had its place in the marking off of the year into birthdays, Christmas, school and holiday time. It helped, along with the other events, in the gradual relating of the timelessness of childhood to the rigidly time-conscious adult world. Once really with us, Uncle Chookie was scarcely there. He liked to stand in windows, coat peaked out at the back because of his stooping shoulders, watching. If we came past, chasing one another in some game, he appeared to be watching us. If we were not there, he might be watching the birds on the lawn, or the clouds. He ran his hand stiffly over the spine of the cat; at meals he hardly spoke. And my mother did not make any plans while he was with us. "I won't be going anywhere much just now—while I've got Chookie with me, you know," she would apologize on the telephone. Then she would come into the room where he stood, and, her head consideringly on one side, ask him what he would like to eat, the way she would come into a room and ask you what you fancied when you were sick in bed. "I think I'll get the man to fillet us a couple of nice soles, shall I? They would be nice for lunch," she would say. "Would you like them fried, or would you rather I did them with a white sauce?"

He would sigh and stare back at her with that anxious, affronted look that came to his face whenever he was spoken to, as if being addressed were a burden on him, a responsibility he didn't feel he could take. "I don't mind, Bab. Fried will do for me. With a bit of lemon . . . I don't mind. Fried or boiled. I don't mind how I take it."

And they would stand held in the anxiousness of each other's eyes for a moment—you almost expected to see them sway, their eyes were so dark and big and fascinated—before my mother murmured heavily, "Right, then. Right," and went off to the kitchen.

The only time Uncle Chookie ever really made the fortnight

131

his own was when he sang for us. On top of the highly polished upright on which my brother Bernard and I practiced "Für Elise," there was an untidy pile of popular music—albums of songs from the Kern and Gershwin and Rodgers-and-Hart musicals that came so thick and splendid from New York in the Thirties, and "selections" from London and Broadway successes. My mother, who, difficult though it is to believe now, must still have been a young woman and interested in such things, had mastered a kind of hop and thump in the bass that was known at the time as "syncopation." We liked to stand around her after supper, following her curious hobbling-out of the tunes with much thin volume but little "voice"; my sister Katie, at fifteen, managed quite sweetly on the lower notes, but disappeared entirely out of normal hearing range, perhaps into that suprahuman register that dogs are said to be able to hear, on the higher ones.

My mother's brother was attracted by this gathering around the piano. He would be drawn to it, rather than consciously join us of his own free will; one moment he would be sitting in his chair, the next we would feel his coat sleeves, smell his linen-cupboard odor, among us. And he would start to sing, and we would gradually stop. He would sing on alone, in a slightly husky, mellow voice, and when one song was finished, go on to another. My mother would turn the pages and change the tune without speaking or moving her head, as if she were participating in a spell. We would fall back, literally. First our voices went, and then we ourselves, moving away from the piano to perch on the arms of chairs or lie down on the old, molting leopard-skin rug, to listen. Uncle Chookie, who apparently could bear to speak only under cover of the conversation of others, and who fell instantly silent—died out in the middle of a sentence, in fact—if he heard his own voice speaking out loud, would sing on for half an hour in the center of everyone's absolute silence

132

and attention. He, who looked at everything from a bus ticket to a fork as if it presented some menacing challenge to him, would glance at the music sheet now and then to verify a coming note or a word of the lyric, as if the printed sheet were to him, as it would be to anyone else, merely a piece of paper. He was casual. Standing up singing alone in an attentive room, he met our eyes.

I remember particularly a song from an English revue called "Clowns in Clover"; you could be sure that if he had not joined us at the piano before, he would do so when we reached the point in the "selection" where this song began. We children would waver through the revue's "chorus" numbers, a novelty number, and what was, I think, a kind of tango, and then, with the first notes of this particular song, his voice would be there:

> "I've got those Little Boy Blues,
> My heart's right down in my shoes,
> Just for that little boy who's
> For-getting me . . ."

I realize now that this must have been a curiously inappropriate song to be sung by Uncle Chookie—one so obviously meant for a Gertrude Lawrence or a Bea Lillie. Yet we—or at least Bernard and I—did not find it in the least incongruous, so I am sure that, for some equally curious reason, it wasn't. We would have been amazed, too, if anyone had found it funny. It couldn't have been that, either. Children are usually right about these things. Now, of course, I find the contrast between Uncle Chookie and his song ironic, but if children have any sort of innocence of mind left them by the time they are ten and twelve, as Bernard and I were, it is innocence of irony, so we could not have been expected to notice that.

It was when the McKechnies moved away from the house two doors up. We children hung about watching the new people move in. I saw two boys about Bernard's age, with ears like the handles of pitchers, and then a rather strange-looking little girl, younger than I, with a thick neck and a babyish bow in her hair. She called out to me something that I didn't hear properly, because I couldn't understand what it was that she said.

Bernard was not slow in getting to know people. Later in the same afternoon, he came back from playing with the two new boys.

"What's the matter with the sister?" I said. "She said something to me that I didn't hear, and then she slammed the door."

"She's loony," said Bernard, with relish. He rolled his eyes, clutched the front of his hair, and lolled his tongue out.

"You know you're not allowed to use that word," said Kate, looking at him with her customary disgust.

"Her brothers told me she's loony," said Bernard indignantly. "You know what? In their old house, she tore the pages out of the telephone book and stuffed them in the lavatory. You should just hear her—she makes the most awful noises, like an ol' cat." He gave a demonstration, brushing aside Katie's protests with "I'm loony! Ooh, I'm loony! I can't help it, I tell you, I'm loony!"

He and I fell upon each other, shrieking; I lay laughing, but he was too delighted with the idea of pretending to be mad and kept his tongue lolling out at Katie.

"Just you let Mother see you carrying on like that," said Katie. "Just you let her see you making fun of that kid."

"Look, my tongue's got all dry—feel it!" In his interest, Bernard forgot to be mad. When his tongue was comfortably moistened again, he said, "They'll have to send her to a loony bin when she's grown up."

"*Bernard!*" Katie was exasperated.

"Frightened of your Mommy! What will Mommy say?" Bernard taunted her.

Katie got the look on her face of having something behind her back that she didn't want to show anyone. "You know it's not that. You'll just hurt her feelings, that's all." She sat there looking at us.

"Why?" I asked, suddenly feeling awkward.

"Because," she said.

"She'd just say it was unkind to talk that way, that's all," I offered.

Katie shook her head. A hangnail on her thumb caught on the silk of her dress, and she lifted her thumb and bit at it with fierce concentration for a second or two. Then she said, "You know why. Because of Uncle Chookie. Uncle Chookie's in one."

Bernard shot her a fast, aghast, derisive look. *"He's not!"*

"Oh, yes, he is," she said conversationally. "A mental hospital. That's where he always comes from, to visit us. Where d'you think he is all the time, and why don't we ever go to see him?"

"But he's not mad," I said, looking first at Katie and then at Bernard, and seeing Bernard as he had been a minute before, with his tongue hanging out and his eyes rolling. "Uncle Chookie's not mad?"

Katie shrugged. She put her smarting thumb to the warmth of her neck and looked at our stricken faces with a kind of ashamed satisfaction at the sight of her handiwork.

I spent a great deal of time trying to find out if what Katie had told us was true. I did everything but ask. That was impossible. Impossible, too, to speak about it to Bernard, who must have been as bewildered as I, or to Katie, who had accepted it and was apparently calmly going on with her life. It was true, of course, that my mother did not allow us to talk of "loonies," but then we were not allowed, either, to call black people "niggers" or "Kaffirs," nor could we, without reproof, be overheard referring to someone who squinted as "boss-eyed." So how was one to tell?

I went along the road many times to stare, fascinated, at the thick-necked child in the garden two doors away, grunting in the dust where she wandered all day long, shut out of the house like some small, noisome animal. I watched her brothers when they came to play at our house with Bernard. I listened to my mother chattering to the native servant girl above the thick sound of batter being beaten in the kitchen.

I went into the bedroom I shared with Katie and looked at my eyes in the mirror. My mother's eyes. *His* eyes.

And when the voices of the others came out, very jolly around the piano in the evening:

> ". . . heart's right down in my shoes,
> Just for that little boy who's
> For-getting me . . ."

I dropped out of their circle, their jollity, and went off to my room, where I lay on my bed, eyes open in the dark, still hearing it.

One afternoon, when I had finished practicing, I took "Clowns in Clover" out of the pile of music and hid it in a box of my father's old technical books.

I never really found out. Gradually, as I grew older, my mother began to talk as if it were accepted that I knew Uncle Chookie was in a mental hospital—as, I suppose, she had begun to talk before Katie when Katie was my age. And no doubt she expected that, like Katie, I would accept it simply as a piece of rather sad information. She never noticed the blankness with which I met the mention of his name; she never once sensed the hostility I felt—was it toward Uncle Chookie, for linking me inescapably with a world of horror and confusion that I half sensed, half imagined out of my fear, or toward my mother, until now my shield against all that was painful, for exposing me to this ugly awareness by having him for a brother, or toward myself, for carrying in my veins the blood of this gentle, kindly creature?

As we children began to grow up, the yearly visits were dropped. It may have been because my mother's brother, like a prisoner who learns to prefer the safety of prison to the bewilderment of the world outside, no longer wished to come, or maybe my mother felt that with Bernard thirteen, me almost fifteen, and Katie a young lady with suitors about, his presence might be an embarrassment. I remember what must have been the last time he came, though, and the last time I saw him. Immediately I had heard he was expected for the usual fortnight, I announced casually that I would be spending that particular time with a friend with whom I often exchanged visits; I was at the age when girls have violently secretive friendships. But unfortunately he arrived a little earlier than he had been expected, and I had to meet him, after all—at the top of the stairs, in fact, just as I was coming down with my suitcase and my tennis racket in its initialed drawstring cover.

I had thought about him such a great deal and had not seen him for such a long time that the sight of him, like opening one's eyes to the plain, calm daylight of a room that has just been swollen and twisted as the *mise en scène* of a nightmare, shocked me into anticlimax. I stood there at the top of our stairs, and he stood a few steps below, holding an umbrella and a neat, shabby portmanteau, which accentuated the curve of his stoop. Each of us held back, waiting for the other to get out of the way first, like two nervous animals who do not recognize each other's scent. He was afraid, always afraid, and perhaps, for him, it was merely a confirmation of what he *knew*, to find that someone else —one of the others, outside of what he knew—was afraid, too. We met on his ground that day. As I looked at him—a graying, never-old, never-young man—guilt inflamed through all my veins, as adrenalin comes with anger. But all that I had wound about him in my thoughts came up to obscure me from shame; guilt hardened into hostility and revulsion. Without a word, I bolted past him down the stairs.

In the fifteen years since, I have never had a chance to say that word or to smile that smile. He died several years ago, out of sight, as he had lived. But the other day when I turned on the radio, I heard the song, the song from "Clowns in Clover." And I found myself remembering with real pleasure that slightly husky, mellow voice—the voice of Uncle Chookie. So perhaps I have made it all right—if such things are possible between this world and the next—between him and me.

A Wand'ring Minstrel, I

Rupert and Lilo Grant had been expecting them all day. "*With* the three children?" asked the little Polish baroness who came to play tennis.

"But, my dear, what could I do?" Lilo threw up her hands and the plucked ridge of her own eyebrows flew up too, underscoring the painted ones she shaped to her defiant fancy.

"Oh, I *know*," said one of the other women, the corner of her mouth whitening for a moment in that knowing, stoic sense of iniquity into which even the women most indulged by men plunge, like a kind of atavism, when they are championing their own sex against some injustice of the other. "That poor thing never has her children under one roof with her. They're always farmed out—someone takes this one, someone else takes that one."

"Is that so?" somebody's husband asked. "But he's an able fellow?"

"Able, mmh—" With a jerk of her head, Lilo indicated her husband, Rupert, as if to say, "Ask him."

But all Rupert said was "Ah, it's a mess." He did not want to talk about the man who was to be his guest.

Like all Rupert's obscure loyalties, this brought a little rise of irritation, like bile, into Lilo's mouth.

"Mess, all right. That's putting it mildly. He's had three jobs in five months. I mean you can go on being talented just so long.

People get a bit tired of it. Utterly irresponsible, utterly un-reliable."

"So how do they live, for heaven's sake?"

"They don't, my dear. At least not the way a normal woman expects to live."

The men were laughing among themselves about something else. But the women remembered things they had heard, casual meetings.

"She's English, isn't she? Rather pretty? And there's a fat little girl?"

"Oh, of course! They were the people who stayed in the Elsburgs' house while Cissie was away."

"Well, so's he English. Got a DFC or something in the RAF."

"No, a DSO, I remember, the same time as my brother."

"Well, anyway. He brought her out to South Africa and went and had three children and never did any good at all. That girl's never known what it is to have two rooms she could call her own."

"So they spend all their time living in other people's houses, while people are away on holiday and so on?"

"All the time. She packs and unpacks. With three children, can you imagine?"

"I have seen this Mrs. . . ." The baroness paused; the name eluded her. She went on in a kind of detached wonder at the description of a woman's life which she felt she did not under-stand, not out of the impossibility of herself being in such a posi-tion, but out of the barrier of language and background, as she might fail to understand the point of an English joke: "I have seen her at the club. Once she was dancing there, with that tall one—"

"Barron? Barrow? The Colonel Barrow, that's right?" supplied her husband, pleased that he had remembered an English name.

"Oh, poor girl, it's a wonder! She has little enough pleasure, heaven knows."

"Why, only last week—" said Rupert in spite of himself.

Lilo tried for the last sip of her drink, but it was an illusion of the bottom of the glass; there was nothing for her to swallow. "She phoned up before eight one morning. I heard there was something funny about her voice. But you know, she's rather reserved."

"Oh, she's a nice girl," someone affirmed.

"Too fine for him, that's it, I should say."

"So I didn't say anything, I simply called Rupert—she asked for him. So then she says to Rupert in her quiet, controlled way, 'Please, Rupert, I don't want to bother you, but I haven't seen Andrew since the day before yesterday, late in the afternoon. He went to some club celebration that should have been over by six or seven. Would you ask at the club, if you happen to be there for lunch today? It may be that he's been there, or they've seen him.' "

"How awful!" One of the women looked as if she had just seen an abyss, dark and terrible, which—who knows?—one might have opened up under one's own feet, simply by smiling at the wrong man at the wrong moment.

"So you *see*, my girl." An affectionate husband patted his wife warningly on her soft girlish behind as she passed his chair. And the atmosphere of the room changed, as a mirror changes as it is turned in the light; at once they were all easy with chaffing banalities.

They trooped in to lunch. "Cold, I'm afraid," said Lilo. "Without decent servants, hot lunch for more than four's impossible here on a Sunday. Rosie's off."

"Well, we'll warm our blood with some red wine," said Rupert amiably.

"Excellent!" someone murmured.

Rupert called from the darkness of the cupboard where liquor was kept, "What's happened to the other two bottles of Beaune, Lo?"

"Oh, all right, I'm coming," she said, and added in a confidential undertone to her woman friend beside her, "To tell you the truth, I've put most of our decent liquor away, before *he* comes. Not that one wants to be mean—"

"Of course. He drinks like a fish, I believe. So for *her* sake, anyway."

"Exactly. I'll offer him one drink every night before dinner, and that's all. I'm going to warn Rupert, too—you know what men are, no sense. I don't want that poor girl embarrassed in my house."

After lunch the affectionate husband and his young wife left, and the rest of the guests sat about on the terrace among the ash trays and the coffee cups. Lilo and Rupert were easy, thoughtful hosts. "Who'd like a snooze?" she asked. "Plenty of beds upstairs."

"Oh, I don't think so."

"Too nice out here, Lo."

"What's happened to your boarders?"

"Well, I don't know. I said any time they were ready, we'd be here all day anyway. Their rooms are ready for them."

"I'm sure Sigmund likes to sleep," the baroness said, smiling.

The baron shrugged, politely denying his suppressed yawns and the puffiness of his face around the eyes.

"Yes, I know, I know him!" his wife cried delightedly.

"Come on, Sigmund," said Rupert. "Let's go up. I'm dead too."

"Of course," said Lilo. "What about you, Noele?"

Two of the men and three of the women went upstairs, leaving the baroness with her shining, unpowdered face turned to the sun, and the two other men with the Sunday papers behind which they instantly began to breathe deeply and regularly in the slumping anesthesia of food and wine.

It was five o'clock by the time the Douglases came. They arrived just at the point when they had failed the mild expectancy of the household so long that everyone momentarily really had forgotten about them; they produced a pause, a moment of unexpressed confusion when the room full of people was confronted with the living reminder of the couple about whom so much had been said all day. The faces turned toward Sheila Douglas—that curiously English contradiction, dark beauty and primness—and her husband Andrew—filling the doorway behind her with his large sandy-colored presence—tingled with guilt.

The baroness, looking out of her schoolgirl's large eyes as if she peered over a wall, remembered Sheila, but did not think that she had seen the husband before. The baron, sleepily immersed in politics, which worked around his mind as slowly and seriously in South Africa as they had done in Europe, rose from his chair and stood a moment with his heels neatly together; as he sat down again he remembered who these people were and lowered his eyelids as a cat does when settling down to regard something interesting.

Lilo stood introducing everyone to Mrs. Douglas. In between, she fussed aside: "Sheila, my dear, I've put your little Elizabeth in with Eva. I hope you'll approve. . . . One side of the cupboard is cleared for her things, if that will be enough."

The tall, smooth-browed English girl, whose eyes looked as if they had never focused on anything smaller or warmer than open spaces, whose stiff, little-girl neck rose very straight from her neat blouse, smiled slowly and faintly to everyone, looked submission to Lilo, and sank, still very upright, to the edge of the sofa, next to Noele and Bertie Haffner. Noele said brightly, "I'm sorry I take up so much room. The way Lilo feeds you!

I could see myself spreading visibly, all day. . . ." But the young woman merely looked at her quickly, like a child who does not know whether or not to answer, and continued to sit on the edge. Her two hands met each other in her lap.

"Hullo," said Andrew Douglas, from the door. It was an amused hullo—at once a greeting, a reminder, and a challenge. He stood there looking at them all.

"Oh, I'm awfully sorry—Andrew, Baron Varohevsky, Baroness Varohevsky, Noele and Bertie Haffner, and I think you know Archie. And this is Archie's wife, Betty, and Frank Davis."

Andrew Douglas stood at the door, touching a hand to his forehead in salute to them. He was so big, it seemed for a moment that the frame of the door held him there. Did he need holding? Or did they imagine that he swayed slightly, or rather that the way he held himself showed that somewhere inside him something swayed?

"Hi," he said, looking down between his legs. "Hi there!"

A little boy as sandy-haired as himself burst through his parted knees; Lilo's Eva struggled past at the same time. Another small girl, also sandy-haired, came in and went straight and silently to the side of her dark mother, sitting in silence on the edge of the sofa. Noele's blond children, pale-eyed furies, tore in, too.

Andrew grinned down at them. He was one of those handsome fair men whose features, eyes, and markings of hairline and brows have become smudged and neutral-toned in the dissolvent of liquor and fleshiness. Every brandy he took, like an inconsequent drip wearing away the fine edge of a stone, gently smoothed away the clarity with which once his nose had been cut against the planes of his face, washed the green and sharp hazel flecks of his eyes more nondescriptly into each other. His whole face had the effect of being a little blurred to the eye of the beholder, like a print that has been over-enlarged. He had a large mouth with freckled lips—the kind of mouth that must always be fresh from the imprint of a kiss, a drink, or a dangling cigarette.

"Swept off my feet. Do you think I look like a swing door?"

"Oh, yes, Dad, be one, be one!"

His small son charged at him and the man whirled his heavy body around with surprising agility.

The children squealed under his flaying arms. He sat down suddenly in a chair, in the midst of them. Their faces were turned expectantly to him. Over their low heads he caught the eye of the little baroness and smiled at her lazily, acknowledging the child in her, too. A suffused brightness came up over her face; caught out, she smiled back.

All conversation in the room had ceased at the entry of the new guests; it seemed impossible to revive it. It was as if the big blunt presence of this man who should, surely, have sensed the weight of the others' disapproval and discussion of him and have felt some measure of unease before them, had thrown them off their social balance by his complete ease. Somewhere, subconsciously perhaps, they had determined that they *would* put him at ease, *for her sake,* if nothing else, in order to save her embarrassment. Now it was he who seemed to be putting them at ease. He sat in his chosen chair looking around at them, moving slightly to shift himself to comfort inside the rather washed-out army-issue shorts which were too tight for him around the waist.

Rupert was busy pouring drinks again, as he had been before lunch. Noele and the baroness had theirs already; Bertie had asked for gin and tonic, the baron a vermouth. When Rupert asked Sheila Douglas what she would have, she started, and, sitting nervously forward, said almost inaudibly, "Oh—thank you— a small gin and lime juice, please, if you have it." Her large, dark, blank eyes were fixed on her husband in a kind of taut, warning expectation. He looked up in answer to Rupert's question, felt

145

himself interrupted, like a tap on the shoulder, by the intensity of the girl's look, and could not escape it, met it good-naturedly, ironically, but not with the weight of his full attention; meanwhile he was waggling a foot to amuse the little Eva.

Suddenly the English girl said stiffly, "I wish you wouldn't." The remark fell with the prim clarity of a stone into a puddle. Everyone in the room was instantly remote with embarrassment, except Andrew Douglas and the children around him. He leaned his head back against his chair, looking lazily questioningly from his wife to Rupert. "Just a small brandy. And water, Rupert, please." He lowered his head in an imaginary charge at the little Eva, who crouched back squealing delightedly.

His wife sat with every line of her body drawn up, looking at him. Noele Haffner managed a light polite remark to the baroness, Bertie said something to Frank Davis, but whatever was spoken was merely an undertone to the line of high tension humming from the figure of Sheila Douglas to the heavy blond man relaxed in his chair.

He made no attempt to join in the desultory conversation, but, unlike his wife, who was obviously deaf to the normal, the trivial inconsequentialities about her, he had the look of a man who had half an ear for the talk, tolerantly, even though he could not bring himself to the trouble of contributing. She sat isolated in her reproach.

He finished half his drink, deliberately, almost musingly. Once he found himself looking straight at that pretty, tight English face, the discreetly tinted mouth with the corners of the lips pulled in, the small, narrow-nostriled nose, the well-washed ears just showing beneath the perfectly neat, conventionally cut hair. And Noele Haffner saw the skin under his eyes crinkle in an intimate, insolent, culpable smile that was closer to a wink.

Nothing moved in the face of the English girl. Even the dark lashes remained lowered and steady.

The man heaved himself up out of his chair with a grunt and wandered over to the window, where he put his glass down on the sill. The children were about the floor, getting under his feet. He picked up a toy guitar one of them had left lying on a stool and said, catching one of Noele's blonds by the hair, "What can you sing? D'you know 'Yankee Doodle'?" He stood there, grinning, with the toy in his freckled hands. And, strumming, he began to sing himself, ". . . went to town, riding on a pony."

He pulled a chair around and sat down to it. The children giggled. "Oh my darlin', oh my darlin', oh my darlin' Clem-en-tine," he sang softly. And then with a thump and a flourish on the tuneless strings, he burst into "Camptown Races" with a minstrel accent and gestures in the best and most exuberant tradition.

The children came and stood around him, as if he were a freak, with all the cruel candor of their curiosity.

"Sing some more," they demanded, as they might have said, "Show us your sores."

Now, he had the low, insinuating drawl of a torch singer; the pouches of his faded handsomeness drooped toward his red-grained neck. "It was just one of those things . . . if we'd thought a bit, of the end of it, wh-en we start-ed painting the town . . . we'd have been a-ware, that our love affair was too hot . . . not to cool down. . . ." He broke off, smiling at their puzzled faces: "No? Well, what about this?" and he sang "Abdul the Bulbul Amir."

They were enchanted: the small Eva moved her head with a gasp of distress when Ivan Petruski Skavar was slain; the breathing of the boys was heavy as in the act of identifying themselves with cowboys in a film. After four or five verses, the baroness came and stood with an arm about each of the blond Haffners. Frank Davis leaned forward with his elbows on his spread knees, his emptied glass dangling like a transparent lily between his hands. Noele Haffner crossed one tightly stockinged leg over the other and sat back, the corners of her mouth twitching. Smiling, Rupert got up to replenish Davis' glass, and, in answer to a frowning, parenthetic sh-sh! from Lilo, almost tiptoed.

"Did you ever know that song of the French, perhaps?" said the baroness when the ditty was over. "I heard it when I was with my father in Paris during the Occupation—how was it?" And shyly, she lifted her hand and conducted her own thin voice for a bar or two.

Andrew Douglas sat with his full lips amusedly together, gravely, the guitar still in his hands. Then he struck an excruciatingly tuneless chord on the thing and began to sing, in good French, the song of which she was thinking.

"But you sing awfully well!" said the girl Betty.

He inclined his head to her, mockingly obsequious, goodnatured.

"A damned sight better than the stuff they put over the radio," Frank Davis admitted.

Bertie Haffner was looking at Douglas appraisingly. He said suddenly, "You know, I think we were once on a party together in Cairo. End of '44 or beginning of '45. Of course . . . But you were half the size then, man—"

"And *your* waistline?" his wife Noele cut in indignantly. "Have you forgotten your ten pounds around the middle?"

"Oh, I know, I know." Bertie laughed, putting his hand gently on his crumpled waistband.

"Sing 'Alouette'! Please!" Betty pleaded. "I adore 'Alouette.'"

The big blunt hand handled the toy guitar as if it were a Stradivarius, in an elaboration of care that counterpointed his performance with burlesque. The voice went from "Alouette" into one of those childish songs with a refrain in which a noise is substituted for one of the words: "A fly flew in the window . . .

he—" Andrew Douglas rolled his veined green eyes, blew noisily through his freckled lips—"there, and he—" the children shrieked with laughter and made the noise for him—"there, and he flew right out again." The grownups made a discreetly laughing audience.

"Do you think that's a song to sing to children?" The English girl had her hands clenched in her lap now. Her face, firm and pretty and unchanged, unaware of its inability to change, regarded him as she must have learned, ten years ago, when she was a school prefect, to regard one of the girls who had let down the honor of the house. Her slim defenseless back, stiffened only by the starch of gentility, bastioned her against the people in the room.

A flicker of interest passed to her; but eyes were on the entertainer; there was even, perhaps, a slight irritation at the interruption. Noele Haffner turned to the young woman with a smile of intercession and appeal that instantly withdrew feebly, like a foot that has been put in the wrong doorway.

In the interval of three sound thrums, between verses and refrain, Andrew Douglas grinned at his wife, a warm, impervious, shamefaced, flirtatious grin—the grin with which he had looked at her for the first time eight years ago across a bar in London. His underlip gleamed with the saliva of song; his eyes swam a little with the second brandy which Rupert had given him.

The Grants' Eva went and hitched herself up onto the arm of his chair, in a claim of intimacy; the man's big hand left the guitar a moment to steady her (that was the gesture, too, with which he always had put out his hand to stroke the hair of a passing girl behind the back of the girl with whom he might be dancing).

Immediately his own daughter left her mother's side and wriggled up onto his lap in possession. He played the guitar held above her small head. He passed from the mildly bawdy to the sentimental ballad now, while everyone had another drink, and the children began to have the look in their eyes that comes just before sleep.

He was singing an old Gilbert and Sullivan air—". . . a wand'ring minstrel, I, a thing of shreds and patches . . ."—when Lilo became conscious that something had altered in the composition of the room, and saw that the English girl, the young wife with the neat black curls and straight back, must have left the room some minutes before, unnoticed by anyone; had gone, ignored, past the backs of their chairs and out of the door, up to the two rooms which did not belong to her.

Happy Event

There were so many things in life you couldn't ever imagine yourself doing, Ella Plaistow told herself. Once or twice she had said it aloud, too, to Allan. But mostly it grew, forced its way up out of the silences that fell upon her like a restraining hand during those first few days after she had come home from the nursing home. It seemed to burst through her mouth in a sudden irresistible germination, the way a creeper shoots and uncurls into leaf and stem in one of those films which telescope plant growth into the space of a few terrifying vital seconds.

Silence followed it again. In her mind, if she had spoken inwardly, to herself; in the room, if she had spoken aloud. The silence that covers the endless inward activity of shuffling for a foothold, making out of a hundred-and-one past justifications and pressures the accommodations of a new position for oneself. It was true, of course. You start off as a child (it was so long ago, there have been so many slight shifts, this way and that, that it is difficult to remember when), pretending to think the blond doll prettier than the brunette, so that your loved sister may fall into the trap of choosing the one you don't want for yourself. You go on, by one day finding your own tongue glibly acquiescing to a discussion of your best friend's temperament with someone whom you know to be her disliked enemy. And before you know where you are, you have gone through all the sidlings and inveiglings of taking somebody's work for less than it is worth, throwing someone into an agony of jealousy for the sake of a moment's vanity, pretending not to see an old lover lest he should not seem impressive enough in the eyes of the new one. It is impossible to imagine yourself doing any of these; but once done . . . Like ants teeming to repair a broken anthill, like white corpuscles rushing to a wound, all the forces that protect oneself from oneself have already begun their quick, sure, furtive, uneasy juggling for a new stance, a rearrangement for comfort into which amorphous life seems to have edged you.

"It's your *body* that objects," said Allan. "Remember that. That's all. There's some sort of physical protest that's got nothing to do with you at all, really. You must expect it. It'll pass off in a week or so."

And of course he was quite right. She certainly didn't have any regrets. They had two children, a girl and a boy (the wrong way round, as they said—the girl was the elder—but it's dangerous to have everything too much the way you want it!) who were just old enough to be left with their grandmother. Allan's new partner was thoroughly reliable, the bond on the house was almost paid off; at last there was nothing to stop Allan and Ella —they had booked to go to Europe, in the spring of next year. So to have allowed themselves to be stopped by this—! To be, instead, this time next year, caught up in chemists' bills and diapers and wakeful nights all over again! No, they had brought up their babies, had loved and resented them and were content with them, and all through eight years had planned for this time when they would suddenly lift themselves clear out of whatever it was that their lives had settled into, and land, free of it, lightly in another country.

Because it was something that Ella could never have dreamed she would ever do, in a week or two the trip to the nursing home slipped away into the unimportance of things that might never have happened. She was busy planning next winter's clothes for the children—it would be winter in South Africa while she and

Allan were in spring in Europe—and getting the garden into shape, because they hoped to let the house for the period they were to be away, and if they wanted a decent tenant, the place must look attractive. She was just beginning to feel really strong again—undoubtedly that business had left her a little weak—and it was just as well, since she had so much to do, when, of course, servant trouble started.

The old house-cum-garden boy, Thomasi, began quarreling with Lena, the native maid whom Ella had thought herself lucky to engage two months ago. Lena, a heavy, sullen, light-colored Basuto, represented in her closed-in solemnity something that challenged irritation in Thomasi. Thomasi was a Basuto himself—Ella had the vague conviction that it was best to have servants who belonged to the same tribe, rather as she would have felt that it would be better to have two Siamese cats instead of one Siamese and one tabby, or two fan-tailed goldfish rather than one plain and one fancy. She always felt puzzled and rather peevish, then, when, as had happened often before, she found that her two Basutos, or two Zulus, or two Xosas did not necessarily get on any better than one would have expected two Frenchmen to get on simply because both were French, or two Englishmen simply because both were English.

Now Thomasi, barely five feet tall and with that charming, ancient, prehuman look of little dark-skinned men with bandy legs, was maddened by the very presence of Lena, like an insect circling angrily around the impassive head of some great slow animal. He quarreled with her over dusters, over the state of the kitchen sink, over the bones for the dog; he went about his work shaking his head and rumbling with volcanic mutterings.

"If you've got anything to say, come out and say it," Ella said to him, irritated herself. "What's the matter now?"

"That woman is too lazy, madam," he said in his high, philosophical, exasperated voice.

It was difficult to think of old Thomasi as something quite like oneself, when he rose to his hind legs. (Yes, one had the feeling that this was *exactly* what happened when he got up from polishing the floor. Of course, if he had been dressed in a tailored American-drape hop sack instead of the regulation "kitchen boy" outfit that was a cross between a small boy's cotton sailor suit and a set of underwear, he might not have looked any funnier than any of the small, middle-aged Johannesburg men behind their directors' desks.) "Look, Thomasi, she does her work. I'm satisfied with her. I don't want you to go making trouble. I'm the missus, and she works for me, not you, you understand?"

Then, later in the day, Ella would relent. Having shown Thomasi the hand of authority, she could approach him on the other level of their association: that of common concern for the house that they had "run" together for nearly six years, and whose needs and prides and inanimate quirks both understood perfectly.

"Thomasi?"

"Missus?" She might be strolling in the garden, pretending that she was not seeking him out. He would go on wielding the grass shears, widening and snapping like the sharp bill of some great bird imprisoned in his hands.

"What has she done?"

"Well, I tell her the dog he mustn't have the small bone. Yesterday I tell her. Now she doesn't say nothing when I tell her. This morning I see she give the chicken bone to the dog. All that small bone, you know, the missus keep for the cats. Now when I say why you give that bone to the dog, the dog he's going to get sick, she just look me . . ."

The coffee cups left unwashed from the night before.

The iron left switched on while she went to her room after lunch.

154

And too many friends in her room at night, too many.

"I think she makes the kaffir beer," said Thomasi.

But at this complaint Ella was ready to discredit all the others, again. This was Thomasi trying to cook something up. If the girl brewed kaffir beer in her room, Thomasi would be her first customer, not the informant seeking to get her into trouble.

"Listen, Thomasi, I don't want to hear any more of these tales and grumbles, you understand? I'll see if Lena works properly or not, and I don't want you interfering with her."

As she would give her children a handful of sweets each to equalize some difference between them, Ella cleared out a cupboard that needed clearing anyway, and gave Thomasi an old shirt of Allan's, Lena a cheap blue satin nightgown that she had bought to take to the nursing home and that she somehow felt she didn't want to wear again. "I must keep the peace," she said to Allan. "I'm not going to go training another new girl now. I must stick it out with this one until we go. She's a perfectly nice girl, really—a bit sulky, that's all. But you know what an old devil he can be when he wants to. I shouldn't be surprised if what's behind it is that he fancies her, and she's not interested. Shame, he looks such a little old wizened imp of a thing next to her, she's such a hulking, big-breasted Juno."

But the gifts did not quiet for long whatever it was that inflamed Thomasi's malice. The following month, on a Monday morning, Ella found Thomasi alone in the kitchen, cooking the greasy, metallic-tasting fried eggs that were his idea of a white man's breakfast. Lena, he said, bearing his message from across that neat stretch of grass and crisscross wash line that was the no man's land between the lives of the white people in the house and the black people in their back-yard quarters, said she was sick this morning. She would do the washing tomorrow.

"Are those for the master . . . ?" Ella indicated the eggs but lacked the courage to complain. "What's wrong with Lena?"

Over the frying pan, Thomasi gave a great shrug of disbelief and contempt.

"What does she say?"

Thomasi turned around to the young woman in the soiled pink dressing gown, the dark line of her plucked and dyed white-woman's eyebrows showing like pen strokes on the pastel of her fair-skinned face, unmade-up, faintly greasy with the patina of sleep. His brow drew in, intricately lined, over his little yellowish eyes; he said with exaggerated poise and indifference, "I don't know how she's sick. I can't say how a person she's sick when there's noise in her room all night. When people is talking there, late. Sometime I think: She got someone staying there, or something? Talking, and late, late, a baby crying."

Ella went out, over the stones and the grass, across the yard to the native girl's room. The grass was crisp with dew and the chill struck through the old sandals she liked to wear instead of slippers; long threads of spider web danced between the clotheslines. She knocked on the door of the little brick room; the window was closed and curtained. She knocked again and called softly, "Lena?"

"Ma'm?" The voice came after a pause.

Ella opened the door with difficulty—natives usually tampered with the doorknobs of their rooms, making them removable, as an added protection against intruders—and, finding it would open only halfway, edged her way in. The room had a warm animal smell, like the inside of the cupboard where old Lixi, the tabby, lay with her kittens at her belly, purring and licking, purring and licking. The air in here had nothing to do with that other air, wet and sharp with morning, just outside: it was a creature air, created by breathing beings. Although the room was small, Lena in her bed seemed far away. The bed was raised high on bricks, and it was half curtained, like a homemade four-poster. Some sort of design, worked in red or purple thread, trailed round the hems of the material. Lena lay, her head turned to the angle of her raised arm on the pillow. She seemed to be taking some communion of comfort from her own tender exposed armpit, close to her face.

"Are you sick, Lena?" said the white woman gently.

The black woman turned her head back and forth once, quickly, on the pillow. She swallowed and said, "Yes."

"What do you feel?" said Ella, still at the door, which she now saw could not open properly because of a cupboard made of boxes which was pushed half against it.

"My stomach, ma'm." She moved under the fringed traveling rug that was her blanket.

"Do you think you've eaten something that's made you sick?" said Ella.

The girl did not answer. Ella saw her big slow eyes and the white of her teeth come out of the gloom.

"Sometime I've got a cold in my stomach," the girl said at last.

"Is it pain?" said Ella.

"I can do the washing tomorrow," said the voice from the great, hemmed-in agglomerate of the bed.

"Oh, it doesn't matter," said Ella. "I'll send Thomasi out with something for you to take. And do you want something to eat?"

"Only tea, thank you, ma'm."

"All right then."

She felt the woman's slow eyes watching her out of that room, which curiously, despite its poverty, its soapbox cupboards fretted with cutout newspaper edgings, the broken china ducks, and the sword fern draped in stained crepe paper (the ornaments and the fern were discards from the house), had something of the richly charged air of grand treasure-filled rooms of old houses heavy with association, rooms much used, thick with the overlaid echoes of human concourse. She thought, for some reason, of the kind of room in which one expects to find a Miss

Havisham. And how ridiculous! These two whitewashed servants' rooms (some white people called them "kyas," as one calls
a dog's house a kennel, wanting to keep in their minds the now-
vanished mud huts which the word indicated) neatly placed
out of the way between the dustbin and the garage! What had
they to do with Dickens or flights of fancy or anything else, in
fact, except clean, weatherproof, and fairly decent places for the
servants to sleep? They belonged to nothing and nobody, merely
were thrown in along with the other conditions of work.

On the kitchen step Ella stopped and shook each foot like a
cat; her feet were sopping. She made a little exclamation of
irritation with herself.

And when she had dressed, she sent Thomasi out to the room
with a dose of chlorodyne ready-mixed with water in one of the
old kitchen glasses. She got her younger child Pip ready for
Allan to take to nursery school, and saw that her daughter
Kathie had some cake to take for her school lunch, in place of
the sandwiches which Lena usually made.

"Darned nuisance, mmh?" Allan said (suppressing a belch,
with distaste, after the eggs).

"Can't be helped, I suppose," Ella said. "I wouldn't mind so
much if only it wasn't Monday. You know how it is when the
washing isn't done on the right day. It puts the whole of the
rest of the week out. Anyway, she should be all right by tomorrow."

The next morning when Ella got up, Lena was already doing
the washing. "Girl appeared again?" called Allan from the bathroom. Ella came in, holding one of Pip's vests to her cheek to
see if it was quite dry. "She doesn't look too good, poor thing.
She's moving terribly slowly between the tub and the line."

"Well, she's never exactly nimble, is she?" murmured Allan,
concentrating on the slight dent in his chin, always a tricky place
to shave. They smiled at each other; when they smiled at each

other these days, they had the conspiring look of children who have discovered where the Christmas presents are hidden: Europe, leisure, and the freedom of the money they had saved up were unspoken between them.

Ella and Allan Plaistow lived in one of the pleasantest of Johannesburg suburbs: gently rolling country to the north of the city, where the rich had what amounted to semicountry estates, and the impecunious possessors of good taste had small houses in an acre or two of half-cultivated garden. Some of the younger people, determined not to be forced back into real suburbia through lack of money, kept chickens or bred dogs to supplement the upkeep of their places, and one couple even had a small Jersey herd. Ella was one of their customers, quite sure she could taste the difference between their, and what she called "city," milk.

One morning about a week after the native girl Lena had delayed Ella's washday, the milk delivery cart was bowling along the ruts it had made for itself along the track between the dairy and the houses in the Plaistows' direction, when the horse swerved and one wheel bowed down the tall grasses at the side of the track. There was a tinny clang; the wheel slithered against something. Big Charlie, the milk "boy," growled softly at the horse, and climbed down to see. There, as if it had made a bed for itself in the long grass the way an animal turns round and round before sinking to rest, was a paraffin tin. Big Charlie stubbed at it once with his boot, as if to say, oh, well, if that's all . . . But it gave back the resistance of a container that has something inside it; through his toes, there came to him the realization that this was not merely an empty tin. It was upside down, the top pressed to the ground. He saw an edge of blue material, stained with dew and earth, just showing. Still with his foot, he pushed hard—too hard, for whatever was

159

inside was light—and the tin rocketed over. There spilled out of it a small bundle, the naked decaying body of what had been a newborn child, rolled, carelessly as one might roll up old clothing, in a blue satin nightgown.

It did not seem for a moment to Big Charlie that the baby was dead. He gave a kind of aghast cluck, as at some gross neglect—one of his own five doubled up with a bellyache after eating berries, or the youngest with flies settling on his mouth because the mother had failed to wipe the milk that trickled down his chin from her abundance when she fed him—and knelt down to make haste to do whatever it was that the little creature needed. And then he saw that this was hardly a child at all; was now closer to those kittens he was sometimes ordered by his employers to drown in a bucket of water, or, closer still, to one of those battered fledglings found lying beneath the mimosa trees the night after a bad summer storm.

So now he stood back and did not want to touch it. With his mouth lifted back over his teeth in a superstitious horror at the coldness of what had been done, he took the crumpled satin in the tips of his fingers and folded it over the body again, then dropped the bundle back into the paraffin tin and lifted the tin onto the cart beside him.

As he drove, he looked down now and then, swiftly, in dismay to see it there still, beside him. The bodice of the nightgown was uppermost, and lifted in the firm currents of the morning air. It was inside out, and showed a sewn-on laundry label. Big Charlie could neither read nor write, so he did not know that it said, in the neat letters devised for the nursing home, E. PLAISTOW.

That, of course, was how Ella came to find herself in court.

When she opened the door to the plainclothes detective that afternoon, she had the small momentary start, a kind of throb in some organ one didn't know one had, of all people who do not steal or lie and who have paid their taxes: an alarm at the sight of a policeman that is perhaps rooted in the memory of childhood threats. The man was heavily built and large-footed and he had a very small, well-brushed mustache, smooth as the double flick of a paintbrush across his broad lip. He said in Afrikaans, "*Goeie middag. Mevrou Plaistow?*" And when she answered in English, he switched to the slow official English learned for his police qualifications. She led him into the living room with a false air of calm and he sat on the edge of the sofa. When he told her that the Evans' milk boy had found a dead native baby in a paraffin tin on the veld, she made a polite noise of horror and even felt a small shudder, just back of her jaws, at the idea, but her face kept its look of strained patience: what had this gruesome happening to do with *her?* Then he told her that the child was found wrapped in a blue satin nightgown bearing her name, and she rose instantly from her chair in alarm, as if there had ben a sudden jab inside her.

"*In my nightgown?*" she accused, standing over the man.

"Yes, I'm afraid so, lady."

"But are you sure?" she said, withdrawing into anger and hauteur.

He opened a large brief case which he had brought with him and which she had imagined as much a part of his equipment as his official English or the rolled-gold signet ring on his little finger. Carefully he spread out the blue satin, which still kept, all refracted by creases, the sheen of satin, despite the earth stains and some others caused by something that had dried patchily—perhaps that birth fluid, *vernix caseosa,* in which a baby is coated when it slips into the world. The sight filled her with revulsion: "Oh, put it away!" she said with difficulty.

"You recognize it as your own?" he said—pronouncing the word as if it were spelled "racognize."

"It's mine all right," she said. "It's the one I gave to Lena a few weeks ago. But good God—?"

"It's a native girl, of course, the one you gave it to?" he said in his unvarying singsong. He had taken out his notebook.

Now all sorts of things were flooding into her mind. "That's right! She was sick, she stayed in bed one day. The boy said he heard a baby cry in the night—" She appealed to the policeman: "But it couldn't be!"

"Now if you'll just tal me, lady, what was the date when you gave the girl the nightgown . . ." Out of the disorder of her quicker mind, his own slow one stolidly sorted this recollection from that; her confused computation of dates and times through the measure of how much time had passed between the day Pip chipped a tooth at nursery school (that, she remembered distinctly, happened on the same day that she had given Thomasi a shirt and Lena the nightgown) and the morning the washing had not been done, became a statement. Then she went, haltingly because of her nervousness, into the kitchen to call Lena and Thomasi. "Thomasi!" she called. And then, after a pause: "Lena." And she watched for her, coming across the yard.

But the two Africans met the fact of the policeman far more calmly than she herself had done. For Africans there is no stigma attached to any involvement with the forces of the law; the innumerable restrictions by which their lives are hedged from the day they are born make transgressions commonplace and punishment inevitable. To them a few days in prison is no more shaming than an attack of the measles. After all, there are few people who could go through a lifetime without at least once forgetting to carry the piece of paper which is their "pass" to free movement about the town, or without getting drunk, or without sitting on a bench which looks just like every other bench but happens to be provided exclusively for the use of people with a pale skin. All these things keep Africans casually going in and out of prison, hardly the worse—since it is accepted that this is the ways things are—for a cold, buggy night in the cells or a kick from a warder.

Lena has not a pleasant face, thought Ella, but thought too that perhaps she was merely reading this into the face, now. The woman simply stood there, answering, in an obedient Afrikaans, the detective's questions about her identity. The detective had hitched his solid rump onto the kitchen table, and his manner had changed to the impatient one customarily used for Africans by all white persons in authority—a manner that arose perhaps quite legitimately in defense against the circumlocution of the rather poetic Bantu languages, with their delicate formality, and has now hardened into indiscriminate use. The woman appeared weary, more than anything else; she did not look at the detective when he spoke to her or she answered. And she spoke coldly, as was her custom; just as she said, "Yes, madam, no, madam," when Ella reproached her for some neglected chore. She was an untidy woman, too; now she had on her head a woolen *doek* again, instead of the maid's cap Ella provided for her to wear. Ella looked at her, from the *doek* to the colored sandals with the cut thongs where they caught the toes; looked at her in a kind of fascination, and tried to fit with her the idea of the dead baby, rolled in a nightgown and thrust into a paraffin tin. It was neither credible, nor did it inspire revulsion. Because she is not a *motherly* figure, Ella thought— that is it. One cannot imagine her mother to anything. She is the sort of woman, white or black, who is always the custodian of other people's children; she washes their faces and wipes their noses, but they throw their arms around somebody else's neck.

And just then the woman looked at her, suddenly, directly, without a flicker of escape, without dissimulation or appeal,

163

not as a woman looks to another woman, or even a human being to another human being; looked at her out of those wide-set, even-lidded eyes and did not move a muscle of her face.

Oh, but I don't know her, I know nothing about her. . . . Ella recoiled, retracting to herself.

"She'll have to come along with me," the detective was saying, and as the woman stood a moment, as if awaiting some permission, he told her in Afrikaans that she could go to her room if she wanted anything, but she must be quick.

Ella stood near the door watching her servant go slowly across the yard to the little brick room. Her own heart was pounding slowly. She felt a horrible conflict of agitation and shame—for what, she did not know. But if I go after her, she seemed to answer herself, what can I say to her? Behind Ella, the detective was questioning Thomasi, and Thomasi was enjoying it; she could hear from the quick, meaningful, confidential tones of Thomasi's voice that he was experiencing all the relish of a gossip who finds himself at last in the powerful position of being able to influence the lives of those who have forced him out into the cold of a vicarious recorder.

Ella said suddenly to the detective, "Will you excuse me now, please—" and went away through the house to her bedroom. She was standing there still, some minutes later, when the detective called from the front door, "Thank you very much, lady, hey? We'll let you know—" and she did not come out but called back, as if she were at some task she could not leave for a moment, "I'm sorry—will you find your way out. . . ."

But she could not forbear to bend apart the slats of the venetian blind in time to see the back of Lena, in one of those cheap short coats—jeep coats, they were called, beloved of suburban African girls—getting into the police car. It's unbelievable, she told herself; she didn't look any fatter than she does now. . . . And she did the whole week's washing. . . .

The moment Ella heard the car drive away, she went to telephone Allan. As she dialed, she noticed that her fingers were fumbling and damp. I'm really upset, she thought; I'm really upset about this thing.

By the time the court case came to be heard, the quiet, light-colored Lena lying in her bed that day with her head turned to her arm for comfort, standing obediently before the questioning of the detective in the kitchen, was changed in Ella Plaistow's mind into the ghoulish creature who emerged out of discussion of the affair with friends and neighbors. A woman who could kill her own baby! A murderer, nothing less! It's quite awful to think that she handled Pip and Kathie, other women sympathized. It just shows you, you never know who you're taking into your home. . . . You never know, with *them*. . . . You can send them to a doctor to make sure you aren't harboring someone who's diseased, but you've no way of finding out what sort of person a servant is. Well, Thomasi didn't like her from the first, you know, Ella always said at this point. Ah, Thomasi, someone would murmur, now he's a good old thing.

So that when Ella saw the woman Lena in court, there was something disquieting and unexpected about the ordinariness, the naturalness of her appearance: this was simply the woman who had stood so often at the stove in Ella's red-and-white kitchen. And where was the other, that creature who had abandoned her own newborn child to the cold of the veld?

Embarrassment precluded all other feelings, once the white woman found herself in the witness stand. Ella had never, she said again and again afterward, felt such a fool in her whole life.

"You are, of course, a married woman?" said the magistrate.

"Yes," said Ella.

"How long have you been married?"

"Eight years."

"I see. And you have children?"

"Yes, two children."

"Mrs. Plaistow, am I to understand that you, a woman who has been married for eight years and has herself borne two children, were not aware that this woman in your employ was on the point of giving birth to a child?"

Of course, the man must have thought her quite moronic! But how to explain that one didn't go measuring one's servant's waistline, that she was a very big, well-built woman in any case, and that since she must have been well into her pregnancy when she started work, any further changes in her figure were not noticed?

He made such a *fool* of me, Ella protested; you can't imagine how *idiotic* I felt.

The case dragged on through two days. The woman herself said that the child had been born dead, and that since no one knew that she was pregnant, she had been "frightened" and had hidden the body and then left it on the veld, but post-mortem findings showed strong evidence that the child might have lived some hours after birth, and had not died naturally. Then there was Thomasi's statement that he had heard an infant cry in the night.

"In your opinion, Doctor," the magistrate asked the government medical officer, in an attempt to establish how much time had elapsed between the birth and death of the infant, "would it be possible for a woman to resume her normal day's work thirty-six hours after confinement? This woman did her employer's household washing the following day."

The doctor smiled slightly. "Were the woman in question a European, I should, of course, say this would be most unlikely. Most unlikely. But of a native woman, I should say yes—yes, it would be possible." In the silence of the court, the reasonableness, the validity of this statement had the air of clinching the matter. After all, everyone knew, out of a mixture of hearsay and personal observation, the physical stamina of the African. Hadn't everyone heard of at least one native who had walked around for three days with a fractured skull, merely complaining of a headache? And of one who had walked miles to a hospital, carrying, Van Gogh-like, in a piece of newspaper, his own ear—sliced off in a faction fight?

Lena got six months' hard labor. Her sentence coincided roughly with the time Ella and Allan spent in Europe, but though she was out of prison by the time they returned, she did not go back to work for them again.

*T*here were two men in the town—a deaf man and a drunkard.

The one was a watchmaker and the other a doctor, and they never met except when the watchmaker consulted the doctor about his stomach ulcer, or the doctor's watch needed cleaning, but they belonged together in the mind of twenty-year-old Kate Shand. Extraordinary to think in what unimaginable partnerships one may exist in the minds of others, with what faces one's own may be bracketed forever, through some categorical connection, of which one will never know, in the memory of a third person.

The association between the watchmaker and the doctor in Kate Shand's mind began when she and her brothers were children. For the Shand children there were two kinds of people. There were people their mother had a lot of time for, and people she had no time for. The definitions were not only expressive but literal. The people she had a lot of time for she would allow to delay her endlessly, talking to them on street corners when she met them out shopping, visiting them when they were ill, stretching telephone conversations far beyond her normal brusque limits; the people she had no time for took up no more than the duration of a curt nod, or a half sentence of dismissal should their names come up in conversation.

Both the watchmaker and the doctor were in Mrs. Shand's favored category. The deaf watchmaker, Simon Datnow, was employed by Kate's father in his jeweler's shop. "I've got a lot of time for Simon," Mrs. Shand would say consideredly, with a "mind you," a sage reservation in her voice. That was because, on the whole, she did not care for relatives, and this man was, in fact, one of the procession of Lithuanian and Russian relatives whom Marcus Shand had "brought out" to South Africa, before Kate was born, in the early Twenties and whom, ever after, he regarded with a surly indifference quite out of character with his gentle nature—a churlishness created by the conflict in him between family feeling for them and a resentment against them for being the kind of people he would not have expected his wife to like. For though he winced under his wife's scorn of his relatives, there was a perverse pride in him that he should have succeeded in marrying a wife who *would* scorn them. They were used to sleeping, these foreigners (Mrs. Shand said), on top of the stove. They did not bathe more than once a week. They ate disgusting food—salted fish and soup made of beetroot. At that time the Shand kitchen still had a coal range; the children pictured these strange aunts and cousins huddled together on the sooty surface after the fire had been raked out in the evening, greasy-fingered, like Eskimos. It would not have surprised Kate, William and Dykie to hear that the aunts chewed their husbands' boots to soften them.

Simon Datnow was not actually a blood relation of Marcus Shand, but merely the brother of one of Mr. Shand's sisters' husbands. The husband was dead and Simon had "come out" with his sister-in-law as a kind of substitute protector. Perhaps it was because there was no blood tie to rein his resentment with guilt that, if Mrs. Shand liked Simon most, Mr. Shand liked him least of the immigrant relations. It seemed to annoy Marcus Shand that, after the first year, the deaf watchmaker really owed him nothing; had, unlike the others, nothing in particular for which to be grateful to him. Simon Datnow had paid back the passage money which Mr. Shand had advanced, and he was a skilled watchmaker whose equal Mr. Shand could not have hoped to find in South Africa. Kate, whenever she entered her father's shop, always remembered the watchmaker as she used to see him from the door—sitting in his little three-sided glass cage with the inscription WATCH REPAIR DEPARTMENT showing in gold leaf like a banner across his bent head. As Kate grew up, the gold leaf began to peel, and behind the faint loop of the first P you could see his left ear more and more clearly. In that ear, from time to time, a new hearing aid, flesh-colored, black or pearly, would appear, but usually, when he was working, he did not wear one. He would put it on only when you approached to speak to him, and in the moment before you did speak, the moment when the device dropped into contact with his ear, you would see him wince as the roar of the world, from which he had been sealed off like a man dropped in a diving bell to the floor of the ocean, burst in upon him.

A curved bite had been sawed out of the work table at which he sat, and the edge of the wood had long since been worn smooth by the rub of his body as he leaned forward over his work, and it seemed to Kate that he fitted into the table as the table fitted into its glass walls. Before him were tiny, shallow receptacles and metal work platforms a few inches square on which the delicate tweezers and probelike instruments with which he worked stalked like timid, long-legged insects among specks of red jewel and minute wheels, and springs that looked like a baby's hair you had run through thumb and fingernail. Tiny glass bells protected the innards of watches on which he was not working. She felt she dared not breathe too near the exposed ones, lest they took off on the current and sailed into some crack in the scored and worn table top. Yet the instruments that worried at them delicately, that picked them up and dipped them into a dewdrop of oil or spirit and finally fitted

171

them together, were controlled by a pair of blunt, curled hands with broken nails like plates of horn imbedded in, rather than growing from, chapped fingers. The skin of these hands was permanently tarnished from contact with oil and metal, and, in winter, was swollen and fissured with dreadful chilblains. The WATCH REPAIR DEPARTMENT was in the draftiest corner of the shop, and it was then that the watchmaker, blue-nosed and pale above his gray muffler, reminded Kate of one of those zoo animals which, denied the lair of its natural habitat, shudders out the cold months in a corner of its cage.

In the summer the watchmaker worked in his shirt sleeves, with shiny expanding armbands to pull the cuffs up out of the way, and a constant trickle of sweat making his short, graying hair spring out slowly into curl from its confinement of pomade. Summer and winter, most days he looked up only when Marcus Shand came stumping over to shove at him a watch for diagnosis, bellowing, "Loses twenty-five minutes in twenty-four hours" or "Oiling and cleaning. See if it's in working order." "What?" the deaf man would say in his half-inaudible voice, frowning vacantly and fumbling for his "machine"—as he always called his hearing aid—while he held back from the force of his employer in nervous distaste. Shand would shout in impatient repetition, so that half of what he said would not be heard by the watchmaker, and the other half would thunder in upon him as his aid was switched on. The force of this half-sentence would strike the watchmaker like a blow, so that for a moment he was bewildered and unable to understand anything. Then Shand would become more impatient than ever and shout twice as loud. Because of this communication at cross purposes, Marcus Shand tended to phrase everything he had to say to his watchmaker as shortly as possible, and to dispense with all graces of politeness, and so almost all that came to Simon Dat-

172

now of the outside world for eight hours a day was an assault of surly questions and demands.

Because his watchmaker and relation by marriage was sensitive to the tick of a watch but not an undertone of the human voice, Marcus Shand got into the habit of abusing Simon Datnow in mumbled asides, before his very face. It was a great comfort to Shand to be able to abuse someone with impunity. Yet although it was true that he was able to say abusive things without being heard, it was, of course, not possible for these not to show on his face while he said them; and so it was that Simon Datnow felt the revilement more cuttingly than if it had come to him in words, and a wall of thick, inarticulate hostility, far more impenetrable than that of deafness, came to exist between the two men.

It infuriated Mrs. Shand that the only person whom her husband should have the courage to abuse should be someone only half of this world, and, as a result, too uncertain of his ground to take a stand upon it. She herself had tried, and, in fact, went on trying all her life, to get her husband to stand up to *her*. But no; the only person before whom Marcus would dare raise the timid flag of his spirit was a man who couldn't trust himself to interpret the challenge clearly. Mrs. Shand retaliated by championing Simon Datnow. Datnow, she gave her children to understand, was a natural gentleman, a kind of freak incidence among the immigrant relations. His drudgery became an ideal of conscientious service; his enforced remoteness from the world, an ideal of contemplation. The bewildered, impotent rage that showed in his eyes—the repressed daze of savagery in the eyes of the bull who cannot see where the darts have lodged in the nerves of his shoulders—before the rudeness of her husband which he could not hear, she interpreted as the self-control of a superior being. The meek aspect which his deaf-

173

ness imposed upon him as he went about the town during his lunch hour seemed to her the quality that should inherit the earth. Even the stomach ulcer from which he suffered as a result of the tension of his work and the fragmentary intensity of his communication with the world came, through their mother, to be associated in the minds of the Shand children with a quality of exceptional sensitivity.

When Kate was small she would sometimes stand for a long time with her face close to the glass cage, smiling respectfully at the watchmaker when he smiled his slow, saliva-gleaming smile back at her, and nodding her interest when he held up some part of a watch, a piece of metal confetti, for her to see. At the approach of her father she would go still—taking cover from the crude and puzzling aspect of him which showed when he spoke to Simon Datnow. This gruff man with the thick strings of vein rising against his collar had nothing to do with the father who would put his cheek to hers and ask, humbly, for a kiss.

One day, a week before Christmas in the year when Kate was nine years old, she was hanging about her father's shop. In the burning midsummer December of South Africa, the gold-mining town was seedily festive with borax snow in the shop windows, red and blue lights strung round the Town Hall, and the beery voices of miners in sports blazers slapping one another on the back outside the bars. The jeweler's shop was very busy. Kate ran errands for her father and the young Afrikaans sales girl, and drank lukewarm lemon squash in the room behind the shop where cardboard boxes and straw and sheets of tissue paper for packing were kept, and the mice were so impudent that anything edible disappeared while you turned your back.

At this time of year the watchmaker was constantly interrupted at his work by requests to fit gleaming new watch straps to customers' watches, or to make minor adjustments to necklaces that were too long, or to mend silver bracelets with faulty catches. In order to get his watch repairing done, he came to work early in the morning, before the shop was open, and stayed behind long after it was closed. And all day, while the bustle of customers and the rustle of parcels and the ring of the cash register filled the shop around him, he was bent over his table, trying to do several things at once, often under the harassing, impatient eye of Marcus Shand or the salesgirl. His lunch sandwiches remained uneaten. Once, a mouse from the back room ventured into the shop to gnaw at them. His morning and afternoon tea turned pale and scummy in the cup. On the crowded table before him, the tiny viscera of his watches got mislaid beneath the metal straps, the necklaces, the bracelets. He looked like a worried mouse himself, gray-backed, rustling furtively over his jumble of work.

On this particular day he was so busy that the face of the little girl, who had wandered over to watch him through the glass, did not penetrate his concentration. She watched him a minute or two, nevertheless. He fitted a tiny spring into the intricacy of a watch's belly; over it went a wheel; into some pin-sized holes, three chips of ruby. Then he put out his long tweezers to peck from its spirit bath something that proved not to be there. He felt about with the tweezers, looked in another dish; at last he lifted his eyebrow so that the jeweler's loop in his left eye socket fell out into his hand. He stood up from his stool and looked carefully and methodically under every glass bell, in every dish. He rummaged systematically through the cardboard box lid where he kept the filings, little twirls of yellow and silver metal like punctuation marks, from the watchstraps, the necklaces, the bracelets. He paused a moment, as if deliberating where he should look next. And then, the light of a solution, a calm relief relaxed his face. Slowly, he stood back, creaking his stool away behind him over the cement floor. Then he grasped his work table firmly, palms up under its top, and brought it over, crashing and slithering all its conglomeration of contents on top of himself.

He stood there amid the wreckage with his hands hanging at his sides. His eyes glittered and his mouth was clenched, so that the skin in which the growing beard showed like fine blue shot was white above and below his stiffened lips. He was breathing so loudly that it could be heard right across the sudden silence of the shop full of people.

Before the shock of that silence broke, Kate ran. Her running broke the silence; she heard, as she pulled the heavy back door of the shop closed behind her, babble and movement spill out. She went trembling across the dirty yard which the shop shared with several other contiguous with it, and sat on a rotting packing case against the wall of the lavatory. It was dank there, with the solitude of dank places. She stayed a long time, playing with some old letterheads puffy with rain.

When she went back into the shop again, there was a cheerful delegation from a mine, in the part of the shop known as the jewelry department, choosing a canteen of cutlery for presentation to a retiring official. Behind the WATCH REPAIR DEPARTMENT the watchmaker was putting the last of his tiny containers back at the angle at which it had always stood; only the glass bells were missing, and they must have been swept away by Albert, the African cleaner. The face of the watchmaker, behind the gold-leaf letters, was pale and calm.

Presently, he looked up and beckoned to her across the shop, and, hesitantly, she went to him. He gave her one of the three-cornered buns filled with poppyseed that he had brought for his tea and that he knew she loved. Holding it between finger and thumb, she took the bun into the back room and hid it in a corner, for the mice.

Mrs. Shand had even more time for the doctor than she had for the watchmaker. When Kate, or William, or Dykie were ill, and Mrs. Shand was expecting Dr. Connor on his morning round of calls, she would have a plate of fresh scones baked ready for tea from before ten o'clock. And if he happened to come earlier, while the Shand house was still in the uproar of cleaning which not even consideration for the patient was allowed to interrupt, Amos and Fat Katie, the servants, and their shining vacuum cleaner and buzzing floor polisher were banished at his approach, trailing the cords of their machines behind them. Mrs. Shand would stand smiling, with her hands on her hips, while the doctor did his examination of the patient. Even if she had been voicing the gravest misgivings about the nature of the child's malady to her sister or mother over the telephone ten minutes before, Mrs. Shand always seemed to be transformed into a mood of levelheaded confidence the moment the doctor appeared. Her attitude became jocular and skittish: "Show Doctor the old tum-tum, darling. Really, Dykie, must you wear these pajamas? Why *do* they take fancies to the most unsuitable things, sometimes? Children, oh, children! . . ."

Then, the moment the examination was completed, Mrs. Shand and the doctor would disappear into the living room, talking in an intimate undertone, and the child, fevered with self-importance and the desire to know if the pain really might be appendicitis, would lie cross and rigid, straining to separate the murmuring voices into words. If the other children were at home, they would hang about the passage outside the living room, and now and then the door would open suddenly and their mother's face would appear, requesting more hot water or another jug of milk. There would be a glimpse of the living room, blue with cigarette smoke, fragrant with tea, the doctor sitting in the big armchair—and then the door would shut firmly again. When Dr. Connor rose to leave, Mrs. Shand would accompany him all the way down the garden path and then stand talking over the gate, or at the window of his car.

She would come slowly back up the path to the house after he had driven off, holding carefully in her hand the prescription he had written. Slowly through the house and into the bedroom where her child lay. The child seemed almost a surprise to her. "Well, there you are, darling," she would say absently. "No school for you for a few days. Now I must go down to the chemist and get this made up. And you're to stay in your bed and not jump about, do you hear? Dr. Connor says . . ." Then she would go to the telephone and speak to her mother and her sister again. "Well, he's been. That's what I like about him—when you need him, he's there at once. And, of course, it's just as I thought—a real chill on the stomach, that's all, and he recognized it at once. Good old Robert Eldridge. I'd trust him with my life any day, in spite of his faults."

Their mother always talked about Dr. Connor by the two imposing Christian names which she had seen on his degree diplomas in his consulting rooms—Robert Eldridge. For years Kate thought of this form of address vaguely as some sort of designation; it was like speaking of the Major, or the General Manager, or the Editor. The "faults" in spite of which Mrs. Shand—and, indeed, half the town—trusted Robert Eldridge were, of course, his drunkenness. He was not merely addicted to drink; he was dejectedly chained to it, as the great sheepish dog whom he resembled might be chained to a kennel. He did not drink at parties or with friends, but only in his own company, in solitary, irregular and frequent bouts—sometimes every week, sometimes at intervals of several months, sometimes every day for a month. Once he was sober for more than a year; once he was scarcely sober at all for a year. Unless he had had a particularly long bout and was in very bad shape indeed, he did not drink at home, but drove out into the veld with his African garden boy and a case of raw South African brandy— the cheapest brand; he did not care what he drank. There he would stay for two or three days. The brandy ensured oblivion, and the African, who asked no questions and offered neither protest nor sympathy nor arguments for reformation, ensured survival. For the odd thing was that this wretched man—who crept away to drink himself not into euphoria but into stupor and delirium, shamefully, like a sick animal following the instinct to hide its sickness from the sight of others of its kind— wanted to survive. The desire was so strong in him that it seemed to protect him from harm. He drove his car when he was drunk and did not kill himself, and he operated on his patients when he was drunk and did not kill them. So it was that he came to bear, for the people of the town, the legend of a charmed life, and they were not afraid to entrust themselves to him.

He lived alone with his old mother in a large, neglected house that had the stunned, withdrawn atmosphere of walls, furniture, possessions which have absorbed the unhappy stare of silent inmates. Here, in the living room with the empty vases, he had sat in morose penitence with his unreproachful mother. Here, in the consulting room where he examined his patients beneath a pale photograph of his first wife in a Suzanne Lenglen tennis outfit (his wives had come and gone without any sympathy from anyone), he had, in desperate times, concealed brandy in bottles bearing the labels of medicaments. And here, in the hall,

179

where years of dust had turned the black shaggy curls of a mounted wildebeest head into a powdered wig, he had lain at the foot of the stairs whole nights, unable to get up to his room.

The house was silent, yet spoke of all this. Kate, when she was thirteen, heard it. She was going to Dr. Connor's house every day at the time to have a course of penicillin injections for an outbreak of adolescent boils. She was filled with a bewildering self-disgust because of the boils (her body was punishing her, or being punished; she was guilty, that she knew, though she did not know of what), and there was something in this house of Dr. Connor's that recognized instantly, found common cause with, self-disgust. The wildebeest head, the vases, the pale dead girl in the bandeau claimed kinship with her. You are not alone, they said; there is a whole side of life along with which your feeling belongs. The claim filled her with dismay and a sense of struggle against some knowledge being forced upon her that she did not want. For the first time, the bony, prematurely white head of Dr. Connor, bent over his big, clean hands as they snapped the top off an ampule and plunged into it the needle of a syringe, did not seem to her the image of succor and skill and reassurance that it had been all those other times, the times of measles, of tonsillectomy, of the broken arm. He was a mouth-breather with a loose, wet, kindly lower lip; but today there was no comfort in that audible intake and outlet of breath. To-day the uninhabited blue eyes—she had not noticed before that there was no one there—filled her with an indignant, frightened questioning. Where was he gone, and why did everyone go on pretending he was still there? Why, why, why? He had been someone to revere, someone for whom her mother had had a lot of time, "in spite of." Yet why must there always be excuses for grownups? Why couldn't they be strong, beautiful, happy? Ly-ing down on the white-covered couch and baring her behind for the needle, she felt her young heart fill with cold cruelty toward the mild-voiced, broken man bending over her.

As Kate Shand grew up, she went less and less often into her father's shop. She was away from the town, of course, first at a boarding school and then at a university. When she did come home, it was always with something of a shock that she saw the shop exactly as it had always been, the watchmaker still at his work in the booth behind the gold-leaf lettering. At seventeen, eighteen she felt the world revolving with her; how could it be that *these* remained static, were found as you had left them, like the castle where the princess pricked her finger and put everything to sleep for a hundred years? She smiled at the watchmaker across the shop, but she did not cross to speak to him, as if to do so would be to fill with substance again the shadow of the little girl who used to stand there, on the other side of the lettering, watching. The little girl who had seen, one hot Christmas time, the work table turn over shuddering to the ground, as if some beast that slept beneath industry and submissiveness stirred in impotent protest.

Once the childish ills were behind her (the Shand children had run through the whole alphabet of them, from croup to whooping cough, under Dr. Connor) Kate did not need a doctor again for many years, but her mother often did; and, home from the university one vacation, Kate was irritated to hear that Mrs. Shand had "just been over to see Robert Eldridge." "Good God, Mother! Why can't you go to a *doctor?*"

"That's all right. I'd rather have him than any of these fancy young men."

Dr. Connor still drove about in the car that people gave way to as if it were a sacred cow wandering about the streets, was still accepted without comment, back under the photograph in the consulting room in the old house, after his periodical disappearances.

In books, worms turned, drunkards ended violently in the gutter, the world moved; in the small town, Kate felt, everything held back tolerantly to the pace of—well, for example, those two men for whom her mother had such a lot of time, two men who apprehended the world from a remove, the one looking through glass into an aquarium where silent, mouthing fish swam up to him incomprehensibly and swam away, the other through the glassiness of his own eyes, through which he saw even his own hands, as if he had escaped from them, going on mechanically stitching flesh and feeling pulses.

When Kate graduated and her mother, with her usual capability, announced that she had used her influence with the school board (there were people on it who had a lot of time for *her*) and that a post awaited Kate in a local school, all the reasons the girl gave why she would not, could not, ever live in the town again were the logical, rational ones which children have always used in the process of severing themselves from their parents. But, oddly, for Kate, even as she argued them, pleaded them, they were not true. She was not thinking about the greater academic opportunities, the wider social choice, the cultural stimulation of the city to which she would go; and even if she had dropped the clichés and bluntly substituted for them more money, more men, more pleasure, she would have been no nearer the real reason why she had to go. This reason—and it was a kind of panic in her—had taken shape for her, slowly, out of all her childhood, in the persons of those two men whom she had known, really, so slightly—the deaf man and the drunkard. Why them? Two harmless and handicapped people who, as her mother often said, had never done a scrap of harm; whom, as a child, Kate had automatically respected because they belonged to the people for whom her mother had a lot of time.

And yet, at twenty, it was because of *them* that Kate knew she could not come back to live in the town. They belonged together in her mind, and from them, from the shards of their images there, she must turn away, to live.

hen she was in Northern Rhodesia—that is, during her first two months in Africa—she said to her husband, "But they're like *oxen*. If they're all going to be like that, I just don't see how I'm going to manage." She was talking of the hotel servants, the Nyasa and Rhodesian Africans with the skin of such thick blackness that they seemed to live behind it as certain animals take shelter in a protective hide: it seemed impossible to get at them through that murky opacity; it obscured their facial reactions, for her, as if their eyes gleamed out from a perpetual night.

There was the elderly bedroom boy who made up the beds with honeycomb-weave covers still heavily damp from the laundry; the whole of the dim, gauze-obscured room smelled moldy as a result. There were the tall waiters in dirty white robes that suggested Islam, who sauntered in giggling groups about the dining room, had an English vocabulary that consisted solely of the names of drinks on the hotel wine and spirit list, and, one morning, brought to the table a mixture of tea and coffee in one pot. And there was the anonymous presence everywhere, along with the ants, all over the hotel grounds and about the red sand streets of the little town, of the skinny, hornyfooted ones of no particular calling who hacked away with their scythes at the scrubby jungle, which, the moment their backs were turned, crawled back over the earth that had been claimed from it. When she sat on the gauze-enclosed veranda which darkened the bedroom like an eyeshade and saw one of these men swinging away at the tough grass outside, or (bored, bored, and with two hours to get rid of before her husband could be expected to come in from his round of visits to the scattered copper mines) she walked down the road to the Indian shops to buy fruit and saw others, resting with their dust-gray legs in the air under the red flowering trees, look up at her mildly without seeing her as she passed, she thought, baffled, uneasy: Like *cattle.*

"Oh, it'll be quite different in Johannesburg," said Hank, stroking her beautiful hair. "Darling, this is the wilds. These poor guys are recruited practically straight out of the trees."

She accepted the caress, but she continued to look at him accusingly; she did not need to remind him in so many words of Mrs. Wilks, who had been with her in her New York apartment for four and a half years before she married—Mrs. Wilks, who cooked and cleaned and pressed and shopped for her; Mrs. Wilks, at whom she had yelled when she was irritable and on whose crooked shoulder she had wept when she wanted some man she couldn't have.

He knew only too well what she had given up; in fact, he would never, he felt, cease to marvel and rejoice that she had thrown it all over for him—the friends in the theater, the publishers who discussed their forthcoming lists with her over lunch, the artists who wouldn't show their pictures until she had approved the order of hanging, the parties and the admiration, the atmosphere of fun and luxury and neurosis that had put together her terrifying little person. In many ways it had been a wonderful life; although he had never lived it, he understood that. And it had also been a hateful life, and he could understand that, too. And he knew that between the hatefulness and the wonder he stood, he and his job on another continent. What it was that he stood for, for her, he could only dimly guess, out

186

of the fact that he was an American himself, though not her kind of American, not one of those who, like her, was the privileged embodiment of all those longings which publicity had made articulate in America: as if the magazines, the radios and the cameras had listened in to the confused sleep of millions who were troubled in the new world by hunger-dreams of the old world, and had created out of these half-valid dreams an ideal American desire and an ideal American fulfilment—wealth, beauty, if not fame itself, then a chance to be bracketed, within a gossip column, at lunch along with the famous. Not (though it is fashionable, with a sneer, to call it that) quite the American dream, but the garbled version of it that one would expect eavesdropping magazines, radios and cameras to pick up and impose upon a people.

All this, then, she had lost. And yet, once they were actually in Africa, it was not, as he had expected, the absence of these things that became a problem, but something to which he had never given a thought. It was not the reminder of the theater, or the publishers, or the parties that brought an anxious apprehension of approaching homesickness to his Pat's eye; it was the mention of Mrs. Wilks. For it came to Pat with the inescapable, stodgy logic of a growing, day-to-day apparence that the New York life had been granted her by Mrs. Wilks: Mrs. Wilks had freed her to live it; a Mrs. Wilks was necessary in order to free one to live anywhere. Hank felt that, although his wife was too intelligent and sophisticated to be romantic and had not quite expected to be the memsahib, she had also somehow failed to imagine what urban Africans would be like. She had sense enough to realize that the Africans who would work for her in her home in Africa would not be anything like the few Negroes she had known, from time to time, in New York. Nor would her acquaintance at home with a Negro writer or two help her much. But, for the rest, only these two negative suppositions dropped into the dark gap between Dr. Ralph Bunche and the anonymous noble savage.

Once in Johannesburg, all her uneasiness at the example of the Africans in Rhodesia was justified. With the help of a friend in the American community, Hank had got a fine new apartment ready for them to move into when they arrived. There, where the furniture and pictures from New York were duly unpacked and disposed, three "native girls" (as the South African women called them) passed in and out in less than a month. One was cheerful, ironed and cleaned meticulously, but could not read or write. "Can't even take a *call* and get the name right," said Pat, whose mode of life had given her a great respect for the place of the telephone in human relationships. The next looked like a scared rabbit, said "Yes" when she had failed to understand instructions and should have said "No." The third made coffee by boiling up the grains in a mixture of milk and water, and, as she had a cold, wiped her nose along the back of her hand.

So it was that Hank was greatly relieved when the wife of a consulting engineer with whom he had had some business dealings, recommended Rebecca.

Hank, taking advantage of the empathy generated by a cocktail party, had confided his fears about Pat's domestic problem to the engineer's wife. As he spoke, he glanced up across the room to where his beautiful girl stood, grimacing animatedly while she described something to an admiring circle, and the engineer's wife followed his gaze diagnostically, as if they were two doctors in consultation over a patient's treatment. "My Sarah's got someone for you, I'm sure," she said. "I'll ask her about her cousin Rebecca who came to me last year when Sarah was ill. She's a first-rate girl. Your wife won't have to lift a finger. You'll see."

"Oh, I like that," said Pat, with her lovely, big, bold laugh, when he crossed the room to tell her. He loved that rakish laugh of hers; it became her bizarrely, as she might have worn a workman's cap on her perfumed hair. "I like that very much, darling. . . . Not even this littlest one?" And she held up the little finger of her left hand, manacled with the ring a famous playwright had had made for her in the course of a friendship which had ended before Hank knew her, and into the importance of which he was afraid to inquire. "Oh, bring on Rebecca. And quick." She was a little drunk; Hank found it endearing that, despite her life in New York, it took only two drinks to make Pat a little drunk.

Rebecca had worked in white people's houses for nineteen years—since she was seventeen and had left her first baby in the care of her grandmother—and she thought she knew what they wanted of you, by now. She didn't pretend to understand them; that she'd given up after the first year, of course. But she certainly thought she knew what they wanted, and how much and how little of yourself you should get away with giving them. She had known all kinds. Once, at the beginning, she had worked in a miner's house in one of the Reef gold-mining towns, and had been beaten, along with his wife and children, when he got drunk. They had eaten their dinner in the kitchen with a minimum of dishes and knives and forks. Then she had come to Johannesburg and worked for a woman who had given her old curtains and a rug for her room in the back yard, and taught her how to cook and use a sewing machine. These people spoke about her to other white people as "our Rebecca"; called her in to get her present off the children's tree at Christmas. They ate in a special small room off the kitchen, called the dining room, with a starched white cloth on the table (changed twice a week unless something was spilled) and a slightly larger variety of cutlery. When she left them because she had been offered a job with more money, the woman wore a cold and injured air. She spoke no longer to her friends of "our Rebecca," was heard to remark, "They have no sense of gratitude. You think of them as one of the family, but you don't understand that, all the time, *you* mean nothing to them, nothing at all. We've *clothed* that picannin of hers since she's been with us. All the children's really good things that they've grown out of."

The next house was a very large one. (It amused Rebecca to remember, after years of familiarity with a string of houses in the northern suburbs of Johannesburg, how the only building to which this house seemed possible of comparison on that first day when she saw it was the hospital where she had once visited a sick uncle; it was the only other building of such size and confusion she had ever been in.) There were six servants, two staircases, many doors, long periods of quiet and comparative idleness broken by an evening or week end of noise and blaze of lights and clamor of washing up that first confused, then excited and finally exhausted her.

The madam of the house interviewed her the day she was engaged, but never appeared in the kitchen. The master of the house called her politely by the name of her predecessor. The son of the house noticed her after three weeks when he rang alarmingly long from his room, and wanted to know what idiot had put starch in the collar of his sports shirts. She was terrified to have to admit that she had done it, but the cook-housekeeper, who was as skilled as any product of Whitehall or Washington in the diplomatic wiles between those who have some service to sell and those who have need to buy it, assured the girl that she had nothing to fear from *him*; he would not, by any chance, want his mother to get to know that he had burned a hole in his eiderdown last week, or that, if the houseboy Willie hadn't felt through the pockets of his gray suit, eight pounds would have gone with it into the vats at the dry cleaner.

Along with subtleties of this nature, Rebecca also learned at this house that there were a great many more knives and forks and spoons than she had yet seen; and she even came to know what they were all for. Soon she was able quite serenely to set out, rather like the keys on the enormous piano in the room with the yellow satin curtains, the hors d'oeuvres knives and forks, the fish eaters, the steak knives and forks, the butter knives, the fruit knives, the round compote spoons, the pointed grapefruit spoons, the shovel-shaped ice-cream spoons, and even, with equal confidence, on great occasions, the special little forks for eating oysters, whose pearly handles seemed to be made out of the same stuff as the inside of the oyster shells themselves. She did it all faultlessly, in time, even to the tiny silver dish of salted almonds before each place mat, the protocol of wineglasses, the rose petal in each fingerbowl. She could fold napkins into water lilies; she could shave off from a pound of cold butter perfect curls, or pat it into thick coins with the imprint of a shamrock pressed upon each one. And what is more, in time, she did it all ceasing to wonder why eating should be made so difficult or the washing up so much. She neither envied, nor admired, nor resented, nor questioned; and later, when the kitchen was swabbed down and left to the cockroaches, she sat in the room of Rosa, the cook-housekeeper, with the other Africans, and, along with them, dipped into a great pot of meat and mealie meal.

For the first few years of her working life Rebecca was like a person who has known only extremes of climate—intense heat or utter cold. Nothing can be done about either experience to bring it closer, through a norm, to comprehension of the other. Her natural state, in the location on the outskirts of Johannesburg where she had been born, was one of such poverty that money was discounted. As a child, apart from the bare essentials of food and shelter which her grandmother had managed to give her through a levy of pity on her sons (Rebecca was illegitimate and her mother had run away when she was a year old), she had had to depend solely on what she was given—hand-me-downs from white families for whom her uncles worked, pennies begged, fruit discarded by Indian vendors, toys thrown away by other children. Money had no value for her because she never had been able to find out what relative sums of it would buy. A five-shilling box of chocolates and a shining new motorcar were equally out of reach.

In the first house of wealth in which she worked she met the opposite state, of superabundance, with almost exactly the same equipment of adjustment. At home there was nothing; so money had no value. Here there was everything; so again money had no value. She wasted magnificently: soap lay in water until whole cakes melted away, irons were left on until they burned out, fruit rotted because she left it to rot and ordered more to replace it. This fine, high-handed disregard went almost unnoticed in that first house, where the mistress concerned herself hardly at all with the kitchen, but in the next house in which Rebecca worked it caused her dismissal. She had been reprimanded, but her actual dismissal came the morning she gave the dog a drink of water in a china bowl. The mistress of the house found it, splattered with mud, in the yard. The bowl was one of a set of four she had discovered in an antique shop in Brussels. It was crackle ware, quite plain, and if Rebecca had given her choice of it for the dog a thought at all, in a house so full of bowls and vases and second and third dinner services, she would have found it less pleasing to her and therefore likely to be less precious than the assortment of cheap flowered china meant for use in the kitchen.

But by the time Rebecca came to work for Pat and Hank McCleary all this was nearly nineteen years away, and she was too much of an old hand to make such obvious blunders. In fact, so far as she could tell, she was too much of an old hand to make any blunders at all any more. She left a good job to come to the McClearys because they, in their foreign ignorance, offered her nearly a third more money than she was getting. Then, too, the McClearys had no children, and she was getting to an age and a standing when she no longer wanted to be expected to amuse children. She had had her fill of the joy and chagrin of children without ever having experienced her own, of course; they were with her grandmother.

To Rebecca, all people who came from outside South Africa fell under the vague heading of "English." Vast distances of ocean, an end to the mass of land on which she had her orbit, and the existence of other masses of land were not comprehensible to her. Oh, she had worked for people who traveled overseas, but when she remarked that her madam had gone to London, her mind did not take the leap of the journey beyond the idea of Cape Town or some other South African town from which she knew people, her own people. So it was that when she was told that her new employers were Americans, she was neither curious about them nor did she expect to find them any different from other "foreigners" for whom she had worked. She arrived at the apartment with her neat clothes and her neat suitcase and her neat roll of bedding secured in a red leather strap, confident and experienced, a polite, heavy-faced woman who answered questions without subservience and in a fair English. She was met at the door by a beautiful girl with a shiny nose, wearing a man's fugi silk shirt beneath the tails of which bare legs showed to the thigh; it looked as if there was nothing under the shirt, but the fact was that it hid a pair of almost legless shorts. This was Pat's favorite house dress, and it did not startle

Rebecca particularly, because another thing she had learned about was the pleasure white women with many dresses took in going about in the sort of makeshift clothing one might be ashamed to have to resort to when one was very poor.

When Rebecca had gone upstairs to unpack her things in the servant's quarters provided on the roof of the building, Pat flew to the telephone. She, who usually spoke so extravagantly, prodigal with adjectives and exaggeration, smiling fit to beatify the world, frowning fit to damn it, was almost terse with guarded seriousness. "Can't say much yet," she said to Hank, "but I have hopes. This may be it. This woman may be *very good*."

As for Rebecca, upstairs in the small, cold cubicle which was the accommodation customarily built for African servants, she was discovering sheets laid out upon the bed. In nearly twenty years no mistress had ever provided such a thing. Sheets! Rebecca felt that there was something suspicious about this. When she went into the apartment again she thanked Pat in the tone of laconic politeness with which a servant would receive the usual provision of an iron bedstead and mattress.

There were one or two other odd things about the Americans, Rebecca discovered. They would not let her call them "Madam" and "Master" but insisted that she say "Mrs. McCleary" and "Mr. McCleary"; she found this very awkward, after years of other usage. She constantly found herself saying, "The master—" (catching Pat's eye) "—Mr. McCleary says . . ."

But they wanted it that way, and that way they should have it. "Mr. McCleary" too had a habit of coming into the kitchen after Rebecca had cooked something particularly to his liking, and saying, "Bec, that was a darned good pie." Sometimes he even slapped her on the back as he said it. Extraordinary. Of course, she had worked for nice people before, where the master would drop a half crown into her palm the morning after a dinner party, saying, "Here. For last night." That was the usual *bonsella*—tip—given as a reward for extra work; this young white man's friendly slap of commendation was a bonsella of a different kind. It gave her the same sort of feeling that she got when one of her friends admired the dress she wore on her day off.

Yet the McClearys were not what Rebecca would have called easy to work for. Measured by her nineteen-year standards, they would have fallen into the category of those to whom she had to give the most rather than the least of what she calculated you could get away with. For the beautiful young white woman had, in her green eyes, a similar calculation—what the masters might hope to get away with in their demands on those who served them. The dinner parties were frequent. The silver abundant, heavily chased, and endlessly to be cleaned. Dresses were equally abundant, and equally endlessly to be ironed. The same high standards of finish were required for both silver and dresses. But, looking the beautiful white woman in the eye from under the low lids of her own brown ones that were like two peeled hard-boiled eggs—glossy, bluish—beneath their tracery of broken veins, Rebecca measured up to the white woman's standards without yielding an inch beyond the limit of her own. She had never worked so well before—that she knew. Still, even if what this woman got out of her was the margin of service she had kept in reserve from others, it was simply that: something she had not gone so far as to yield, before, but not something beyond what she had calculated was her limit.

She had even learned to use Pat's coffeemaker, which kept hot coffee constantly on tap. The simplicity of this machine and the impossibility of teaching Rebecca's predecessors how to use it without breaking it had driven Pat to tears and cynical exasperation. "There you are, darling," said Hank. "She even makes coffee just the way you like it." It was, of course, no mean consolation to Pat, in a town where, wherever you went, you were offered cups of milky Indian tea. The only thing was, Rebecca never seemed to sense *when* you wanted to have a cup of hot coffee brought to you. If you told her, three times a day, or every hour, she would bring it to you on the dot, but she never simply walked in bearing a steaming cup, just when you happened to be dying for it. At home, often, Mrs. Wilk's hand would come round the bathroom door with one of the lovely Italian cups (they had been broken in transit to South Africa, and, of course, you couldn't get such things there) while Pat lay in her bath. And always when she came home exhausted, and was twisting her cramped toes in the pleasure of release from the shoes she had just kicked off, there was Wilks and the coffee.

Now, when Pat came back from an abortive but equally exhausting shopping trip in this wretched town of Johannesburg, where, truly, as she often stated as a fact to Hank, there was nothing on earth you'd really want to buy, she'd say, as she slammed her way through the apartment into Rebecca's presence, shedding gloves, keys, parcels: "God, I'm dead. Ab-solutely dead." Rebecca would look up from her ironing or her cooking and greet her respectfully, and then carry on with whatever it was she was doing. Pat would pad into the living room in her stockinged feet and wait, lighting a cigarette. She could hear Rebecca moving about in the kitchen. But Rebecca did not appear. There was no coffee borne in in an unobtrusive hand. And Pat would not ask. It was silly, of course; she had only to say, Rebecca, please make me some coffee; Rebecca, *always* make coffee for me when I come home tired. But she wouldn't. That wasn't what she wanted; it wasn't what would *do*. After a while she would call out sulkily, "Any calls, Rebecca?" and the servant would appear, dutifully, with her message pad, and go back, dutifully, to her work.

It was the same when Pat gave a cocktail party and finger supper to some of the dull, kindly people who had "taken up" Hank and her (she supposed there might be some interesting

196

people in Johannesburg, but, dependent upon Hank's business connections, they didn't seem to have met them). Rebecca worked hard and obediently, but she didn't say a word when she saw the splendid center piece Pat had created with a wicker cornucopia ordered by mail from a decorator shop at home, and filled to the traditional spilling overflow with South African fruits. Then the guests came and ignored Hank's really dry martinis and drank their eternal harsh brandy-and-soda and talked about a local presentation of a play that had been magnificently done in New York four years ago. It was one of Mateus' best plays—Mateus Hanitz was the playwright who had given Pat the ring on her little finger—and it filled her with a kind of amused depression to hear these people on a remote continent discuss it as if the Johannesburg players had interpreted one single line the way Mateus had intended it.

When the guests had gone, she could not even allow herself the comfort of confessing this depression to Hank, since she didn't want to remind him about Mat, who was a perfectly marvelous person, but not Hank's kind of person at all. Hank said, "Why so down-in-the-mouth? Let's have a beer before we go to bed." His wife was staring at her cornucopia, plenty in the midst of a table of remains, and she did not answer. She was remembering, with a spasm of irritation that vented her depression, how Rebecca, who had worked with her on the preparation of food all day, hadn't even admired the thing.

Hank followed the direction of his wife's eyes to the table, but not the direction of her mind. "Rebecca'll have a nice little job of clearing up to do tomorrow," he said. "Still, she won't fuss, will she?"

"Hell, no," said Pat. "She doesn't grumble." She yawned, her eyes watering, and added, "She's got about as much enthusiasm as a piece of boiled fish."

Next day, Hank came home early in the afternoon to find

Rebecca washing all the paintwork in the apartment. "Pat?" he said. "Pattie, don't you think you're riding her a bit hard? She worked like a trouper all day yesterday and half last night."

Pat had not combed her hair. She wore an old velvet dressing gown in the torn hem of which she tried to wrap her bare, cold feet, whose soles were stained with polish picked up from the floor. Hank knew this mood, when Pat expressed the disgruntledness she felt inwardly by trying to make herself look outwardly ugly. As it happened, she was one of those girls whom sluttishness suits and makes more exciting. The polished uniformity of her American beauty was gone. Her big, pale mouth without paint, the Medusa-like disarray of her neglected hair, the patches of color from the rise of her blood beneath her skin, the coarsening of that skin around the mouth and nose—she did not know that these gave her beauty a new heat of life; the eternal fascination of the opposing forces of death and quickening, of decay and bloom, showed in that face. "Oh, all right," she said listlessly, and then shouted through the open doorway to the other room, "Hey, Rebecca! You can leave the rest till tomorrow, if you like."

Hank sat down creakily on a low wicker table and moved his large, young feet, shod in pigskin with soles like rubber mattresses, in a Charleston. The rubber squealed on the polished floor.

Pat did not frown at him, but her right eyebrow quivered slightly, like a cat's tail.

Hank. He really hardly knew her at all. Sometimes this was charming, she adored it, it made things possible with him that hadn't ever been possible with anyone else. But at other times, it was wearying. Now, for instance. Those others, her friends in New York, they knew her to the bone, because they knew themselves. Oh, *vive la petite différence* and dear Hank. Hank was always on the trail, but somehow never caught up and found her out.

"What'll we do?" he said now.

She shrugged.

"Like to drop in on someone?" he said.

She asked, "Who?"

He spread out his ten fingers, smiling.

She said, "Who, for instance?"

He looked embarrassed, as if he were responsible for the elements which made up the population of Johannesburg. "There isn't anyone much. The Crutches—here last night. Nicky Trew—but I think he's out of town till Thursday. Caroline?"

Pat did not even trouble to pull a face. She picked up a thick strand of hair and closed her teeth on the end of it.

"Well, let's call the De La Reys—see what they're doing."

"Hell, no," said Pat. "Not the De La Reys."

"But, darling, you always say they're the only people you really like in Johannesburg."

She drew her head back into her neck and narrowed her eyes at him. "That's just it. They are. The *only* ones. That's just why I couldn't stand to see them again tonight. Everytime we want to go see someone, or ask someone to go out with us, it has to be the De La Reys. No, darling, not the De La Reys. I couldn't stand it."

He said, out of a miserable silence, "Do a show?"

"That play, perhaps?" she said, pouncing. "That play that they were all bleating about, 'so good that they could see it again.'"

He did not answer.

She looked at him. "Or some damned movie we've seen in New York a year ago?"

She looked so sulky, so attractive to him, that he was about to walk over and kiss her unreasonable, sarcastic mouth when Rebecca appeared at the doorway.

Rebecca always waited to be spoken to; it was as if she had decided that hers would never be the responsibility for opening verbal negotiations of any kind. She did not fidget while she waited; she was, it often appeared to Pat, without nerves.

"Well, Rebecca?" said Pat wearily.

Rebecca knew, too, that weariness that comes upon white women from doing nothing. She asked respectfully, "Is Madam going to be in for dinner? What must I cook?"

Pat turned her head away, half into the cushion behind her. "Rebecca," she said, "why can't you call me by my name?"

"Yes, Mrs. McCleary," said Rebecca. She did not sound impatient, only bored, like a mother who is forced into entering into a child's game.

There was a pause. Rebecca stood calmly.

"Shall we go out somewhere, on our own, to eat?" said Hank. "What do you say, darling? Let's get dressed and go out, just the two of us."

"If there was somewhere to go *to*," said Pat, showing a feeble flicker of interest, in spite of herself.

Hank was always alert in some part of his mind for remarks like this from her. He had stock interpretations for them, but the frequency with which he had to employ these interpretations did not blunt the hurt they did him. Of course, she was thinking of "21" or the Colony. (He had never been to either, but they belonged in his imaginary context of high living.) Had he known it, he was wrong again: she was thinking of a small place near the old Theatre de Lys, in the Village. There you drank Calvados and knew everybody.

"Oh, all right," said Pat suddenly. "Let's go."

Hank sighed. "O.K., Rebecca," he said. "No cooking."

"Yes, Mas—Mr. McCleary," said Rebecca, and went unhurriedly back to the kitchen.

His wife made no move, but said, from the sofa, "Funny how she can't learn. 'Is Madam going to be in for dinner?' "

"It's just that she thinks it's more respectful, honey," said Hank.

Pat sat up slowly and gave her special coarse laugh. "Respectful! Christ, why should she *respect* me? Just because she works for me? I don't want her damned mealy-mouthed respect. I want to be treated like a human being. I can just imagine what Matthew" (she nearly said Mateus, but quickly substituted the name of another friend) "and Joy and the others would think of me, being bowed down to by black slaves and all that." (These were friends who lent their important names to the sponsor lists of committees concerned with Negro emancipation, and now and then received a single Negro doctor or author at one of their cocktail parties with all the warm dignity with which one would welcome an emissary from another land.)

She rose, and, dragging her feet, trailed through the hall to the bedroom to dress. On her bed she found a dress box, unopened and addressed to her. Listlessly she freed a new gray velvet dress from its wrappings, held it up against her old gown. At once she felt better. She would wear it. She would put it on right away. "Rebecca," she yelled. Rebecca must steam it quickly, to bring up the pile. "Rebecca! My new dress has come, see?" Pat said to her with a brilliant smile.

"Shall I press it?" said Rebecca.

Pat dropped the dress over the woman's arm. "Just steam it. And you can give the belt a very light press, on the wrong side."

"Yes, Mrs. McCleary."

"It's a beautiful dress, isn't it, Rebecca?" said Pat, already smearing a layer of pale-green greasepaint on her eyelids.

But Rebecca had gone to the kitchen.

While Pat dressed and made up, her spirits continued to rise.

201

Indeed, there are few people who would not have got pleasure out of the sight, in a mirror, of that lovely face taking on adornment, even if the face was not, as it was for her, their own. While she was in the bathroom, Rebecca brought the velvet dress back to the bedroom and laid it carefully on the bed. Then she went out.

Pat came back into her room and regarded the dress with satisfaction a moment before she slid it gently over her head. Hank drew up the zipper for her. The dress fitted magnificently. Really, it looked as good as anything you could get in New York. Hank, wriggling first one shoulder, then the other, in under the braces that held up the trousers of his best dark suit, confirmed this admiringly. She put on a pink velvet hat, and took it off again. She was quite excited; the lump of excitement rose at the back of her throat as she flitted from dressing table to pier glass, from wardrobe to bed. At last, she was ready. She looked, she felt, almost as good as she had looked at home.

She walked out into the hall, hesitated at the living-room door, and went on into the kitchen. Rebecca was putting two cold chops and the remains of the lunchtime salad into a paper bag, a dinner she would share, upstairs in her room, with her current man, a newspaper delivery worker.

The white woman stood in the doorway, smiling. She was beautiful. She was beautifully dressed. The smile was one of justifiable pleasure in the knowledge of the power of beauty, the smile that, in a room full of such smiles, was striking enough to make the artists, the writers, the television producers and the playwrights turn their heads in homage.

Rebecca was glad to be off early, for once. She raised her yellowed eyes a moment in abstracted acknowledgment of her mistress's presence. "Good night, M'am," she said, and gave the sink a quick wipe with a swab before she picked up the paper bag and her key and went out, locking the kitchen door behind her.

Pat heard her husband calling in the hall, "Pat? Dar-ling?"

But she stood there, before the door the servant had closed behind her, the fur on her arm sinking lower and lower, all the excitement in her blood ebbing flatly, like the fizz in a drink left standing.

"Pat?" said Hank at her shoulder. She turned slowly. She was either angry or on the verge of tears—he did not know which. The prospect of either mood, at this moment on a perfectly ordinary evening, baffled him equally. So he said nothing, but ushered her through the door with a smile.

In the car, as they stopped in obedience to the first traffic lights, she said out of the silence, "She didn't even say it was a nice dress."

"Who?" said Hank, astonished, unable to imagine what she was talking about.

Pat did not turn her head. "Rebecca," she said.

"Darling!" he said, laughing.

As they drove, the lights made a pattern like moire on the smooth surface of the street. "You know I can't stand it," she said wildly. "I must be loved. I can't stand it if I don't have love and warmth around me, if people don't care about me." She was remembering nights in New York he could not know about, when, suddenly, in a taxi, or as she stepped into her own door- way, the laughter and the repartee she had just left seemed to mock her, as if she heard its echo above her own grave, and she forgotten, lost to it. Nights germinating in the very height of their stimulation and pleasure that seed of dismal fear; nights because of which she had chosen him, and his job on another continent. "I want love," she was saying with passion. "Someone who says, how pretty you look, Mrs. McCleary; how young; how beautifully you do things. . . . You do see, don't you? Loved and cared for and wanted. That's how I want to feel all the time."

The Cicatrice

*T*he new wife saw them first, and recognized her predecessor, Hannah, at once, even though she had never seen her before except in the photograph.

Hannah was coming down the pavement on the arm of Count Bianci, an arm bent at a foreign-looking angle in the ridiculous parody of exaggerated gallantry which old Marcus delighted to use. Hannah and Bianci were coming from their first lunch together since her return from Italy, and the empty pavement outside the Chinese restaurant in the lower end of the city aimed them at Hannah's former husband and his new wife like a missile.

To cross the street deliberately in the middle of the block was impossible; there was nothing to cross for but the shuttered warehouses of merchants on the other side. The two couples seemed to pause for a second of eternity, hanging fire, but in fact their legs went on walking, bearing them down upon one another.

"I never wanted to meet her!" said the new wife, stifled, before her husband, Jo, who did not have particularly keen sight, had even seen that it was his first wife and his old friend Marcus Bianci whom they were about to encounter. And as the girl beside him spoke, he saw.

"Don't be silly," he said, and banished the instant when she might have turned and run, stopped dead, anything.

At the other end of the pavement, Hannah said, "Oh, God . . ."

"So? It's nothing. It's got to happen sooner or later, just as well get it over . . ." Marcus swaggered her along, his head turned lingeringly to her profile in a magnificent example of what she and Jo had always called "Marcus' only-woman-in-the-world act." And it was just as well, for at once she was clinging to Marcus the way a child will almost strangle its mother in embarrassment or fear, inhibiting its own escape by making it impossible for the woman to bear it away to safety. The new wife saw her striding along very close and absorbed with her companion, laughing up into his smile and using her white-gloved hands as she talked.

And it seemed that as they drew close, the first thing the girl saw about Hannah was the scar; in all Hannah's tall elegance, her beautiful clothes, her long, pointed feet in the handmade shoes from Spain, her wide hat as dark as her brilliant eyes, it was the scar that the other saw; and the scar seemed Hannah's greatest elegance. Of course the new wife had seen it in the photograph. Jo still had all Hannah's letters that she had written to him during the war—when he had moved into the new house with the new wife he had taken them out of one of the mover's packing cases before her, and had put them away at the top of the cupboard where he had decided to keep the suits and flannels that he no longer wore. In silence, she had watched him, silent, and after a moment of hesitation that was somehow conveyed to her by the angle of the back of his head as he peered up to the shelf, he took the photograph out of the packet of letters and looked at it himself, half offering it to her, the way one indicates a willingness to share a newspaper or a book. She had come to stand under his arm, obediently. They had studied the face of Hannah for a moment. "Of course the scar spoils her," Jo had said.

The new wife knew the story of the scar. Everybody who had ever heard of Hannah and Jo knew it. It had happened as the result of a motor accident on their honeymoon; driving down to the coast at night, Jo had dropped asleep at the wheel and the car had turned over into a deep culvert. A piece of glass from the windscreen had slit Hannah's mouth on the left side from corner to chin, diagonally. And of course, it did not spoil Hannah in the least. Even in the photograph, one could see that. Hannah herself had refused to have a plastic operation to smooth away the cicatrice.

"It will not make me what I was," she would say in her regretful, half-amusing, half-acid way. "If I cannot be what I was, I do not want to be what the plastic surgeon may fancy to make of me. I would rather keep it, like a wrinkle or the gap of a lost tooth. I hate cars that look as if they've never been driven, perpetually having the dents knocked out of their fenders and shining with new finish, people who keep running to psychiatrists to have all evidence of the scratches of experience rubbed out of their souls."

What Hannah meant by "what I was"—beautiful or merely attractive—no one would ever know, so no one knew, either, whether *she* believed she was spoiled, or whether, like poor people who cease to weep over a maimed child the moment they realize the possibilities for it of a stand on the street corner, she had long ago come to understand that it is easier to be a woman who is beautiful despite the flawing of a scar than it is to qualify for the standards of a flawless beauty.

Now they were bunched together blocking the pavement in that expanse of empty street like survivors of a shipwreck huddled on an enormous beach. Bianci stood by in a courtly fashion, with the polite, prim look people keep on their faces when they are waiting to be introduced; Hannah held her neck arched a little, her head drawn back, smiling elaborately, warmly, as if, though her arms remained one bent through Bianci's, the other pressing her handbag to her side, they were extended in a gesture of welcome, acceptance—the stage gesture with which the bountiful lady takes the young people to her heart.

The new wife looked unblinking into that smile. She stood there quietly, her handbag held in front of her in her two hands, the way a schoolgirl holds a hat. Her look seemed to say: I do not know you, yet. I do not have to greet you until I know you.

The eyes of Hannah and Jo met over her head; of course it was not the first time Jo had seen Hannah since her return from Europe. He had gone to meet her at the airport when she arrived early on Friday morning. ("Why must you go?" the new wife had said, with the faintest possible emphasis on "you." "Well, it seems the only decent thing," he had answered; "it's dismal to find no one to meet you, and it's at such an awkward time, it's not likely that any of her friends will make it." When he had come home on Friday evening, they had not mentioned where he had been; it was as if, like Orpheus, he had gone down to escort Eurydice back through the shades—but this one, his new wife, was his real, his earthly love, belonging to ordinary, warm life.)

The "hullo" between Hannah and Jo was a sketchy thing, a mere signal in the air rather than a sound: the way husbands and wives bypass these formalities through familiarity. Jo cleared his throat and said, "You two haven't met, really, have you? . . . This is Gypsy. Gyp, Hannah. And Count Bianci—Marcus."

The girl managed a very slow stiff smile which did not even part her lips. And then it was gone and she was looking at Hannah again, completely expressionlessly. The acknowledgment, such as it had been, seemed to have been dragged out of her by Hannah, by the brilliant, frank smile that Hannah had turned to her at the exchange of names. The full charm of Hannah came out of herself, her body, even, like a strong perfume wafted into life by a movement of clothing. Jo saw, fascinated, the beauty, the coaxing of that greeting; Hannah's face,

Hannah's manner saying: Come, you are a charming girl, I am
delighted to see; I am *sure*. I wish you joy, I take it gracefully, I
am sure I shall like you as a person. Don't be shy, don't be frightened, we are all civilized grownups, are we not?

And while Hannah looked and spoke ("I am so glad to meet
you. How do you do, Gypsy?") no one, not the new wife, not
Jo, not Bianci even, though he was in contact with her body
through her arm, knew of the horrible spasm of terror and
despair that contracted inside her for one unbearable moment.
Her head was thrust down brutally into darkness—the eternal,
smothering darkness of what has been lost. And her jealousy was
like the shocking sight of the beating heart of some small animal,
exposed through dissection, and still alive in the cold pain of
the air.

He's mine, the voice clamored in that terrible place inside
herself where people were fighting, where everything writhed
and staggered from wall to wall. He's mine. He belongs to me.
Nobody else can have him. He's mine.

". . . Marcus said we'd better go there because I haven't been
to China, so at least I shouldn't be able to say, oh, but you should
taste the way they do it *there!*" she was saying, laughing, pulling
a face at herself, culpable.

"You know how it is with her whenever she's been overseas,"
Marcus appealed to Jo. And he parodied the expressiveness of
Hannah's face: "If she's been to Italy, the macaroni's too short
here. When she went to New York, the chewing gum here wasn't
sticky enough for her."

The idea of Hannah chewing gum! Only Marcus could put his
finger so unerringly on the impossibly ludicrous. Jo laughed
delightedly in the joy of Marcus, which he had forgotten, and
Hannah laughed too, for the situation threw Marcus and her into
a kind of act together, and she must play foil for him as he "fed"
her. Quite naturally and unintentionally now, a question shifted

the talk from Marcus, Jo, and Hannah to Hannah and Jo. Jo said, "I forgot to ask. Did you meet Bella and Leslie in Florence? I wondered. Did you hear what happened about the flat the day they left?"

"Did I hear indeed? I was blamed for the whole thing. You see, when they cabled me to Genoa—no, it was Venice—" And she recounted the story, with nods and interjections from Jo: "Well, they told me—" "That wasn't what I was told—"

All her life people had said of Hannah: she can talk her way out of anything. And now that seemed literally true; hand over hand, her animation, her zest, her attractiveness, her easy command of herself lifted her out of disadvantage; she climbed over the faces of Jo and the new wife and the old friend, away out of the situation where she—spoiled child who never really believed her doll would be taken away from her, who had played some perverse game of rejection with Jo until she had goaded him to divorce her, and then had never thought that he would ever struggle sufficiently free of her to marry someone else—found herself indeed bereft, indeed replaced, pushed out on the lonely corner of the triangle. But she was as agile as ever; she proved it again, as she had proved it many times before: the ability to come out on top that they had impressed upon her so admiringly, so long. She produced it as obediently as a circus animal does its trick. Like the seal with his ball, of whom it is difficult to say whether he has enjoyed his skill, or whether it came to him mechanically at the crack of an invisible whip.

The new wife stood there with nothing to say and nothing to give. Marcus retired to the side of the stage, unobtrusive, but there to catch his partner if—unthinkable thing, seeing her spangled up there—she should fall. And then, quite suddenly— the dreadful timelessness of such a meeting contracting the instant it was over into the ordinary dimensions of a few minutes' encounter—they had parted. With the polite scuffle of good-bys

(Marcus bowed to the new wife, who looked as if she didn't know what to do with such a gesture; lifted two fingers in an old easy signal to his friend Jo) the two couples had re-formed and got rid of each other, got past. The heels of the new wife sounded quickly away down the pavement behind Marcus and Hannah; sounded in Hannah's ears like the scamper of a mouse.

Hannah was breathing deeply. Marcus saw the tanned shiny skin in the neckline of her dress swell with the rising pressure of her breasts, saw, quite distinctly, the one or two freckles flecking that hollow. It brought out in him not desire, but, oddly enough, a sudden homesickness—homesickness for one of those Italian Riviera beaches where he had lain, summer after summer, before the war, in the scent of the sun on his newly shaven skin. He squeezed Hannah's arm; he had never felt such kinship with her before. And he saw, as a man sees a trickle of blood on the face of the comrade with whom he has come through a battle, sweat under the powder between her eyebrows. She pulled her lips down swiftly, one against the other, the way women even the thickness of their lipstick. And there too, on her upper lip, there was sweat. But once back in repose, the corners of her mouth indented in a high, nervous smile. After a minute she turned to him and her eyes were so dark, so flooded with intensity that they had no color and were bright as black water in sunlight.

"Stood there like a child hanging around while its parent has a gossip! Sullenly waiting to be yanked off—no will, no volition. Did you see?"

"Yes," said Marcus.

She was breathing so hard she had to breathe through her mouth. "God, I feel so excited," she said.

He nodded, making an understanding mouth.

"You know?"

"Of course," he said.

"Like a puppy dog on a string. Stop when the master stops. Wait to be allowed to go on."

He shrugged. But it was still not enough for Hannah. "Wasn't it so?" she insisted again.

"Well, what do you expect?" he said, deprecating. He disposed of the new wife, kindly, with a half movement of his hand, as if she were not even worth the full gesture. "She seems a nice enough little girl."

"Of course," said Hannah. She was laughing. "But you would have thought I was the one in the strong position. Any one would have thought I was the one who had ousted *her*."

They both laughed, at Hannah.

"Simply stood there staring at my scar. Did you see? Like a rude child, I'm telling you. Never took her eyes off it."

"Well, I suppose she was embarrassed, poor girl."

"Why should she be? Why more embarrassed than anyone else? I felt like saying, I won't *eat* you. And poor Jo . . ."

"I told you, it's a good thing it's over," said Marcus in an aging man's voice.

It seemed to spurt Hannah up into youth and gaiety. "Darling old M," she said, "she probably thinks you're my new lover. A wicked foreigner, picked up in a casino."

"Now, now," said Marcus.

"She's pretty, you know. Well, of course. Very tiny. Did you see how I towered over her? Well, that's good. Jo'll feel more masterly; he'll be able to be protective toward her."

Marcus knew she was talking to herself; she did not want any response but his presence.

Then she turned to him, challenging, proud, really beautiful now as if she were afire inside with her own arrogance, and she said in a different voice, the voice of a conspirator, the voice of a child seeking the approval of a father, a voice that was every

212

contradiction she herself was: "Was I all right?" She was clutching his arm, looking excitedly down at him.

He looked at her ruefully, admiring. "Oh, you," he said.

She was watching his eyes with her own shrewd, distrustful, inescapable ones. "But my behavior. Was it all right? Did I behave well?"

He shook his head slowly in the absolute assurance of it.

"Perfect. You carried it off—magnificently. You managed well. You were very good."

She smiled at him slowly; he watched the curve of her mouth back from her teeth, the flush of her cheeks, the softening lines around her eyes, and, last, was held by the dance of the eyes themselves. They were the eyes of the old warrior who hears at last and yet again the bells of another triumph.

Driving his car with the stranger who was his new wife sitting silent beside him, Jo heard the bells too, but to him they tolled something different. He saw the head of the girl at his side, who was faithful, affectionate, reliable, commonplace—Hannah had made him see that in the ten minutes she stood beside her. The dog virtues, he thought. Hannah had made all that perfectly clear, simply by being there.

And he, who ten minutes before had seen all Hannah's charm, the great desirability she had for him, unimpaired despite all that had happened, had now for the first time an entirely new feeling toward Hannah. Now it was dead, completely dead; he no longer loved her, and for that, and for the other, at last he hated her.

The Smell of Death and Flowers

*T*he party was an unusual one for Johannesburg. A young man called Derek Ross—out of sight behind the "bar" at the moment—had white friends and black friends, Indian friends and friends of mixed blood, and sometimes he liked to invite them to his flat all at once. Most of them belonged to the minority that, through bohemianism, godliness, politics, or a particularly sharp sense of human dignity, did not care about the difference in one another's skins. But there were always one or two—white ones—who came, like tourists, to see the sight, and to show that they did not care, and one or two black or brown or Indian ones who found themselves paralyzed by the very ease with which the white guests accepted them.

One of the several groups that huddled to talk, like people sheltering beneath a cliff, on divans and hard borrowed chairs in the shadow of the dancers, was dominated by a man in a gray suit, Malcolm Barker. "Why not pay the fine and have done with it, then?" he was saying.

The two people to whom he was talking were silent a moment, so that the haphazard noisiness of the room and the organized wail of the gramophone suddenly burst in irrelevantly upon the conversation. The pretty brunette said, in her quick, officious voice, "Well, it wouldn't be the same for Jessica Malherbe. It's not quite the same thing, you see . . ." Her stiff, mascaraed lashes flickered an appeal—for confirmation, and for sympathy because of the impossibility of explaining—at a man whose gingerish

215

whiskers and flattened, low-set ears made him look like an angry tomcat.

"It's a matter of principle," he said to Malcolm Barker.

"Oh, quite, I see," Malcolm conceded. "For someone like this Malherbe woman, paying the fine's one thing; sitting in prison for three weeks is another."

The brunette rapidly crossed and then uncrossed her legs. "It's not even quite that," she said. "Not the unpleasantness of being in prison. Not a sort of martyrdom on Jessica's part. Just the *principle.*" At that moment a black hand came out from the crush of dancers bumping round and pulled the woman to her feet; she went off, and as she danced she talked with staccato animation to her African partner, who kept his lids half lowered over his eyes while she followed his gentle shuffle. The ginger-whiskered man got up without a word and went swiftly through the dancers to the "bar," a kitchen table covered with beer and gin bottles, at the other end of the small room.

"*Satyagraha*," said Malcolm Barker, like the infidel pronouncing with satisfaction the holy word that the believers hesitate to defile.

A very large and plain African woman sitting next to him smiled at him hugely and eagerly out of shyness, not having the slightest idea what he had said.

He smiled back at her for a moment, as if to hypnotize the onrush of some frightening animal. Then, suddenly, he leaned over and asked in a special, loud, slow voice, "What do you do? Are you a teacher?"

Before the woman could answer, Malcolm Barker's young sister-in-law, a girl who had beeen sitting silent, pink and cold as a porcelain figurine, on the window sill behind his back, leaned her hand for balance on his chair and said urgently, near his ear, "Has Jessica Malherbe really been in prison?"

"Yes, in Port Elizabeth. And in Durban, they tell me. And

now she's one of the civil-disobedience people—defiance campaign leaders who're going to walk into some native location forbidden to Europeans. Next Tuesday. So she'll land herself in prison again. For Christ's sake, Joyce, what are you drinking that stuff for? I've told you that punch is the cheapest muck possible—"

But the girl was not listening to him any longer. Balanced delicately on her rather full, long neck, her fragile-looking face with the eyes and the fine, short line of nose of a Marie Laurençin painting was looking across the room with the intensity peculiar to the blank-faced. Hers was an essentially two-dimensional prettiness: flat, dazzlingly pastel-colored, as if the mask of make-up on the unlined skin *were* the face; if one had turned her around, one would scarcely have been surprised to discover canvas. All her life she had suffered from this impression she made of not being quite real.

"She *looks* so nice," she said now, her eyes still fixed on some point near the door. "I mean she uses good perfume, and everything. You can't imagine it."

Her brother-in-law made as if to take the tumbler of alcohol out of the girl's hand, impatiently, the way one might take a pair of scissors from a child, but, without looking at him or at her hands, she changed the glass from one hand to the other, out of his reach. "At least the brandy's in a bottle with a recognizable label," he said peevishly. "I don't know why you don't stick to that."

"I wonder if she had to eat the same food as the others," said the girl.

"You'll feel like death tomorrow morning," he said, "and Madeline'll blame me. You are an obstinate little devil."

A tall, untidy young man, whose blond head outtopped all others like a tousled palm tree, approached with a slow, drunken smile and, with exaggerated courtesy, asked Joyce to dance.

217

She unhurriedly drank down what was left in her glass, put the glass carefully on the window sill, and went off with him, her narrow waist upright and correct in his long arm. Her brother-in-law followed her with his eyes, irritatedly, for a moment, then closed them suddenly, whether in boredom or in weariness one could not tell.

The young man was saying to the girl as they danced, "You haven't left the side of your husband—or whatever he is—all night. What's the idea?"

"My brother-in-law," she said. "My sister couldn't come because the child's got a temperature."

He squeezed her waist; it remained quite firm, like the crisp stem of a flower. "Do I know your sister?" he asked. Every now and then his drunkenness came over him in a delightful swoon, so that his eyelids dropped heavily and he pretended that he was narrowing them shrewdly.

"Maybe. Madeline McCoy—Madeline Barker now. She's the painter. She's the one who started that arts-and-crafts school for Africans."

"Oh, yes. Yes, I know," he said. Suddenly, he swung her away from him with one hand, executed a few loose-limbed steps around her, lost her in a collision with another couple, caught her to him again, and, with an affectionate squeeze, brought her up short against the barrier of people who were packed tight as a Rugby scrum around the kitchen table, where the drinks were. He pushed her through the crowd to the table.

"What d'you want, Roy, my boy?" said a little, very black-faced African, gleaming up at them.

"Barberton'll do for me." The young man pressed a hand on the African's head, grinning.

"Ah, that stuff's no good. Sugar-water. Let me give you a dash of Pineapple. Just like mother makes."

For a moment, the girl wondered if any of the bottles really did contain Pineapple or Barberton, two infamous brews invented by African natives living in the segregated slums that are called locations. Pineapple, she knew, was made out of the fermented fruit and was supposed to be extraordinarily intoxicating; she had once read a newspaper report of a shebeen raid in which the Barberton still contained a lopped-off human foot—whether for additional flavor or the spice of witchcraft, it was not known.

But she was reassured at once. "Don't worry," said a good-looking blonde, made up to look heavily sun-tanned, who was standing at the bar. "No shebeen ever produced anything much more poisonous than this gin-punch thing of Derek's." The host was attending to the needs of his guests at the bar, and she waved at him a glass containing the mixture that the girl had been drinking over at the window.

"Not gin. It's arak—lovely," said Derek. "What'll you have, Joyce?"

"Joyce," said the gangling young man with whom she had been dancing. "Joyce. That's a nice name for her. Now tell her mine."

"Roy Wilson. But you seem to know each other quite adequately without names," said Derek. "This is Joyce McCoy, Roy—and, Joyce, these are Matt Shabalala, Brenda Shotley, Mahinder Singh, Martin Mathlongo."

They smiled at the girl: the shiny-faced African, on a level with her shoulder; the blond woman with the caked powder cracking on her cheeks; the handsome, scholarly-looking Indian with the high, bald dome; the ugly light-colored man, just light enough for freckles to show thickly on his fleshy face.

She said to her host, "I'll have the same again, Derek. Your punch." And even before she had sipped the stuff, she felt a warmth expand and soften inside her, and she said the names

219

over silently to herself—Matt Sha-ba-lala, Martin Math-longo, Ma-hinder Singh. Out of the corner of her eye, as she stood there, she could just see Jessica Malherbe, a short, plump white woman in an elegant black frock, her hair glossy, like a bird's wing, as she turned her head under the light while she talked.

Then it happened, just when the girl was most ready for it, just when the time had come. The little African named Matt said, "This is Miss Joyce McCoy—Eddie Ntwala," and stood looking on with a smile while her hand went into the slim hand of a tall, light-skinned African with the tired, appraising, cynical eyes of a man who drinks too much in order to deaden the pain of his intelligence. She could tell from the way little Shabalala presented the man that he must be someone important and admired, a leader of some sort, whose every idiosyncrasy—the broken remains of handsome, smoke-darkened teeth when he smiled, the wrinkled tie hanging askew—bespoke to those who knew him his distinction in a thousand different situations. She smiled as if to say, "Of course, Eddie Ntwala himself, I knew it," and their hands parted and dropped.

The man did not seem to be looking at her—did not seem to be looking at the crowd or at Shabalala, either. There was a slight smile around his mouth, a public smile that would do for anybody. "Dance?" he said, tapping her lightly on the shoulder. They turned to the floor together.

Eddie Ntwala danced well and unthinkingly, if without much variation. Joyce's right hand was in his left, his right hand on the concavity of her back, just as if—well, just as if he were anyone else. And it was the first time—the first time in all her twenty-two years. Her head came just to the point of his lapel, and she could smell the faint odor of cigarette smoke in the cloth. When he turned his head and her head was in the path of his breath, there was the familiar smell of wine or brandy breathed down upon her by men at dances. He looked, of course, apart from his eyes—eyes that she had seen in other faces and wondered if she would ever be old enough to understand—exactly like any errand "boy" or house "boy." He had the same close-cut wool on his head, the same smooth brown skin, the same rather nice high cheekbones, the same broad-nostriled small nose. Only, he had his arm around her and her hand in his and he was leading her through the conventional arabesques of polite dancing. She would not let herself formulate the words in her brain: I am dancing with a black man. But she allowed herself to question, with the careful detachment of scientific inquiry, quietly inside herself: "Do I feel anything? What do I feel?" The man began to hum a snatch of the tune to which they were dancing, the way a person will do when he suddenly hears music out of some forgotten phase of his youth; while the hum reverberated through his chest, she slid her eyes almost painfully to the right, not moving her head, to see his very well-shaped hand—an almost feminine hand compared to the hands of most white men—dark brown against her own white one, the dark thumb and the pale one crossed, the dark fingers and the pale ones folded together. "Is this exactly how I always dance?" she asked herself closely. "Do I always hold my back exactly like this, do I relax just this much, hold myself in reserve to just this degree?"

She found she was dancing as she always danced.

I feel nothing, she thought. *I feel nothing.*

And all at once a relief, a mild elation, took possession of her, so that she could begin to talk to the man with whom she was dancing. In any case, she was not a girl who had much small talk; she knew that at least half the young men who, attracted by her exceptional prettiness, flocked to ask her to dance at parties never asked her again because they could not stand her vast minutes of silence. But now she said in her flat, small voice the few things she could say—remarks about the music and the pleasantness of the rainy night outside. He smiled at her with bored tolerance, plainly not listening to what she said. Then he said, as if to compensate for his inattention, "You from England?"

She said, "Yes. But I'm not English. I'm South African, but I've spent the last five years in England. I've only been back in South Africa since December. I used to know Derek when I was a little girl," she added, feeling that she was obliged to explain her presence in what she suddenly felt was a group conscious of some distinction or privilege.

"England," he said, smiling down past her rather than at her. "Never been so happy anywhere."

"London?" she said.

He nodded. "Oh, I agree," she said. "I feel the same about it."

"No, you don't, McCoy," he said very slowly, smiling at her now. "No, you don't."

She was silenced at what instantly seemed her temerity.

He said, as they danced around again, "The way you speak. Really English. Whites in S.A. can't speak that way."

For a moment, one of the old, blank, impassively pretty-faced silences threatened to settle upon her, but the second glass of arak punch broke through it, and, almost animated, she answered lightly, "Oh, I find I'm like a parrot. I pick up the accent of the people among whom I live in a matter of hours."

He threw back his head and laughed, showing the gaps in his teeth. "How will you speak tomorrow, McCoy?" he said, holding her back from him and shaking with laughter, his eyes swimming. "Oh, how will you speak tomorrow, I wonder?"

She said, immensely daring, though it came out in her usual small, unassertive feminine voice, a voice gently toned for the utterance of banal pleasantries, "Like you."

"Let's have a drink," he said, as if he had known her a long time—as if she were someone like Jessica Malherbe. And he took her back to the bar, leading her by the hand; she walked with her hand loosely swinging in his, just as she had done with young men at country-club dances. "I promised to have one with Rajati," he was saying, "Where has he got to?"

"Is that the one I met?" said the girl. "The one with the high, bald head?"

"An Indian?" he said. "No, you mean Mahinder. This one's his cousin, Jessica Malherbe's husband."

"She's married to an Indian?" The girl stopped dead in the middle of the dancers. "Is she?" The idea went through her like a thrill. She felt startled as if by a sudden piece of good news about someone who was important to her. Jessica Malherbe—the name, the idea—seemed to have been circling about her life since before she left England. Even there, she had read about her in the papers: the daughter of a humble Afrikaner farmer, who had disowned her in the name of a stern Calvinist God for her anti-nationalism and her radical views; a girl from a back-veld farm—such a farm as Joyce herself could remember seeing from a car window as a child—who had worked in a factory and educated herself and been sent by her trade union to study labor problems all over the world; a girl who negotiated with ministers of state; who, Joyce had learned that evening, had gone to prison for her principles. Jessica Malherbe, who was almost the first person the girl had met when she came in to the party this evening, and who turned out to look like any well-groomed English woman you might see in a London restaurant, wearing a pearl necklace and smelling of expensive perfume. An Indian! It was the final gesture. Magnificent. A world toppled with it—Jessica Malherbe's father's world. An Indian!

"Old Rajati," Ntwala was saying. But they could not find him. The girl thought of the handsome, scholarly-looking Indian with the domed head, and suddenly she remembered that once, in Durban, she had talked across the counter of a shop with an Indian boy. She had been down in the Indian quarter with her sister, and they had entered a shop to buy a piece of silk. She had been the spokeswoman, and she had murmured across the counter to the boy and he had said, in a voice as low and gentle as her own, no, he was sorry, that length of silk was for a sari, and could not be cut. The boy had very beautiful, unseeing eyes, and it was as if they spoke to each other in a dream. The shop was small and deep-set. It smelled strongly of incense, the smell of the village church in which her grandfather had lain in state before his funeral, the scent of her mother's garden on a summer night—the smell of death and flowers, compounded, as the incident itself came to be, of ugliness and beauty, of attraction and repulsion. For just after she and her sister had left the little shop, they had found themselves being followed by an unpleasant man, whose presence first made them uneasily hold tightly to their handbags but who later, when they entered a busy shop in an attempt to get rid of him, crowded up against them and made an obscene advance. He had had a vaguely Eurasian face, they believed, but they could not have said whether or not he was an Indian; in their disgust, he had scarcely seemed human to them at all.

She tried now, in the swarming noise of Derek's room, to hear again in her head the voice of the boy saying the words she remembered so exactly: "No, I am sorry, that length of silk is for a sari, it cannot be cut." But the tingle of the alcohol that she had been feeling in her hands for quite a long time became a kind of sizzling singing in her ears, like the sound of bubbles rising in aerated water, and all that she could convey to herself was the curious finality of the phrase: *can-not-be-cut, can-not-be-cut.*

She danced the next dance with Derek. "You look sweet tonight, old thing," he said, putting wet lips to her ear. "Sweet."

She said, "Derek, which is Rajati?"

He let go her waist. "Over there," he said, but in an instant he clutched her again and was whirling her around and she saw only Mahinder Singh and Martin Mathlongo, the big, freckled colored man, and the back of some man's dark neck with a businessman's thick roll of fat above the collar.

"Which?" she said, but this time he gestured toward a group in which there were white men only, and so she gave up.

The dance was cut short with a sudden wailing screech as someone lifted the needle of the gramophone in the middle of the record, and it appeared that a man was about to speak. It turned out that it was to be a song and not a speech, for Martin Mathlongo, little Shabalala, two colored women, and a huge African woman with cork-soled green shoes grouped themselves with their arms hanging about one another's necks. When the room had quietened down, they sang. They sang with extraordinary beauty, the men's voices deep and tender, the women's high and passionate. They sang in some Bantu language, and when the song was done, the girl asked Eddie Ntwala, next to whom she found herself standing, what they had been singing about. He said as simply as a peasant, as if he had never danced with her, exchanging sophisticated banter, "It's about a young man who passes and sees a girl working in her father's field."

Roy Wilson giggled and gave him a comradely punch on the arm. "Eddie's never seen a field in his life. Born and bred in Apex Location."

Then Martin Mathlongo, with his spotted bow tie under his big, loose-mouthed, strong face, suddenly stood forward and began to sing "Ol' Man River." There was something insulting, defiant, yet shamefully supplicating in the way he sang the melodramatic, servile words, the way he kneeled and put out his big hands with their upturned pinkish palms. The dark faces in the room watched him, grinning as if at the antics of a monkey. The white faces looked drunk and withdrawn.

Joyce McCoy saw that, for the first time since she had been introduced to her that evening, she was near Jessica Malherbe. The girl was feeling a strong distress at the sight of the colored man singing the blackface song, and when she saw Jessica Malherbe, she put—with a look, as it were—all this burden at the woman's feet. She put it all upon her, as if *she* could make it right, for on the woman's broad, neatly made-up face there was neither the sullen embarrassment of the other white faces nor the leering self-laceration of the black.

The girl felt the way she usually felt when she was about to cry, but this time it was the prelude to something different. She made her way with difficulty, for her legs were the drunkest part of her, murmuring politely, "Excuse me," as she had been taught to do for twenty-two years, past all the people who stood, in their liquor daze, stolid as cows in a stream. She went up to the trade-union leader, the veteran of political imprisonment, the glossy-haired woman who used good perfume. "Miss Malherbe," she said, and her blank, exquisite face might have been requesting an invitation to a garden party. "Please, Miss Malherbe, I want to go with you next week. I want to march into the location."

Next day, when Joyce was sober, she still wanted to go. As her brother-in-law had predicted, she felt sick from Derek's punch, and every time she inclined her head, a great, heavy ball seemed to roll slowly from one side to the other inside her skull. The presence of this ball, which sometimes felt as if it were her brain itself, shrunken and hardened, rattling like a dried nut in its shell, made it difficult to concentrate, yet the thought that she would march into the location the following week was perfectly clear. As a matter of fact, it was almost obsessively clear.

She went to see Miss Malherbe at the headquarters of the Civil Disobedience Campaign, in order to say again what she had said the night before. Miss Malherbe did again just what *she* had done the night before—listened politely, was interested and sympathetic, thanked the girl, and then gently explained that the movement could not allow anyone but bona-fide members to take part in such actions. "Then I'll become a member now," said Joyce. She wore today a linen dress as pale as her own skin, and on the square of bare, matching flesh at her neck hung a little necklace of small pearls—the sort of necklace that is given to a girl child and added to, pearl by pearl, a new one on every birthday. Well, said Miss Malherbe, she could join the movement, by all means—and would not that be enough? Her support would be much appreciated. But no, Joyce wanted to *do* something; she wanted to march with the others into the location. And before she left the office, she was formally enrolled.

When she had been a member for two days, she went to the headquarters to see Jessica Malherbe again. This time, there were other people present; they smiled at her when she came in, as if they already had heard about her. Miss Malherbe explained to her the gravity of what she wanted to do. Did she realize that she might have to go to prison? Did she understand that it was the policy of the passive resisters to serve their prison sentences rather than to pay fines? Even if she did not mind for herself, what about her parents, her relatives?

The girl said that she was over twenty-one; her only parent, her mother, was in England; she was responsible to no one.

She told her sister Madeline and her brother-in-law nothing. When Tuesday morning came, it was damp and cool. Joyce dressed with the consciousness of the performance of the ordinary that marks extraordinary days. Her stomach felt hollow; her hands were cold. She rode into town with her brother-in-law, and all the way his car popped the fallen jacaranda flowers, which were as thick on the street beneath the tires as they were on the trees. After lunch, she took a tram to Fordsburg, a quarter where Indians and people of mixed blood, debarred from living anywhere better, lived alongside poor whites, and where, it had been decided, the defiers were to forgather. She had never been to this part of Johannesburg before, and she had the address of the house to which she was to go written in her tartan-silk-covered notebook in her minute, backward-sloping hand. She carried her white angora jacket over her arm and she had put on sensible flat sandals. *I don't know why I keep thinking of this as if it were a lengthy expedition, requiring some sort of special equipment,* she thought; *actually it'll be all over in half an hour. Jessica Malherbe said we'd pay bail and be back in town by four-thirty.*

The girl sat in the tram and did not look at the other passengers, and they did not look at her, although the contrast between her and them was startling. They were thin, yellow-limbed children with enormous sooty eyes; bleary-eyed, shuffling men, whom degeneracy had enfeebled into an appearance of indeterminate old age; heavy women with swollen legs, who were carrying newspaper parcels; young, almost white factory girls whose dull, kinky hair was pinned up into a decent simulation of fashionable style, and on whose proud, pert faces rouge and lipstick had drawn a white girl's face. Sitting among them, Joyce looked—quite apart from the social

228

difference apparent in her clothes—so different, so other, that there were only two possible things to think about her, and which one thought depended upon one's attitude: either she was a kind of fairy—ideal, exquisite, an Ariel among Calibans —or she was something too tender, something unfinished, and beautiful only in the way the skin of the unborn lamb, taken from the belly of the mother, is beautiful, because it is a thing as yet unready for this world.

She got off at the stop she had been told to and went slowly up the street, watching the numbers. It was difficult to find out how far she would have to walk, or even, for the first few minutes, whether she was walking in the right direction, because the numbers on the doorways were half obliterated, or ill-painted, or sometimes missing entirely. As in most poor quarters, houses and stores were mixed, and, in fact, some houses were being used as business premises, and some stores had rooms above, in which, obviously, the storekeepers and their families lived. The street had a flower name, but there were no trees and no gardens. Most of the shops had Indian firm names amateurishly written on homemade wooden signboards or curlicued and flourished in signwriter's yellow and red across the lintel: Moonsammy Dadoo, Hardware, Ladies Smart Outfitting & General; K. P. Patel & Sons, Fruit Merchants; Vallabhir's Bargain Store. A shoemaker had enclosed the veranda of his small house as a workshop, and had hung outside a huge black tin shoe, of a style worn in the twenties.

The gutters smelled of rotting fruit. Thin *café-au-lait* children trailed smaller brothers and sisters; on the veranda of one of the little semidetached houses a lean light-colored man in shirt sleeves was shouting, in Afrikaans, at a fat woman who sat on the steps. An Indian woman in a sari and high-heeled European shoes was knocking at the door of the other half of the house. Farther on, a very small house, almost eclipsed by the tentacles of voracious-looking creepers, bore a polished brass plate with the name and consulting hours of a well-known Indian doctor.

The street was quiet enough; it had the dead, listless air of all places where people are making some sort of living in a small way. And so Joyce started when a sudden shriek of drunken laughter came from behind a rusty corrugated-iron wall that seemed to enclose a yard. Outside the wall, someone was sitting on a patch of the tough, gritty grass that sometimes scrabbles a hold for itself on worn city pavements; as the girl passed, she saw that the person was one of the white women tramps whom she occasionally saw in the city crossing a street with the peculiar glassy purposefulness of the outcast.

She felt neither pity nor distaste at the sight. It was as if, dating from this day, her involvement in action against social injustice had purged her of sentimentality; she did not have to avert her gaze. She looked quite calmly at the woman's bare legs, which were tanned, with dirt and exposure, to the color of leather. She felt only, in a detached way, a prim, angry sympathy for the young pale-brown girl who stood nursing a baby at the gate of the house just beyond, because she had to live next door to what was almost certainly a shebeen.

Then, ahead of her in the next block, she saw three cars parked outside a house and knew that that must be the place. She walked a little faster, but quite evenly, and when she reached it—No. 260, as she had been told—she found that it was a small house of purplish brick, with four steps leading from the pavement to the narrow veranda. A sword fern in a paraffin tin, painted green, stood on each side of the front door, which had been left ajar, as the front door sometimes is in a house where there is a party. She went up the steps firmly, over the dusty imprints of other feet, and, leaning into the doorway a little,

230

knocked on the fancy glass panel of the upper part of the door. She found herself looking straight down a passage that had a worn flowered linoleum on the floor. The head of a small Indian girl—low forehead and great eyes—appeared in a curtained archway halfway down the passage and disappeared again instantly.

Joyce McCoy knocked again. She could hear voices, and, above all the others, the tone of protest in a woman's voice.

A bald white man with thick glasses crossed the passage with quick, nervous steps and did not, she thought, see her. But he might have, because, prompted perhaps by his entry into the room from which the voices came, the pretty brunette woman with the efficient manner, whom the girl remembered from the party, appeared suddenly with her hand outstretched, and said enthusiastically, "Come *in*, my dear. Come inside. Such a racket in there! You could have been knocking all day."

The girl saw that the woman wore flimsy sandals and no stockings, and that her toenails were painted like the toes of the languid girls in *Vogue*. The girl did not know why details such as these intrigued her so much, or seemed so remarkable. She smiled in greeting and followed the woman into the house.

Now she was really there; she heard her own footsteps taking her down the passage of a house in Fordsburg. There was a faintly spicy smell about the passage; on the wall she caught a glimpse of what appeared to be a photograph of an Indian girl in European bridal dress, the picture framed with fretted gold paper, like a cake frill. And then they were in a room where everyone smiled at her quickly but took no notice of her. Jessica Malherbe was there, in a blue linen suit, smoking a cigarette and saying something to the tall, tousle-headed Roy Wilson, who was writing down what she said. The bald man was talking low and earnestly to a slim woman who wore a man's wrist watch and had the hands of a man. The tiny African, Shabalala, wearing a pair of spectacles with thin tortoise-shell rims, was ticking a penciled list. Three or four others, black and white, sat talking. The room was as brisk with chatter as a birds' cage.

Joyce lowered herself gingerly onto a dining-room chair whose legs were loose and swayed a little. And as she tried to conceal herself and sink into the composition of the room, she noticed a group sitting a little apart, near the windows, in the shadow of the heavy curtains, and, from the arresting sight of them, saw the whole room as it was beneath the overlay of people. The group was made up of an old Indian woman, and a slim Indian boy and another Indian child, who were obviously her grandchildren. The woman sat with her feet apart, so that her lap, under the voluminous swathings of her sari, was broad, and in one nostril a ruby twinkled. Her hands were little and beringed—a fat woman's hands. Her forehead was low beneath the coarse black hair and the line of tinsel along the sari, and she looked out through the company of white men and women, Indian men in business suits, Africans in clerkly neatness, as if she were deaf or could not see. Yet when Joyce saw her eyes move, as cold and as lacking in interest as the eyes of a tortoise, and her foot stir, asserting an inert force of life, like the twitch in a muscle of some supine creature on a mudbank, the girl knew it was not deafness or blindness that kept the woman oblivious of the company but simply the knowledge that this house, this room, was her place. She was here before the visitors came; she would not move for them; she would be here when they had gone. And the children clung with their grandmother, knowing that she was the kind who could never be banished to the kitchen or some other backwater.

From the assertion of this silent group the girl became aware of the whole room (*their* room), of its furnishings: the hideous "suite" upholstered in imitation velvet with a stamped design of triangles and sickles; the yellow varnished table with the

pink silk mat and the brass vase of paper roses; the easy chairs
with circular apertures in the arms where colored glass ash trays
were balanced; the crudely colored photographs; the barbola
vase; the green ruched-silk cushions; the standard lamp with
more platforms for more colored glass ash trays; the gilded
plaster dog that stood at the door. An Indian went over and said
something to the old woman with the proprietary, apologetic,
irritated air of a son who wishes his mother would keep out of
the way; as he turned his head, the girl saw something familiar
in the angle and recognized him as the man the back of whose
neck she had seen when she was trying to identify Jessica Malherbe's husband at the party. Now he came over to her, a squat,
pleasant man, with a great deal of that shiny black Indian hair
making his head look too big for his body. He said, "My congratulations. My wife, Jessica, tells me you have insisted on
identifying yourself with today's defiance. Well, how do you
feel about it?"

She smiled at him with great difficulty; she really did not
know why it was so difficult. She said, "I'm sorry. We didn't
meet that night. Just your cousin—I believe it is?—Mr. Singh."
He was such a remarkably commonplace-looking Indian, Jessica Malherbe's husband, but Jessica Malherbe's husband after
all—the man with the roll of fat at the back of his neck.

She said, "You don't resemble Mr. Singh in the least," feeling
that it was herself she offended by the obvious thought behind
the comparison, and not this fat, amiable middle-aged man, who
needed only to be in his shirt sleeves to look like any well-to-do
Indian merchant, or in a grubby white coat, and unshaven, to
look like a fruit-and-vegetable hawker. He sat down beside her
(she could see the head of the old woman just beyond his ear),
and as he began to talk to her in his Cambridge-modulated
voice, she began to notice something that she had not noticed
before. It was curious, because surely it must have been there

all the time; then again it might not have been—it might have been released by some movement of the group of the grandmother, the slender boy, and the child, perhaps from their clothes—but quite suddenly she began to be aware of the odor of incense. Sweet and dry and smoky, like the odor of burning leaves—she began to smell it. Then she thought, It must be in the furniture, the curtains; the old woman burns it and it permeates the house and all the gewgaws from Birmingham, and Denver, Colorado, and American-occupied Japan. Then it did not remind her of burning leaves any longer. It was incense, strong and sweet. The smell of death and flowers. She remembered it with such immediacy that it came back literally, absolutely, the way a memory of words or vision never can.

"Are you all right, Miss McCoy?" said the kindly Indian, interrupting himself because he saw that she was not listening and that her pretty, pale, impassive face was so white and withdrawn that she looked as if she might faint.

She stood up with a start that was like an inarticulate apology and went quickly from the room. She ran down the passage and opened a door and closed it behind her, but the odor was there, too, stronger than ever, in somebody's bedroom, where a big double bed had an orange silk cover. She leaned with her back against the door, breathing it in and trembling with fear and with the terrible desire to be safe: to be safe from one of the kindly women who would come, any moment now, to see what was wrong; to be safe from the gathering up of her own nerve to face the journey in the car to the location, and the faces of her companions, who were not afraid, and the walk up the location street.

The very conventions of the life which, she felt, had insulated her in softness against the sharp, joyful brush of real life in action came up to save her now. If she was afraid, she was also

234

polite. She had been polite so long that the colorless formula of good manners, which had stifled so much spontaneity in her, could also serve to stifle fear.

It would be so *terribly rude* simply to run away out of the house, and go home, now.

That was the thought that saved her—the code of a well-brought-up child at a party—and it came to her again and again, slowing down her thudding heart, uncurling her clenched hands. *It would be terribly rude to run away now.* She knew with distress, somewhere at the back of her mind, that this was the wrong reason for staying, but it worked. Her manners had been with her longer and were stronger than her fear. Slowly the room ceased to sing so loudly about her, the bedspread stopped dancing up and down before her eyes, and she went slowly over to the mirror in the door of the wardrobe and straightened the belt of her dress, not meeting her own eyes. Then she opened the door and went down the passage and back again into the room where the others were gathered, and sat down in the chair she had left. It was only then that she noticed that the others were standing—had risen, ready to go.

"What about your jacket, my dear. Would you like to leave it?" the pretty brunette said, noticing her.

Jessica Malherbe was on her way to the door. She smiled at Joyce and said, "I'd leave it, if I were you."

"Yes, I think so, thank you." She heard her own voice as if it were someone else's.

Outside, there was the mild confusion of deciding who should go with whom and in which car. The girl found herself in the back of the car in which Jessica Malherbe sat beside the driver. The slim, mannish woman got in; little Shabalala got in but was summoned to another car by an urgently waving hand. He got out again, and then came back and jumped in just as they were off. He was the only one who seemed excited. He sat forward, with his hands on his knees. Smiling widely at the girl, he said, "Now we really are taking you for a ride, Miss McCoy."

The cars drove through Fordsburg and skirted the city. Then they went out one of the main roads that connect the gold-mining towns of the Witwatersrand with each other and with Johannesburg. They passed mine dumps, pale gray and yellow; clusters of neat, ugly houses, provided for white mineworkers; patches of veld, where the rain of the night before glittered thinly in low places; a brickfield; a foundry; a little poultry farm. And then they turned in to a muddy road, along which they followed a native bus that swayed under its load of passengers, exhaust pipe sputtering black smoke, canvas flaps over the windows wildly agitated. The bus thundered ahead through the location gates, but the three cars stopped outside. Jessica Malherbe got out first, and stood, pushing back the cuticles of the nails of her left hand as she talked in a businesslike fashion to Roy Wilson. "Of course, don't give the statement to the papers unless they ask for it. It would be more interesting to see *their* version first, and come along with our own afterward. But they *may* ask—"

"There's a press car," Shabalala said, hurrying up. "There."

"Looks like Brand, from the *Post*."

"Can't be Dick Brand; he's transferred to Bloemfontein," said the tall, mannish woman.

"Come here, Miss McCoy, you're the baby," said Shabalala, straightening his tie and twitching his shoulders, in case there was going to be a photograph. Obediently, the girl moved to the front.

But the press photographer waved his flash bulb in protest. "No, I want you walking."

"Well, you better get us before we enter the gates or you'll find yourself arrested, too," said Jessica Malherbe, unconcerned.

"Look at that," she added to the mannish woman, lifting her foot to show the heel of her white shoe, muddy already.

Lagersdorp Location, which they were entering and which Joyce McCoy had never seen before, was much like all such places. A high barbed-wire fence—more a symbol than a means of confinement, since, except for the part near the gates, it had comfortable gaps in many places—enclosed almost a square mile of dreary little dwellings, to which the African population of the nearby town came home to sleep at night. There were mean houses and squalid tin shelters and, near the gates where the administrative offices were, one or two decent cottages, which had been built by the white housing authorities "experimentally" and never duplicated; they were occupied by the favorite African clerks of the white location superintendent. There were very few shops, since every license granted to a native shop in a location takes business away from the white stores in the town, and there were a great many churches, some built of mud and tin, some neo-Gothic and built of brick, representing a great many sects.

They began to walk, the seven men and women, toward the location gates. Jessica Malherbe and Roy Wilson were a little ahead, and the girl found herself between Shabalala and the bald white man with thick glasses. The flash bulb made its brief sensation, and the two or three picannins who were playing with tin hoops on the roadside looked up, astonished. A fat native woman selling oranges and roast mealies shouted speculatively to a passer-by in ragged trousers.

At the gateway, a fat black policeman sat on a soapbox and gossiped. He raised his hand to his cap as they passed. In Joyce McCoy, the numbness that had followed her nervous crisis began to be replaced by a calm embarrassment; as a child she had often wondered, seeing a circle of Salvation Army people playing a hymn out of tune on a street corner, how it would feel to stand there with them. Now she felt she knew. Little Shabalala ran a finger around the inside of his collar, and the girl thought, with a start of warmth, that he was feeling as she was; she did not know that he was thinking what he had promised himself he would not think about during this walk—that very likely the walk would cost him his job. People did not want to employ Africans who "made trouble." His wife, who was immensely proud of his education and his cleverness, had said nothing when she learned that he was going—had only gone, with studied consciousness, about her cooking. But, after all, Shabalala, like the girl—though neither he nor she could know it—was also saved by convention. In his case, it was a bold convention—that he was an amusing little man. He said to her as they began to walk up the road, inside the gateway, "Feel the bump?"

"I beg your pardon?" she said, polite and conspiratorial.

A group of ragged children, their eyes alight with the tenacious beggarliness associated with the East rather than with Africa, were jumping and running around the white members of the party, which they thought was some committee come to judge a competition for the cleanest house, or a baby show. "Penny, *missus*, penny, penny, *baas!*" they whined. Shabalala growled something at them playfully in their own language before he answered, with his delightful grin, wide as a slice of melon. "The bump over the color bar."

Apart from the children, who dropped away desultorily, like flying fish behind a boat, no one took much notice of the defiers. The African women, carrying on their heads food they had bought in town, or bundles of white people's washing, scarcely looked at them. African men on bicycles rode past, preoccupied. But when the party came up parallel with the administration offices—built of red brick, and, along with the experimental cottages at the gate and the clinic next door, the only buildings of

238

European standard in the location—a middle-aged white man in a suit worn shiny on the seat and the elbows (his slightly stooping body seemed to carry the shape of his office chair and desk) came out and stopped Jessica Malherbe. Obediently, the whole group stopped; there was an air of quiet obstinacy about them. The man, who was the location superintendent himself, evidently knew Jessica Malherbe, and was awkward with the necessity of making this an official and not a personal encounter. "You know that I must tell you it is prohibited for Europeans to enter Lagersdorp Location," he said. The girl noticed that he carried his glasses in his left hand, dangling by one earpiece, as if he had been waiting for the arrival of the party and had jumped up from his desk nervously at last.

Jessica Malherbe smiled, and there was in her smile something of the easy, informal amusement with which Afrikaners discount pomposity. "Mr. Dougal, good afternoon. Yes, of course, we know you have to give us official warning. How far do you think we'll get?"

The man's face relaxed. He shrugged and said, "They're waiting for you."

And suddenly the girl, Joyce McCoy, felt this—the sense of something lying in wait for them. The neat, stereotyped faces of African clerks appeared at the windows of the administrative offices. As the party approached the clinic, the European doctor, in his white coat, looked out; two white nurses and an African nurse came out onto the veranda. And all the patient African women who were sitting about in the sun outside, suckling their babies and gossiping, sat silent while the party walked by—sat silent, and had in their eyes something of the look of the Indian grandmother, waiting at home in Fordsburg.

The party walked on up the street, and on either side, in the little houses, which had homemade verandas flanking the strip of worn, unpaved earth that was the sidewalk, or whose front doors opened straight out onto a foot or two of fenced garden, where hens ran and pumpkins had been put to ripen, doors were open, and men and women stood, their children gathered in around them, as if they sensed the approach of a storm. Yet the sun was hot on the heads of the party, walking slowly up the street. And they were silent, and the watchers were silent, or spoke to one another only in whispers, each bending his head to another's ear but keeping his eyes on the group passing up the street. Someone laughed, but it was only a drunk—a wizened little old man—returning from some shebeen. And ahead, at the corner of a crossroad, stood the police car, a black car, with the aerial from its radio-communication equipment a shining lash against all the shabbiness of the street. The rear doors opened, and two heavy, smartly dressed policemen got out and slammed the doors behind them. They approached the party slowly, not hurrying themselves. When they drew abreast, one said, as if in reflex, "Ah—good afternoon." But the other cut in, in an emotionless official voice, "You are all under arrest for illegal entry into Lagersdorp Location. If you'll just give us your names . . ."

Joyce stood waiting her turn, and her heart beat slowly and evenly. She thought again, as she had once before—how long ago was that party?—I feel *nothing*. It's all right. I feel *nothing*.

But as the policeman came to her, and she spelled out her name for him, she looked up and saw the faces of the African onlookers who stood nearest her. Two men, a small boy, and a woman, dressed in ill-matched castoffs of European clothing, which hung upon them without meaning, like coats spread on bushes, were looking at her. When she looked back, they met her gaze. And she felt, suddenly, not *nothing* but what they were feeling, at the sight of her, a white girl, taken—incomprehensibly, as they themselves were used to being taken—under the force of white men's wills, which dispensed and withdrew life, which imprisoned and set free, fed or starved, like God himself.

ABOUT THE AUTHOR

NADINE GORDIMER was born in South Africa, in 1923, and has always lived there. She was a student at the University of Witwatersrand in Johannesburg. She has already established a reputation as a writer of artistry and maturity through the medium of short stories, many of which have appeared in this country in *The Virginia Quarterly, The Yale Review, Harper's, The New Yorker* and a number of other magazines. The first collection of Miss Gordimer's stories, *The Soft Voice of the Serpent*, was published in 1952. A novel, *The Lying Days*, appeared the following year.